Ross McCain hesitated. He took the book, his gut twisting into a dozen knots.

He felt Miss Grimes's gaze on him as he looked at the townspeople. Slowly he untied the ribbon and tucked it in his pocket. He opened the book, a gift from the townspeople, and took time to smooth his long fingers over the yellowed pages. The inscription stared back up at him. The handwriting was bold, handsome—and utterly meaningless to him. He couldn't read a word of it.

Ross straightened his shoulders and cleared his throat. His heart pounded in his chest, and for the first time in years, he felt sweat trickle down his back.

"Miss Grimes," he said, looking out over the crowd, expectant eyes riveted on him, "it is indeed a pleasure to have you here with us today." He glanced down again at the page. Something coiled inside him. He was trapped.

Then he felt Miss Grimes's cool hands against his hot skin. Their gazes locked, and in that instant he knew she'd guessed his secret. Yet there was no scorn, no ridicule, only understanding.

Dear Reader,

This month our exciting medieval series KNIGHTS OF THE BLACK ROSE continues with *The Rogue* by Ana Seymour, a secret baby story in which rogue knight Nicholas Hendry finds his one true love. Judith Stacy returns with *Written in the Heart,* the delightful tale of an uptight California businessman who hires a marriage-shy female handwriting analyst to solve some of his company's capers. In *Angel of the Knight,* a medieval novel by Diana Hall, a carefree warrior falls deeply in love with his betrothed, and does all he can to free her from a family curse. Talented newcomer Mary Burton brings us *A Bride for McCain,* about a mining millionaire who enters a marriage of convenience with the town's schoolteacher.

For the next three months, we are going to be asking readers to let us know what you are looking for from Harlequin Historicals. We hope you'll participate by sending your ideas to us at:

Harlequin Historicals
300 E. 42nd St.
New York, NY 10017

Q. What are your favorite historical settings?

_____

_____

Q. Which Harlequin Historicals authors do you read?

_____

_____

Whatever your taste in reading, you'll be sure to find a romantic journey back to the past between the covers of a Harlequin Historicals novel. We hope you'll join us next month, too!

Sincerely,

Tracy Farrell,
Senior Editor

A BRIDE FOR McCAIN

MARY BURTON

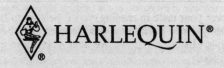

HARLEQUIN®

TORONTO • NEW YORK • LONDON
AMSTERDAM • PARIS • SYDNEY • HAMBURG
STOCKHOLM • ATHENS • TOKYO • MILAN • MADRID
PRAGUE • WARSAW • BUDAPEST • AUCKLAND

ISBN 0-373-29102-7

A BRIDE FOR McCAIN

Visit us at www.romance.net

Printed in U.S.A.

To my agent, Irene Goodman,
and my editor Patience Smith

Thank you for turning my dream into reality.

Chapter One

Sacramento, California
1876

Her fate rested in the hands of a dead man.

The thought made Jessica Tierney's heart race as her hired carriage rolled to a stop in front of a two-story, gray office building. Her gaze traveled up the whitewashed front steps, past the twin stone planters filled with marigolds to the plaque hanging by the front door. It read Cyrus Moore, Attorney-at-Law.

She flexed her fingers until her kid gloves tightened over her knuckles like a second skin. She drew in a steadying breath. This was it. The reading of her father's will.

She'd taken extra care with her toilette this morning, hoping to look more sophisticated. She'd swept her black ringlets into a chignon and chosen a burgundy velvet suit-dress with a parasol to match and a small derby-style hat outfitted with an ostrich plume. She'd pinned a pear-shaped watch pendant just above her right breast and clipped diamonds to her ears.

The carriage driver opened Jessica's door and helped her from the carriage. Years of training at Miss Madeline's Academy for Young Ladies kept her from pushing the man aside, running across the boardwalk and up the stairs into Cyrus Moore's office.

She smoothed her palms over her skirts. "Father, all I need is one small sign that you loved me just a little."

"Excuse me, ma'am?" the driver said.

Automatically, she smiled at him. "Nothing."

"Do you want me to wait, miss?"

"Yes. I don't expect this will take long."

The driver touched his black cap. "Yes, ma'am."

She raised her skirts and climbed the steps. Twisting the brass knob, she opened the door and stepped into an empty receiving room.

No one waited in the room furnished with a large leather sofa, a small desk covered with neat stacks of papers, and vivid oil paintings of clipper ships on the walls. A grandfather clock, made of cherry and sparkling brass, ticked quietly in the corner. The smell of expensive cigars hung in the air.

She looked at the sofa and considered sitting, then changed her mind. Instead, she strolled over to the desk and picked up one of the papers.

Cyrus Moore had been her father's attorney for thirty years and one of the few people he'd trusted. It had been Mr. Moore, not her father, who had communicated with her teachers at boarding school, seen to her allowance and answered her letters.

A small side door opened. A short man with a round belly and a receding hairline entered the room. He glanced up from a thick, leather-bound book and blinked twice. "May I help you?"

She dropped the paper. "I am Jessica Tierney."

He quickly set his book on the desk and tugged his vest down over his belly. "I'm sorry. I should have known. It's just that you've been gone so long, no one really knows what you look like."

Bitterness tightened her chest. "Ten years is a long time."

"My name is Mr. Utley. I'm Mr. Moore's assistant," he said, quickly changing the topic.

She smiled. "A pleasure."

He cleared his throat. "Are your accommodations at the hotel satisfactory?"

"They're fine." Her father's house had never been her home, and she refused to spend one night in it. "Who else is here?"

"Mr. Moore, of course, and William Perry."

Jessica's stomach tightened at the mention of Perry's name. Her father's business partner, and one of the city's social elite, William Perry had persuaded her father to exile her after her mother's death.

"That's all?"

"Yes. I thought you knew."

Jessica straightened her shoulders. "Father and I didn't communicate often."

Truth was they'd not spoken since the day she'd left for boarding school ten years ago. The letters she'd received, including the one summoning her home, had been from Mr. Moore. She'd arrived in

Sacramento two days after her father had died peacefully in his sleep.

"I know Mr. Perry is anxious to proceed with the reading." Mr. Utley quietly opened the door to Moore's office.

A fire crackled in the marble fireplace, flickering on polished wood floors, rugs imported from India and a collection of Chinese vases. Cyrus Moore sat forward in a leather chair in front of the fireplace, drumming his fingers on his knee. The afternoon sun streamed through the window, glistening off his white hair.

Across from him sat William Perry. Meticulously dressed, William crossed his long legs and brushed a piece of lint from his charcoal-gray pants.

Mr. Moore stared at William. "I can't break the seal until Miss Tierney arrives, but rest assured I have the situation under control." As if sensing they were not alone, Mr. Moore looked up. His gaze locked on Jessica and he stood instantly. "Miss Tierney?"

She moistened her lips and smiled. Her rose-scented perfume filled the room. "Yes."

He buttoned his jacket and walked toward her with his hand extended. "The last time I saw you, you were twelve. You've become a beautiful woman."

"Thank you."

He took her hand in his. He seemed unable to tear his gaze away from her eyes. "I must say, your eyes are the most exquisite shade of blue. They remind me of the waters off the Hawaiian Islands. I sailed there once to negotiate a trade agreement for your father.''

''You are very kind.''

He escorted her to a wooden chair in front of his desk. ''Perry,'' he said without turning, ''I believe you know Miss Tierney?''

William studied her intently, but he didn't stand. ''It's about time you got here.''

A tense silence followed as the two glared at each other.

Moore broke the moment, saying, ''Let me express my condolences at the loss of your father.''

William snorted. ''Let's drop the pretense and get on with the reading of the will.''

''Really, Perry,'' Moore said, ''show some tact.''

''Just get on with it.'' Perry rose, walked over to Moore's desk and took one of the other chairs positioned in front of it.

Jessica pulled off her gloves and laid them on her lap. ''Mr. Perry is right. There is no sense offering false sentiments. It's common knowledge that obligation, not love, drove my father to take me in after my mother's death.''

''Simon could be hard,'' Moore said.

Jessica swallowed an unexpected lump in her throat. Her father still had one last chance to redeem himself. ''What's done is done. I'd rather concentrate on the future.''

Moore nodded and sat behind his desk. He placed his spectacles on his nose, then unfolded the will. ''If you two are ready?''

Jessica crossed her fingers. ''Yes, I'm ready.''

William scooted to the edge of his seat. "Get on with it, man."

Moore cleared his throat. "Simon wrote the will after his second wife died in childbirth and he realized he himself was dying."

Jessica nestled trembling hands in her lap. She didn't know her father had remarried. "I understand."

The attorney adjusted his glasses. "Understand also, this will is ironclad."

An unexpected hardness flashed in Moore's eyes before he ripped the red wax seal off the will and unfolded the paper. He read,

"I, Simon Patrick Tierney, do bequeath my entire estate to my daughter, Jessica Elizabeth Tierney—"

"What?" William shouted. "That old bastard can't cut me out like that! I've spent the last fifteen years of my life at his beck and call."

Jessica barely heard William's tirade. Her father, a self-made man, had put his heart, blood and soul into his empire and now he was giving it to her. To her! In his own way, he'd finally told her he loved her.

Moore peered over his spectacles. "I'm not finished."

"What more is there to say?" Jessica said.

"Quiet, let the man finish," William snapped.

Moore arched an eyebrow. "As I was about to continue,

"...provided she marry William Perry within the next thirty days and produce a son within two years. If Jessica does not marry William or produce a Tierney heir in the allotted time, my money will go to Saint Bridget's Orphanage in San Francisco, the only true family I ever had."

A searing pain ripped through her heart. "This can't be," she whispered.

William's face turned red with anger. "This is preposterous! I treated that bastard as if he were my father."

"Is that all there is to the will, Mr. Moore?" Jessica kept her voice calm, refusing to let them know how upset she was.

Moore nodded his head. "Yes."

"So to get the money that is rightfully mine," William persisted, "I've got to marry her—the daughter of an immigrant and a serving wench."

Moore shrugged. "And produce an heir. But remember, the choice to marry is Miss Tierney's alone."

There was a soft knock on the door. Mr. Utley peeked inside the room. "Mr. Moore, Reverend Black is here and insists on performing the ceremony now. He's got a funeral to officiate in one hour."

Jessica jumped to her feet. "Do you mean a marriage ceremony?"

Moore sighed. "Your father requested I have a minister on hand, in case you were anxious to wed William."

"Anxious to marry William?" Jessica cried. "If not for him, I might have had a chance to know my father."

William stood. "Boarding school was exactly what you needed after twelve years with that uncultured mother of yours."

"Boarding school was a prison."

"Don't be dramatic."

"Dramatic! There was no place for me to go on holiday, no family to lean on when I was alone and scared."

"Simon had an empire to build," William said. "He didn't have time to entertain a silly young girl."

"I was his daughter."

"Birthed by an uncultured wench who could barely read or write."

Moore cleared his throat. "Jessica, you don't have to marry William, though you will be penniless if you don't."

Jessica's heart pounded in her chest. The walls closed in around her. "I won't be trapped in a loveless marriage like my mother was. I swore I'd never live that way. Tell the minister his services won't be needed today."

William shook his head. "Don't send him away just yet, Moore. Miss Tierney and I need a moment to talk first."

Moore hesitated. "Certainly." He followed his secretary out of the room and closed the door.

William retrieved a cigar from a silver case on the attorney's desk. "Let's think this through very carefully, Miss Tierney."

"There's nothing to think about," she said. "I'm not marrying you."

William drew the cigar under his nose, savoring the rich tobacco aroma, then bit the tip off and spit it into a large brass spittoon next to the desk. "I can't say I like the circumstances, either, but for the Tierney millions, I'd send my own mother to hell."

"The orphans are welcome to it."

He held the match to the end of the cigar until smoke swirled around his head. "The world can be a very cruel place for a woman alone."

"I'll get by."

"Doing what?"

"I will find a way to survive."

He leaned closer until mere inches separated their faces. "I'm not going to let all that money slip through my hands."

"It already has."

He stubbed out the cigar in a marble ashtray on the desk. "I'm not going to let you walk out of here and take my fortune with you."

"You can't keep me here."

William walked over to the door, turned the key already in the lock and tucked it in his pocket. He faced her. "We will be married by sundown."

"No."

William unbuttoned his jacked and slipped it off. "Your father enjoyed taunting me with his money. I played his foolish little games because I knew there'd be a generous reward if I were patient." He laid his jacket neatly on a chair. "But he couldn't resist one last insult."

Panic swelled in Jessica. "What are you doing?"

He took off his vest. "Collecting what's mine."

"Mr. Moore, Mr. Utley, come in here this instant," she screamed.

Nothing happened.

William smiled. "Mr. Moore doesn't want Simon's money going to those orphans any more than I do." Laughing, he grabbed her by the arm.

She screamed and tried to twist free. "Let go of me."

Still no one came.

"See, my dear? There is only you and me now." William crushed his lips to hers.

Suddenly, anger replaced fear. Her father had stolen her childhood, but William wasn't going to take her future.

Frantically, her fingers skidded over Moore's desk until she touched cold marble. The ashtray. She wrapped her fingers around it, lifted it and slammed it into his head.

William's eyes rolled back and he collapsed onto the thick carpet. He lay motionless.

Jessica's body trembled as she stared at him.

William groaned. His fingers twitched. For an instant, she stood perfectly still, watching him until his body stilled again.

What was she going to do? Mr. Moore couldn't be trusted, she didn't know anybody in town and she was penniless.

She had to get out of Sacramento.

Jessica drew in a steadying breath and picked up William's jacket. As she jabbed her hand into the breast pocket and pulled out the key, her fingers brushed against smooth leather. His wallet. She removed it and snapped it open. Her fingers shook as she fanned her thumb over five rumpled dollar bills.

"No wonder you're so desperate to marry me," she muttered.

Jessica tossed the wallet on the floor next to his unconscious body and tucked the money into her reticule. Her gaze darted around the room. There were no other doors, only four windows. Three faced the street, one the side alley.

Dizzy with fear, she ran to the last one, shoved it open and sat on the windowsill. A narrow laneway separated Moore's office from the neighboring building. There was a five-foot drop from the ledge to the ground.

"Thanks a lot, Father," she mumbled.

Jessica swung her legs over the sill and jumped down. She stumbled and fell hard against the wall of the other building. Her shoulder ached from the blow, but she ran down the alleyway to the gate facing the street. She paused and straightened her hat, then opened the gate and walked to her carriage, as if exiting by way of the alley were the most natural thing in the world. She climbed inside. "Take me to Union Pacific Station."

"Anything you say, miss," the driver answered.

The carriage lurched forward, and she sat back against the cushions. Her heart thundered in her chest and several times she glanced out the window to make sure she wasn't being followed.

Finally, the cab arrived at the train station. She didn't wait for the driver, but climbed out of the carriage. She paid him, and without a word hurried inside.

Dozens of people swarmed around the train standing at the station platform. Mothers held crying babies; a man with a wooden leg sold bruised apples; several men dressed in business suits read papers.

With all the poise Miss Madeline had drilled into her, Jessica slowed her pace. She ignored everyone as she pushed her way forward and marched to the ticket master's office.

Behind the ticket window, a short, barrel-chested man peered over wire-rimmed glasses, watching her approach. The man's hair was slicked back from his face, accentuating bulging eyes and a thick mustache.

Jessica looked through the bars of the window into his small office. "When is the train scheduled to leave?"

"Nine o'clock this morning."

She looked at the clock behind him. "That was three hours ago."

"You asked me when it was scheduled to leave, not when it was gonna leave."

Every nerve in Jessica's body tingled with fatigue and irritation. Thirty minutes had passed since she'd left Mr. Moore's office. Had William Perry awakened and sounded the alarm? Her nerves raw, she resisted the urge to grab the ticket master by the lapels and shake him. "When do you think it's going to leave?"

"Hard to say. It all depends."

"On what?"

"A passenger. We're holding the train for a passenger."

"You're holding a whole train for one person?"

"Yep."

"When's the next train leaving?"

"Tomorrow morning."

Her heart sank. "I must leave today!"

"Nothing I can do."

Jessica forced a smile, willing herself to remain calm. *Never whine. Don't criticize. Always compliment.* Miss Madeline's words washed over her. "I can imagine your job is very difficult. There must be so many angry passengers here today."

"Lady, you don't know the half of it."

"Tell me, who is the person holding up this train? Is he very important?"

The ticket master shook his head. "Ain't a *he,* it's a *she*—a lamebrained schoolteacher named Emma Grimes."

"A schoolteacher! That's insane."

"Don't I know it. But when Ross McCain says hold the train, I hold it."

"Who's Ross McCain?"

"A man you don't want to challenge."

If only she were Emma Grimes, Jessica thought. If only…

At first, she dismissed the notion. She couldn't possibly take another woman's place. It was outlandish. Absurd!

She couldn't stay in Sacramento until tomorrow, either. She thought about William. Likely he was awake now and pounding on Moore's office door, demanding to be released, since she had taken the key. Time was running out for Jessica, her options dissolving.

The idea of impersonating a schoolteacher no longer seemed so outlandish. She could become Emma Grimes for a day—just long enough to get out of California. Then she'd travel to Chicago or Saint Louis and disappear.

The ticket master adjusted his glasses. "So you wanna buy a ticket or not?"

"I'll be back in the morning to buy one."

"Suit yourself."

Jessica walked toward the street, but instead of leaving, waited until two businessmen approached the ticket master's window and distracted him.

Clutching her reticule, she hurried through the crowd. She passed the great iron engine with its cow guard and solitary reflecting lamp, then a baggage car, two freight cars loaded with peaches and grapes, a smoking car and four passenger cars. Finally she saw McCain's car.

The black coach, with polished brass around the windows and doors, was longer than the rest. It seemed to stand alone, connected, yet apart.

Jessica's heart raced as she approached a short man standing by the car. His cap was pushed back on his head and he seemed tired. "Excuse me, is this Ross McCain's car?" she asked.

The conductor looked at her. Hope glimmered in his eyes. "May I help you, miss?"

She smoothed her hands over her skirt. "I understand you're holding the train for me." *Please believe me. Please believe me.* Her mouth went dry. "I'm Emma Grimes."

The conductor's mouth split into a wide grin. "Miss Grimes! I can't tell you how happy I am to see you. I'd nearly given up hope that you were coming. We've just finished firing up the engine and were fixing to leave.'' He turned and called over his shoulder to another conductor, ''Hey, Charlie, did you hear that? Emma Grimes is here! Let's get this train moving.''

One passenger shouted to the conductor, ''Is she the one we've been waiting for?''

''Yep,'' the uniformed man replied.

''It's about time you got here, lady. Remind me to buy you a watch,'' the stranger said, retreating back into his car.

Jessica realized several people had poked their heads out of passenger-car windows to stare at her. She turned away on the chance someone would recognize her.

''I'm sorry I was delayed,'' Jessica said to the conductor. ''My bag was stolen. I've lost everything I own.''

''Not to worry. My name is Ralph Thomas. I work for Mr. McCain, and it's my job to see that you get to Cheyenne.''

She arched an eyebrow. ''Cheyenne, Wyoming?''

The conductor helped her climb the three steps to the small platform at the rear of McCain's coach. He opened the door. ''That's right,'' he said.

''How long does it take to get to Cheyenne?''

''Nine days if our luck holds.''

The thought of traveling to such wild, untamed country made her cringe. ''Oh.''

''I'm just glad you're here now. I didn't want to tell Mr. McCain we didn't have you. He's not the sorta man you want to cross.''

Jessica paused. "Is Mr. McCain here?"

"Oh, no, ma'am. He's meeting you in Cheyenne. From there, he'll escort you to Prosperity, Colorado."

Her courage faltered, and then the image of William Perry flashed in her mind. She swept through the doorway into the car.

The morning sun filtered through the soot-covered windows, revealing a plush blue carpet and matching gold-trimmed curtains. A sturdy table, covered in white linen and flanked by two heavy upholstered chairs, butted against the center window. In the far corner, a woodstove burned brightly near a curtained sleeping berth. The stale smell of cigar smoke clung to the thick velvet draperies and immediately conjured images of Moore's office and William.

"Get yourself settled, miss," the conductor said. "I gotta get this train moving. I'll be back before you know it with your lunch. Mr. McCain told me to take extra good care of you. He's determined to get you to Cheyenne."

Without waiting for her response, he left, slamming the door behind him.

Jessica looked at the plush surroundings. She thought about the nine-day trek ahead of her and the man in Wyoming she didn't want to face. What would he do when he found out she wasn't Emma Grimes?

Suddenly, the train jerked forward, the wheels screeched and began to roll. She stumbled over to the window and pushed back the brocade curtain. She collapsed into one of the chairs by the table as the train slowly lumbered past the platform and away from the station.

The reality of her situation struck home, and for a moment, she couldn't breathe.

Dear God, what had she done?

Chapter Two

The Union Pacific thundered into the small frontier town nine days later at precisely ten o'clock in the morning.

Black smoke billowed from the stack as the train came to a halt, brakes squealing. Jessica braced her legs to steady herself as she stood on the platform at the rear of McCain's car, staring at endless miles of desert and gray sagebrush dotted with a few weathered frame houses and shanties. A party of Indians wearing paint and armed with rifles watched the train as five rough-looking cattlemen drove their long-horned steers past a covered wagon pulled by six oxen. There wasn't a green bush or a flower garden in sight.

Don't let this be Cheyenne, Wyoming. Jessica gripped the railing.

The conductor leaned out the side door and shouted, "Cheyenne, Wyoming!"

She groaned. For nine days she'd worried about where she was going and the man waiting for her. Each time the train stopped to take on water and passengers, she'd considered getting off, but each time she'd been so overwhelmed by the desolate terrain, she'd lost her nerve.

So she'd paced the car endlessly, started but never finished a half-dozen books, and played solitaire until she couldn't look at a deck of cards any longer.

When the train had crossed through the icy Sierras, she'd pinned her hopes on Cheyenne. Certain the town had something to offer, she'd decided to leave the train before McCain arrived. In Cheyenne she'd find a job, a place to stay and she'd live quietly until she decided where to go next.

At least that had been the plan.

"I pray you are a reasonable man, Mr. McCain," Jessica whispered.

Two large tumbleweeds blew past the train, as two drunken cowboys stumbled down the main street toward the tracks. When they were twenty paces from the train, they looked up at her. For a moment they stared in stunned silence.

Finally, the cowboy with a bushy black beard straightened his shoulders and walked up to the train. He took off his hat and smiled, revealing broken, yellowed teeth. "Good morning to you, ma'am."

A crowd began to gather around him as he stared up at her. Jessica wanted to retreat to the safety of the car but didn't want to appear rude. "Sir."

"You're just about the prettiest little thing I ever did see," Bushy Face said.

The other cowboy, slim as a fence post, stumbled through the onlookers up to his companion's side.

"Why, she looks like an angel from heaven. I wonder if she's real."

He started to climb onto the train until Bushy Face grabbed him by the belt buckle and pulled him to the ground. "If anybody's gonna be touching the angel, it's gonna be me. I saw her first."

His friend raised his fists. "I'm willing to fight you for her."

Jessica panicked and scanned the area for help. Her gaze locked onto a solitary man standing near the tracks. The man was powerfully built and quite tall. He wore black work pants, a wide-brimmed hat shadowing his eyes, and a gray range coat that reached to his ankles. Shoulder-length black hair tied back at the nape of his neck emphasized the dark stubble blanketing his jaw.

As if sensing her appraisal, he tilted his head and returned her gaze. Without taking his eyes off her, he strode toward her, his long legs quickly eating up the distance.

Jessica drew back a step. This time the urge to retreat into the safety of the car nearly overwhelmed her. The crowd parted for the man.

He stopped in front of the platform. As the slender cowboy drew back his fist, the stranger shoved him to the ground. "Get away from the car."

Bushy Face stepped back instantly. "We meant no harm. We was just fooling around."

"Do it somewhere else," the stranger said.

"Anything you say," Slim said as he scrambled to his feet.

The stranger watched as the cowboys hurried down the street, and then he turned toward Jessica.

She tensed. "Thank you."

"Who the devil are you?"

She raised her chin to compensate for the butterflies in her stomach. "Emma Grimes," she said quickly.

He tilted his head back, revealing eyes the color of finely cut emeralds—eyes that seemed to look right inside her. Gooseflesh puckered the skin on her arms as he studied every inch of her. His expression darkened and grew angry, but he said nothing. The lingering silence seemed to rake her nerves.

"May I help you?" she managed to murmur.

He stared at her a moment longer. "You shouldn't be outside. It's too dangerous."

"I can take care of myself." The words sounded foolish, ridiculously inadequate.

"Go back inside the train car."

"What gives you the right to tell me what to do?"

"I'm your employer. Ross McCain." Those dangerous, glittering eyes once again assessed her.

Jessica's knees grew weak. She summoned the courage to hold out her hand. "It's a pleasure to meet you."

He ignored it. "I wish I could say the same."

His words sparked her anger, but she decided to obey him. She opened the car door and stepped inside, relieved to be free of his dark scrutiny. Her hands trembled as she paced back and forth.

According to Ralph Thomas, McCain had been a captain in the Confederate army, then, after the war, had moved west. He'd hit upon a silver strike and had parlayed his find into one of the largest mining operations in Colorado.

McCain was a self-made man, hard and uncompromising, with little patience for fools and liars, Mr. Thomas had said. "Ain't no man better to be watching your back," the conductor had told her. "And no man worse to cross."

If she were smart, she'd tell McCain the truth the instant he stepped into the car. "I'm not Emma Grimes," she said, testing the words out loud. "But I can explain." She chuckled nervously. "It's rather humorous if you think about how I got into this situation."

The car door opened. Jessica started and turned. McCain slammed the door behind him. He removed his hat and coat and tossed both in a dusty heap on a nearby settee. Despite the patches on his jacket sleeves, his presence spoke of power.

He pulled off his worn leather gloves finger by finger. Tossing the gloves into his hat, he strode past her to the table in the center of the coach, reached for a small hand bell and rang it. Immediately, Mr. Thomas entered through the opposite door.

"Bring us a pot of coffee, an inkwell and a pen," McCain said. "And signal the engineer to uncouple this car. As soon as we're attached to the Denver Pacific, I want the train to leave."

"Surely, Mr. McCain," the man responded hastily.

McCain brushed a cinder from Jessica's shoulder. "I hope you've got plainer dresses than this."

Her mouth dry, she stared up at him. "Actually, I don't. My bag was stolen before I boarded the train."

He shook his head. "It's probably for the best.

You look like the type of woman who doesn't own anything practical.''

She ignored the comment. "How long will it be before we leave?''

"Twenty minutes.''

"So soon?''

"We're already two days behind schedule, and I'm anxious to get home.''

Before she could press McCain for details, Mr. Thomas returned carrying a tray loaded with coffee, cream and sugar, an inkwell and a pen. He set the tray on the table. "Will there be anything else, Mr. McCain?''

Out of habit, Jessica smiled at him and said, "No, thank you.''

The conductor hesitated. "I take my orders from Mr. McCain, Miss Grimes.''

Jessica realized her blunder. Her cheeks burned with embarrassment as McCain raised an eyebrow. "I'm sorry, Mr. McCain, I've spoken out of turn.''

A hint of a smile touched his lips. "That'll do, Ralph, thanks.''

Jessica sat at the table, eager to hide behind the task of serving coffee. She picked up the porcelain pot and poured the first cup. "How do you take your coffee, Mr. McCain?''

"Black.''

She set the cup and saucer down on the table for him. Pouring herself a cup, she settled back in her chair. She forced herself to relax. "How long will it take for us to get to our destination?''

"Five hours.''

She shifted uncomfortably. "I must say, this has

been a real adventure for me." *Tell him the truth! Tell him!*

"That so?"

She took a sip of coffee. It tasted bitter. "This is a lovely car, Mr. McCain."

McCain didn't respond as he took the seat across from her. "It serves a purpose."

"Do you travel in the car to Sacramento often?" she said, hoping to start a conversation.

"Several times a year."

"I was surprised you sent a whole car for me. That seems rather extravagant."

"Just protecting my investment." Leaning back, he propped his fingers together. His eyes pierced her. "You don't look like a schoolteacher."

Her cup rattled in its saucer, forcing her to put both down on the table.

I can explain! The words stuck in her throat.

Mentally, she counted to ten. Not yet, she reasoned. Not until she was sure he wouldn't send her back to Sacramento and William. She'd do anything to remain free.

She cleared her throat. "What does a teacher look like?"

The creases around his eyes deepened and a hint of a smile teased his lips, but the smile did nothing to soften the hard planes of his face. "Not like you."

She interlocked her fingers around the cup. "Why's that?"

He stared at her. "You look and sound like you belong in one of those fancy, big-city drawing rooms."

"I probably do," she murmured.

He frowned.

"But that doesn't mean I'm not committed to this job," she added quickly. Inwardly, she groaned at the lie. She was getting in too deep.

"Your *commitment* doesn't bother me."

"What then?" Jessica had difficulty meeting his gaze. Instead, she stared at his long tapered fingers as he traced the rim of his cup.

"In a big city you turn heads. In a small town like Prosperity, you'll cause a riot. There are few single women in the territory, and there aren't any in Prosperity over sixteen. Once the men in town get a good look at you, I'll have to contend with more than a few skirmishes."

"I have no interest in marriage," she said honestly. "I shall not be encouraging the men's attentions."

"You're breathing. That's encouragement enough."

"You're overestimating my appeal, Mr. Mc-Cain." Jessica sat as if she were balancing a book on her head.

"Damn, I wish you were a dried-up old prune," he said gruffly. He rubbed the stubble on his chin. "When the men get a good look at you, they'll be hanging around my house like lovesick pups."

"Your house? I'm staying with you?" She felt a shiver of dread.

"Yes. The other two teachers boarded with families in town, and each was married within two weeks. I decided that this time the teacher would live with me so I could keep an eye on her. Peg has already seen that your room has been aired and cleaned.''

''Is Peg your wife?'' she said hopefully.

''My housekeeper. She looks after me and my son, Patrick.''

''I see. Will I meet your wife when we arrive?''

''I don't have a wife.''

''Oh.''

''I'll put you on notice now, Miss Emma Grimes. I'll be damned before another teacher slips between my fingers. You'll complete your two-year contract.''

''Two-year contract?''

''It's what we agreed to.''

The train whistle blew. The car jerked as it was uncoupled from the train.

McCain pulled a folded piece of paper out of his breast pocket, flattened it on the table and pushed it toward her. He held the pen out to her. ''It needs your signature.''

A few lies were one thing, but signing a contract was altogether another matter. ''Why do I need a contract?''

''I want your signature as a bond.''

Jessica hesitated. ''I don't know....''

''If you're unwilling to sign the contract, Miss Grimes, we'll part ways now.'' McCain sat like a tightly coiled spring.

Tell him the truth!

A thousand miles from civilization, with only five dollars to her name, she didn't have many options. The truth was on the tip of her tongue.

''Are you signing or not?'' His eyes burned into her.

''It's just that I'm not accustomed to contracts,'' she hedged.

Tell him! Tell him!

''Decide now, Miss Grimes.''

The sound of gunfire wrenched Jessica from her thoughts. She stared out the window. The two cowboys who'd fought over her earlier stood by the tracks, staring at each other with the tips of their guns smoking.

Through the open window she heard Bushy Face say, ''That'll teach you to hide an ace up your sleeve.''

''Oh, yeah? Well, for your information—'' Slim dropped to his knees, then fell facedown in the dirt.

Bushy Face put his gun in his holster. ''Rot in hell, thief.''

An old woman with gray straw for hair ran up to Slim, kicked him twice, and when he didn't move, took his gun and boots. Other people swarmed around the dead man, taking what they wanted, until he was left with only his long underwear.

Jessica reached across the table to take the pen from McCain. Their fingers touched, sending an unexpected jolt through her arm. She cleared her throat. ''Where do I sign?''

McCain paused before he released the pen. He pointed to the line at the bottom of the paper. She stared at the blank line. Guilt churned inside her. She'd never broken a promise before.

She'd never been this desperate before.

She dipped the pen in the inkwell. This was a

matter of survival. The contract didn't matter, and as soon as she got her bearings, she'd move on to another town. A drop of ink slid off the end of the pen onto the paper.

As Jessica pressed the tip of the pen to the paper, her mind went blank. McCain had her so rattled, she didn't know what name to sign. What was Miss Grimes's first name? Emma? Emily? She looked up at McCain and smiled. Quickly, she wrote the name Emily Grimes.

She set the pen down and pushed the paper toward him. "Satisfied?"

The tightness in McCain's jaw relaxed a fraction. "Why didn't you read it?"

"It's as we discussed in our letters, isn't it?" she said quickly.

"Yes."

"Then I see no problem."

Gingerly, he picked up the paper and studied the signature. He blew on the wet ink until it dried, then carefully folded the paper and tucked it in the breast pocket of his jacket. "I'd have thought a woman with as much schooling as you would have sense enough to read a contract before she signed it."

"I'm a trusting soul."

"Then you're a fool."

Her face flushed, hot with indignation. Common sense told her to be quiet. "I didn't travel a thousand miles to be insulted, Mr. McCain."

"You'd better learn not to be so trusting, Miss Grimes, or you'll never make it out here."

"If you think I'm so unsuitable for the job, then put me off at the next stop." The words were out before she thought. Her breath caught. Was she insane? McCain was not the type of man to take ultimatums lightly.

Laughter flashed in his eyes. "You're green, but you'll learn. Besides, for better or worse, you're stuck with me."

"I don't know if I like the sound of that."

"I'm a good man to have in your corner, Miss Grimes. In fact, I'm going to see to it that you learn to get by out here."

"Surely it can't be that bad? After all, I've done all right so far."

"You've been under my protection since you left Sacramento. My men were under orders to watch over you at all costs. If I turned you loose in Cheyenne, you'd not last the night. Colorado's not any different than Wyoming. It's full of nasty surprises."

"Nasty surprises?"

"Indians, drought, winters so cold you'd gladly go to hell to get warm, and men who'd sell their soul to have a woman like you."

Jessica took several deep breaths. "If you're trying to scare me, it's working."

He chuckled. "Look at it this way—you've got skills few people on the frontier have."

"I do?"

"You can read and write."

"Oh, that."

He leaned back in his chair and stretched out his long legs. "You teach my son and the other children in Prosperity to read, and I'll turn you into a true frontier woman."

"I don't want to be a frontier woman. I like myself just the way I am."

"Colorado's hard country. Nobody leaves it untouched."

His presence enveloped her, overwhelmed her. Fearing her hands would begin to tremble again, she put her cup and saucer back down on the table.

"Tell me about yourself," he said, changing the course of the conversation.

Her color faded a fraction. "Didn't my letters tell you what you needed to know?"

"I judge people best when I hear them speak, watch how they handle themselves."

"Would you like me to tell you more about my studies? I could tell you the books I've—"

"What happened to your family? You never mentioned them in your letters."

Jessica could feel McCain studying her. She was thankful he didn't seem to know a lot about Emma Grimes. She decided she'd tell the truth whenever possible, hoping it would make the lies more believable. "My mother was killed in a carriage accident ten years ago. My father saw to my upbringing."

"What kind of a man allows a woman to venture out into such wild country?"

"My father is dead."

"I'm sorry for your loss," he said automatically. "What was his name? I have a good many contacts in the Sacramento area."

Jessica stopped. She'd said much more than she'd intended. Anxious to turn the tables, she asked, "Were you born in Colorado, Mr. McCain?"

He smiled, as if sensing her ploy. "I'm a Virginian by birth. I moved west after the war."

"You mentioned you had a son, Patrick. How old is he?"

"Eight."

"Where is his mother?"

"Caroline died of lung fever this past spring."

Anger dripped from each of his words. Jessica had struck a chord. Good. Keeping him off balance kept attention off of her. "That must be hard on the boy."

McCain refilled his cup. "He's adjusting."

"That doesn't tell me very much."

McCain's jaw tensed. "That's all you need to know. I want you to concentrate on getting the school up and running so Patrick and the other children get a decent education."

"You put a lot of stock in a good education."

McCain sat back in his chair. "A man who can't read or write is at the mercy of those who can. I don't want that for Patrick or any child in my town."

"How many children are there?"

"Twelve in all."

Twelve children. The railroad car rocked softly as another train coupled onto it. The wheels started to roll forward.

The full impact of what she'd done hit Jessica. Soon twelve children and an entire town would be drawn into her web of lies. The realization made her uneasy and restless.

"You're going to make a big difference in their lives," McCain said.

How could she make a difference in anyone's life? She'd spent the last ten years in an exclusive boarding school, learning to serve tea, paint watercolors and host parties. She had nothing to give these children.

She couldn't go through with this!

She drew in a deep breath. She had to tell him the truth or convince McCain to release her from her contract. "Mr. McCain, I'm worried."

He raised an eyebrow. "About what?"

"I don't think I'm the right person for this job."

"Why not?"

She had to walk a fine line between truth and fiction. "I have a confession to make."

"I don't like the sound of this," he said quietly.

She wrung her hands together and paced back and forth. "It's not as bad as you might think. It's just that I exaggerated my qualifications."

"You can read and write."

"Yes, of course."

"Then you'll work out just fine."

"Even you agree," she rushed to say, "I am really not right for this job. I'm green. A fool, really. I would set a bad example for the children."

"You're staying." His voice was low, deadly.

"But you just said I don't belong here."

"You'll learn to belong."

"But I'm so different from the people out here."

"Different? Or better? I saw the expression on your face when you were standing on the platform looking at those people in Cheyenne."

Shocked at the conclusion he'd drawn, she hurried to say, "That's not it at all. I'm not better. I'm different. The problem isn't them. It's me."

McCain uncoiled himself from his chair. He crossed the room toward her. He paused by the window and lifted one of the tassels on the curtain.

"Prosperity doesn't have a lot to offer, Miss Grimes, but it does have a jailhouse, which is where you'll spend the next two years if you back out on me now."

"What?"

"Break your contract, and when we arrive in Prosperity, I'll march you straight down to the sheriff's office and have him lock you up."

"You can't do that!"

"Lady, I built that town. Everybody in Prosperity, including the sheriff, depends on the McCain mines for their livelihood. So you can be damn sure no one will question me if I want you locked up."

"You cannot intimidate me with threats, Mr. McCain."

He smiled. "I don't threaten. I promise."

"Why can't you just find another teacher who's more suited for the job?"

"It took me two months to find you. In another two months, the snows will make the rails impassable until spring. If you leave now, the children will lose an entire year in the classroom."

Again, her life slipped from her control and there was nothing she could do to stop it. "Perhaps I could recommend someone. I know several ladies—"

"I've got a mine to run and a boy to raise. You signed the contract. I need a teacher. End of story."

"You can't make me stay in Prosperity."

"Try me."

"You'll be keeping me there against my will."

"I'll learn to live with it."

Jessica clenched her fists. She'd escaped William, but she sensed escaping McCain would be much more difficult.

"What's it going to be? Jail or the schoolhouse?"

"You're making a mistake."

"I've made them before. What's your answer?"

She'd traded one prison for another. "The schoolhouse."

He smiled. "Good choice."

Escape.

By three o'clock in the afternoon, when the train arrived in the small town of Greeley, Colorado, escape was more than a fleeting idea to Jessica. As soon as they stopped, McCain got off to check on a horse he'd bought in Cheyenne, and she knew her one chance to flee had arrived.

Jessica watched McCain as he stopped to speak to Mr. Thomas. When he stepped between the cars and out of sight, she hurried to the door and opened it.

A small town, Greeley was made up of frame houses surrounded by green fields. Thanks to an earlier conversation she'd had with McCain, she also knew the town was only twenty-five miles from Fort Collins—an army outpost, and a train stop on the Colorado Central, which linked Denver to Cheyenne and the Union Pacific by rail line.

The idea of staying in Greeley by herself left her

breathless with fear, but she prayed the town was more civilized than Cheyenne. She was running out of time and wasn't in a position to be too choosy. The next stop on the rail line was La Salle, and the next Prosperity, and she had no intention of going to jail or spending the next two years in Prosperity, Colorado.

Jessica glanced from side to side. No one was in sight. She drew in a deep breath and climbed down the three steps to the ground. The air was hot and the dust by the tracks deep, coating her fine leather shoes with a brown film.

She shielded her eyes against the sun. Ahead she saw a small, rough-looking tavern. It seemed a good place to hide and make arrangements for the trip to Fort Collins.

She'd taken three steps when McCain said, "Out for a stroll, Miss Grimes?"

Jessica whirled around. He stood between two rail cars. His arms were folded across his chest, his hat pulled forward, shadowing his unflinching gaze.

She fought an impulse to run, knowing he'd overtake her in seconds. She shrugged. "I was curious about the town."

He captured her arm. "Then why don't I give you a tour?"

She tried to squirm free of his grasp, but could not. "That's really not necessary."

"I think it is." He brushed dust from her shoulder. "You may not realize it yet, Miss Grimes, but you need me just as much as I need you."

"I hardly think—"

"How long do you think you'd last in Greeley? A day? A week?"

She stuck out her chin. "I'm tougher than I look."

"Let's see about that."

Her escape plans ruined, she wanted nothing more to do with the town. "A tour isn't necessary."

"I disagree."

He walked her across the dirt street toward the rustic, two-story tavern. Three men in work clothes piled out the front door as they approached. Each man stopped and stared at Jessica with hard, hungry eyes. She swallowed but held her head high.

One man stepped forward.

McCain's hand slid to his gun. "Don't."

The stranger stared at McCain. Seconds ticked by until finally the stranger dropped his gaze and walked away with his companions.

McCain watched the men walk down the street. Only when he seemed satisfied they were no longer a threat did he speak. "How well do you think you'd have handled those three?"

She swallowed her nausea. "I would have managed somehow."

McCain shook his head. "Sure you would. Let's have a look inside."

When Jessica hesitated, he nudged her over the threshold. The tavern was empty, dark, and the ceiling low. The room was quiet, but what impressed Jessica most was the pungent smell. She pressed her hand to her nose.

McCain drew in a deep breath. "Smells like we're in time for dinner."

Jessica coughed. "You're joking."

"I don't have a sense of humor."

He led her to a small table in a dark corner. McCain held a chair out for Jessica, and reluctantly, she accepted it. Keeping his back to the wall, he took the seat across from her. A half-dozen dark flies swarmed around the table, which was sticky with grease.

Jessica folded her hands in her lap, trying her best to touch as little as possible. "I'm not very hungry, Mr. McCain."

He ignored her and raised his hand, catching the attention of a heavy woman with graying hair. The woman came up to their table.

"What's for supper?" McCain asked.

"Stew."

McCain reached in his pocket, dug out a dollar and slapped it down on the table. "We'll take two bowls and two mugs of coffee."

The woman left, leaving them to wait in silence for their food. Jessica sat erect. McCain lounged back in his chair, stretching out his long legs in front of him.

"This is one of the best places around," McCain said casually.

"The best? I hardly think this is the best Colorado has to offer."

"Choices are few in towns like this."

The innkeeper returned within minutes, her heavy feet shuffling over the wood floor. She carried a tray laden with two bowls of beef stew, half a loaf of bread and a crock of butter that had turned to oil.

When the woman set the bowls on the table, Jessica realized the dish's chief ingredient was flies.

Unable to stand the tavern a moment longer, she stood abruptly and ran outside. McCain was right on her heels when she burst through the front door into the daylight.

Jessica drew in several cleansing breaths. The air had never smelled sweeter. She reached in her reticule, pulled out a delicate lace handkerchief and dabbed the sweat from her forehead.

McCain smiled. "Had enough?"

"That place was vile."

"That's what it's like out here, Miss Grimes. How about we stroll down the center street and have a look at some of the other buildings? There's a mercantile in town."

"No, thank you." She glanced up at McCain's railroad car, longing for its plush, clean interior.

McCain followed her line of sight. "Prosperity's a good deal better than Greeley. My home is clean, and I can guarantee there won't be bugs in your mattress."

"How comforting."

He laid his hands on her shoulders and turned her to face him. His gaze seemed to soak in every detail about her—the lock of hair that had fallen over her forehead, the beads of sweat on her brow, her flushed cheeks. "Don't try to run away again."

"I wasn't trying—"

"I have a short fuse when it comes to liars, Miss Grimes."

She fell silent, overcome by McCain's dark presence.

"Do I have your word you won't try to run away?"

What choice did she have? William Perry had seen to it she couldn't go back to Sacramento, and Colorado's harsh conditions prevented her from traveling alone.

She sighed. "You have my word."

His face softened. "Admit it, Miss Grimes," he said gently, "you do need me as much as I need you."

She stared up at him in silence. There was no reason to argue with him. She did need him.

For now.

Chapter Three

The sun hung low over the Rockies as Jessica stared out of the train window at the crowd of people gathered by the tracks. By the look of it, the entire town of Prosperity had turned out to see the new teacher. Her! She closed her eyes and stifled a groan.

McCain stood behind her. She sensed he was staring. She'd hoped her arrival would be a quiet one and there'd be time to think of a way out of this predicament. She'd never counted on meeting the townspeople so soon or dreamed that her lie would grow so big.

She opened her eyes and took a second look. Prosperity had no train station, only a small shack that served as the ticket office. A mismatched collection of old and new buildings ran alongside wooden boardwalks that flanked the town's only street.

The townswomen wore dresses and sunbonnets made of homespun calico, and most had at least one child in tow. The men wore roughly woven shirts, work pants and scuffed leather boots. The lowest servants in her father's house had dressed better than these people. Yet every man, woman and child grinned with excitement.

The children stood off to the side. Ranging in age from four to sixteen, they were gathered behind a rough, hand-painted sign that read Welcum Techer.

With shame she realized she'd have crossed the street to avoid any one of them if they had approached her in Sacramento. The full weight of her lie pressed against her chest. These people deserved a real teacher, not a fraud and imposter.

Confess now, before it's too late.

"You'll find the people warm and friendly here." McCain's raspy voice shattered the silence.

He was so close, his nearness rattled her senses and made her heart race.

"They all look so eager," she whispered.

"You're going to make a big difference in their lives."

She let the curtain slip from her fingers. How could she make a difference in these people's lives? She didn't have any skills. She'd been trained to be a society wife.

McCain took hold of her elbow and led her out of the car. "Let's meet your neighbors."

Jessica stumbled as she hurried to keep pace with him. An unladylike oath sprang to mind as he pulled her out onto the platform. The instant they emerged, a hush fell over the crowd. Every fiber in her body demanded she run. Only McCain's firm hold on her arm kept her steady. Oddly, he had become a lifeline of sorts.

The women whispered comments to each other,

while the men stared at her, dumbstruck. An army of butterflies fluttered in Jessica's stomach.

"Don't disappoint me, Miss Grimes," McCain whispered as he led her toward the crowd.

Before she could respond, he left her side and climbed down the stairs. He turned, wrapped his long fingers around her narrow waist and easily lifted her from the car. Their gazes locked for an instant as he lowered her to the ground. "Smile," he added, then turned toward the crowd and said, "Folks, I'd like you to meet Prosperity's new teacher, Miss Emma Grimes."

An old man well past his sixtieth year shouted, "She don't look like a teacher. You sure you got the right woman, Mr. McCain?"

McCain scowled. "Yes, Jed."

Jed's white, prickly mustache twitched from side to side as he looked Jessica up and down. "Why'd you have to go and hire a pretty teacher? You're never gonna keep her in the schoolhouse."

McCain pushed the brim of his hat back with his index finger. "We menfolk agreed that no one would court the new teacher for the next two years. Besides, she's signed a contract. Isn't that right, Miss Grimes?"

Jessica's face flushed with anger. He was treating her like an indentured servant.

When she didn't answer, McCain slowly tightened his fingers around her forearm. Anger flashed in his eyes, warning her to concede this small battle of wills. Finally, she relented and said, "Yes."

Jed shook his head. "Ain't much for words, is she?"

"She's tired and anxious to get home," McCain answered.

"Looks like she's gonna be sick."

"Nothing a good night's sleep won't fix."

"I dunno, McCain. If I was a betting man, I'd say she'll quit her job by week's end."

McCain pulled Jessica closer to him. "That's a wager you'll lose."

A heavyset woman with bright red hair, warm brown eyes and three children peering from behind her skirts stepped forward. "Don't you listen to Jed, Miss Grimes. He's just as glad to have you here as the rest of us."

McCain nudged Jessica forward. "Sissy, I'd like you to meet Miss Grimes. Miss Grimes, I'd like to present Sissy and Earl Nevers, and their three children, Daniel, Owen and Elizabeth."

Sissy Nevers took Jessica's hand and shook it. "The pleasure is all mine. My husband and I just couldn't wait to meet you."

Earl, a tall man with a long black beard, wore dirty overalls. He cleared his throat. "Sissy's been on pins and needles since McCain left for Cheyenne."

His wife giggled and held both her hands up in surrender. "I'll admit it. I've barely slept a wink the last few nights. But it means so much to me and Earl that our children are going to learn how to read."

Sissy's eyes burned with the glow of expectancy. Jessica hated the thought of letting her down. "I don't know what to say, Mrs. Nevers."

"Just call me Sissy. That is, if you don't mind.

Everyone calls me Sissy.'' The woman burst into nervous giggles. ''Listen to me prattling on like a fool, but I declare, I can't help it. I'm just so glad to meet you.''

Jessica retreated a step, but McCain pressed his hand into the small of her back and stalled her progress. All she could manage in reply was, ''Thank you.''

Several other people stuck their hands out to her, introducing themselves as they pumped her hand up and down.

I want to leave!

Jessica straightened her shoulders. McCain's threats of prison be damned. She'd call his bluff. She'd tell the truth.

Before she could speak, Elizabeth, Sissy's three-year-old daughter, peeked out from around her mother's skirts and thrust out a fistful of asters. Except for her thick crop of black hair, the girl looked like a miniature version of her mother. ''Miss Grimes, these is for you.''

Frowning, Jessica stared down at the little girl. For a long, tense moment she said and did nothing as all eyes stared expectantly at her. She wanted to run from them all. This was a horrible mistake. She wasn't Emma Grimes, she was Jessica Tierney. But as the single pair of brown eyes looked up at her over the fading blue petals, she felt her chest tighten. She couldn't turn her back on this child. She knelt down, unmindful of the dirt, and extended her hand for the bundle.

''Thank you. They're lovely,'' she said softly.

Jessica stood, clutching the flowers. Everyone was

smiling at her. Even the hard edge around McCain's eyes had softened.

He cleared his throat. "It's getting late. Ready, Miss Grimes?"

Jessica glanced back at the train, then at McCain. "Yes."

"Then let's go home."

Home.

For ten years Jessica hadn't spoken the word. Its meaning held too much pain and loss. She crossed her arms.

"We'll be seeing you at the school tomorrow," Sissy said brightly. "Mr. McCain has given the miners the day off so they can spruce up the schoolhouse. We womenfolk decided to turn the day into a celebration and are having all kinds of food, games and music."

Sissy Nevers's genuine smile made Jessica feel miserable. She didn't want to like Sissy. She didn't want the woman to like her.

"There's gonna be sack races," Owen exclaimed.

Daniel, the oldest of Sissy's three children, puffed out his chest and stepped forward. "Mama's made four apple pies!"

"I don't want you to go to any trouble for me," Jessica said.

Sissy shook her head. "I just hope what we've planned is good enough."

"I'm sure it will be lovely."

The train whistle blew and Jessica looked over her shoulder. A half-dozen people climbed aboard. She'd give the last penny in her pocket to join them.

McCain again pressed his hand into the small of

her back. "Folks, we'll see you tomorrow at the party."

McCain guided Jessica down the wooden board-walk toward the end of town. Two old men sitting in front of the dry goods store pointed at Jessica and talked excitedly. Nearby a little boy chewing on an apple stared at her. In fact, quite a few people were staring. She clutched her parasol closer to her chest.

A tall, lanky man wearing a red wool shirt, gray trousers and black suspenders greeted them when they walked by Thompson's Livery. He removed his muddied gloves and extended his hand to McCain. His gaze flickered over Jessica before he straight-ened his shoulders and sucked in his gut. "It's good to have you back, Mr. McCain."

"It's good to be back. Let me introduce you to Emma Grimes."

"I ain't fit to be meeting no lady right now."

"Nonsense." McCain gently pushed her forward. "Miss Emma Grimes, I'd like you to meet Dave Thompson. He owns and operates the livery here in town. Miss Grimes is Prosperity's new school-teacher."

Dave Thompson rubbed his hand against his pant leg, then slowly extended it to Jessica. She didn't want to take it. Each new introduction pulled her deeper into the deception and further away from her own life.

Jessica drew a deep breath, accepted the man's grimy hand and nodded. "It's a pleasure."

Mr. Thompson blushed. "Pleasure's mine." He ducked his head, then released her hand. He quickly made excuses of more work and disappeared back into the livery.

"Looks like you've given the town something to talk about for the next few months," McCain said evenly.

"I wish I didn't stick out so much. I miss the crowds of a big city. They are so wonderfully impersonal."

"*Lonely* is a better word."

"I'm a big-city girl, Mr. McCain."

"Not for the next two years." McCain nodded down the street. "My home is at the end of town. It's not more than half a mile or so."

"Are you sure you want to keep me on? I know with certainty I'm going to be more trouble than I'm worth."

McCain stared down at her and for a moment said nothing. Beneath the intense look in his eyes, an exquisite ache blossomed inside of her, and for an instant every rational thought in her brain vanished.

"You're worth the trouble," he said.

His voice broke the spell.

"You don't know how truly useless I can be. My father said I wasn't good for anything."

"Everybody's good for something."

"Oh, not me. My teachers at school said they never met a lazier girl than me."

He took hold of her arm and led her down the wooden boardwalk toward the edge of town. "You always talk this much?"

"Yes, constantly, and especially when I'm nervous."

"Great."

They arrived at McCain's home within minutes. Jessica paused while McCain opened the gate of the unpainted picket fence that surrounded the brown yard.

A collection of ladders and sawhorses littered the front yard of the white frame house. The shingles on the roof were bright and unweathered as if they'd just been installed. The house was designed with a wraparound porch, two brick chimneys and floor-to-ceiling windows.

McCain set her bag on the front porch. "The house is nearly finished. I've had carpenters working on it night and day to see that it was finished before you got here."

"You've built a lovely house, Mr. McCain," she said.

Relief flickered in McCain's green eyes before he led her up the steps and opened the front door for her. She stepped past him into the foyer. He shrugged off his coat, hung it up on a peg next to twin ladder-back chairs. A single table hugged the west wall.

Jessica unpinned her hat and set it on the table.

"Where the devil have you been?" The question came from a woman barely four feet tall who'd emerged from a side door off the main hallway. She'd swept up her auburn hair into a tight topknot, accentuating her wrinkled features. She wore a blue wool dress, a gray apron smothered in white flour and men's work boots. "What happened to you? I expected you a couple of days ago," the woman barked.

"We were late leaving Cheyenne," McCain said.

The old woman nodded to Jessica. "Who's this? And where's the schoolteacher?"

"She is the schoolteacher," McCain said. He hung his hat next to his coat.

"You sure you hired the right woman? She don't look like a schoolteacher."

McCain glanced down at Jessica. He flexed his jaw, determination blazing from his eyes. "I got the right woman. Let me introduce you to her."

"What for? I know what her name is. Grimes, ain't it?" The old woman squinted her eyes and studied Jessica from head to toe. She snorted and shrugged her shoulders. "Name's Peg Malone. I run this place."

"It's a pleasure, Mrs. Malone." Jessica extended her hand, but seeing it wasn't going to be accepted, raised it to brush a curl off her face.

"Call me Peg," the old woman said. "Everyone does."

"Where's Patrick? I want Miss Grimes to meet him," McCain said.

"Up in his room. I told him to go up and get ready for bed. Not that he ever listens to me."

He turned to Jessica. "Follow me and I'll show you to your room. Once you've met Patrick, I'll send Peg up with water for a hot bath and a dinner tray."

"If you don't mind, I'll just tag along now," Peg said. "Hate to miss the introductions. We all know how much the boy's been hankering for another teacher." Sarcasm dripped from her words.

McCain glowered at Peg. "Suit yourself."

He guided Jessica up the stairs. "That's your

room,'' he said, jabbing his thumb over his shoulder. ''This one's Patrick's.''

Jessica was more interested in a hot bath than meeting the boy.

''Wonderful.''

McCain knocked briefly, then pushed open the door. In the far corner a boy sat hunched over a block of wood and a whittling knife. Sunlight streamed in through a single window over an assortment of blocks and balls stacked neatly in the corner, a rocking horse and a bookshelf filled with children's books. All the toys and books appeared to be new.

''I'd like you to meet your new teacher,'' McCain said.

Patrick raised his head to reveal a round face smudged with dirt and peppered with freckles. Fresh splashes of mud covered his knickers and shirt. Jade green eyes blazed up at her. ''Don't see why. She'll be gone in a week or two, just like the others.''

''Miss Grimes has come a long way, and I know she's anxious to meet you.''

Patrick shot his father a warning glance. ''I don't want to meet her.''

Clearly, Patrick wanted a teacher as much as Jessica needed a student. Still, he looked so small and forlorn. And he was just a child. Forcing a smile, Jessica walked across the room and sat down on the edge of the bed next to Patrick. She leaned forward to get a better look at his handiwork. ''What are you whittling?''

The boy didn't look up at her. Instead, he continued to work in silence.

"May I look at what you're making?" Jessica coaxed.

"No."

"Patrick," McCain warned, "show Miss Grimes your whittling."

"I don't want to," the boy grumbled.

Peg stepped up behind McCain. "Ever since you left for Cheyenne, he's been worse than usual. A good thrashing would do him some good."

"There'll be none of that in this house, Peg," McCain warned.

Peg shrugged. "Suit yourself."

"Patrick, show Miss Grimes what you're working on."

Patrick flipped his bangs off his forehead and turned his attention to Jessica. "I ain't got no use for her or any other teacher."

"You haven't even met her," McCain said evenly.

"Why should I?" Patrick shouted the words, as he threw his whittling on the bed. Without warning, he rose and shoved all his weight into Jessica. The unexpected blow sent her reeling. She lost her balance and fell forward onto her hands and knees. On her way down, she heard the sound of muslin ripping. On all fours, Jessica drew her fingers into tight fists. Her heart pounding, she suppressed an oath as she stared at the fine grain of the wood floor.

"Patrick!" McCain shouted. He crossed the room in two strides and knelt in front of Jessica. "I expect you to show Miss Grimes respect!"

"I don't want her here!" Patrick jumped to his feet. "I told you, no more teachers."

McCain's eyes hardened. "You'll be getting an education whether you like it or not."

"Well, I don't like it. Just because you're my father doesn't mean I have to listen to you!" Patrick ran from the room and slammed the door behind him.

"I'll give him a thrashing if you like," Peg said.

"Don't lay a hand on the boy, Peg. Let him be," McCain ordered. Suddenly, he sounded tired.

Jessica agreed with Peg, but kept her opinion to herself as she struggled to stand.

McCain took hold of Jessica's elbows and pulled her to her feet. Her heel became embedded in her hem as she rose, causing her to pitch forward into his hard chest. His hands came up to her shoulders as he steadied her. She stared up into his eyes. Her heart pounded in her chest. His touch was strong and gentle, and she discovered she liked having him close.

You're insane, Jessica Tierney! The man had threatened to throw her in jail just hours ago, and here she was acting like a schoolgirl.

Quickly, she unhooked her heel and pushed away from him. She focused on the six-inch-long tear in her hemline.

McCain rubbed his hand over the dark stubble on his chin. "He's never acted that badly before," he said roughly.

Jessica dropped her hem. The sooner she got out of here, the better. "It's all right."

Peg shook her head. "That boy needs to see the business end of a belt."

The sting in Jessica's knees and the rip in her hem

made her want to agree. Instead, she said, "No, just leave him be. I'll have a talk with him in the morning."

"Suit yourself," said the old woman. "I'll bring your dinner tray up." Without another word, Peg left.

"Mr. McCain," Jessica said, "would you show me to my room? I'm tired and I'd like to put an end to this day."

"Certainly." McCain picked up a candle from Patrick's nightstand, then led Jessica out of the room and across the hallway.

McCain nudged open her door with his boot, then lit several other candles by the door. Crossing the room, he knelt in front of the fireplace and began stacking logs in the cold hearth. Jessica set down her reticule and let her gaze sweep over the room.

Everything was unexpectedly inviting. The robin's-egg-blue wallpaper, the twin wing chairs nestled by the fireplace, the large canopy bed and the mahogany writing table were all lovely.

As the kindling began to blaze, McCain stared at the flames. The fire crackled and burned brightly, its light silhouetting his muscular shoulders and powerful legs. When he rose to his feet, he reminded her of a coiled snake. Tense. Tight.

"Be patient with the boy. He'll come around in time," McCain said.

"Yes," she whispered, "in time."

McCain hesitated, as if he wanted to say more. Instead, he walked out into the hallway. "Good evening to you, Miss Grimes. We leave bright and early for the schoolhouse."

Nodding, Jessica closed the door behind her. She'd barely crossed the room when she heard a loud knock. Thinking it was McCain, she smoothed her wrinkled skirt and opened the door.

Peg stood in the hallway, holding a tray covered with a checkered cloth. Without waiting for an invitation, she pushed the door open with her foot and shoved her small frame past Jessica. Setting the tray on the writing table, she pulled off the cloth and unveiled a plate laden with scrambled eggs, fried bacon and warm biscuits.

Jessica wasn't accustomed to such heavy food, but it did smell wonderful. "This looks delicious."

"It ought to be—I cooked it myself. Now sit down and eat before it gets cold." Peg walked over to the hearth and eased into one of the wing chairs. "You don't mind if I take a load off, do you? It's been one hell of a day."

Jessica craved her privacy almost as much as food, but said politely, "No, go right ahead."

Peg stretched out her short legs and massaged her thigh. Closing her eyes, she began to hum.

The aroma of the biscuits and bacon made Jessica's mouth water. She took a bite of a hot biscuit. It wasn't a croissant, but she enjoyed the taste. She took another bite, then another. Before she realized it, she was licking the remains of the gravy from her fingers.

"You've got a healthy appetite," Peg said. "That's good. I don't trust anyone who eats like a bird."

Jessica laughed. "My teachers said my appetite

was very unladylike. One even said I ate like a field hand.''

Peg stared at Jessica, her eyes narrowing a fraction. ''You're not what any of us expected.''

''I've heard that a lot today,'' she said carefully.

The old woman reached in her apron pocket and pulled out a flask. She took a long drink, then held it out to Jessica. ''Want a snort?''

At school she'd had brandy at Christmas and had enjoyed the taste, so Jessica picked up her empty coffee cup and walked over to Peg. She held it out and watched as Peg poured the liquid gold into her cup.

She took a sip, anticipating a treat. Instead, her eyes filled with tears, and several seconds passed before she could speak. ''What is this?'' she wheezed.

Peg held the flask up to her lips and took another drink. ''My own personal stock. I made it last week.''

''It certainly is…unique.''

Peg tucked the flask back in her pocket. ''My fifty-two years ain't been the easiest. I done things I ain't proud of, so I ain't here to judge you. But I'm warning you not to hurt Ross McCain. He's a good man. He pulled me out of the gutter when no one else would, and I'd kill anyone who tried to harm him.''

''I doubt the man can be hurt. He seems made of iron.''

''He was taken in by a pretty face once. It took him years to get over her.''

''I mean McCain no harm.''

"Good." With a groan, Peg rose to her feet. "Now that I've spoke my piece, I'll leave." Her hand was on the doorknob when she turned. "Can you read and write?"

Jessica's chest tightened. Had Peg somehow seen through her lies? "I am a teacher."

"That's not what I asked."

"Yes, I can read and write."

The old woman studied her, then nodded. "Well, that's something."

Chapter Four

Jessica squeezed her eyes tight against the morning light. The clock in the hallway chimed eight times as voices drifted up the stairs. Rolling onto her side, she curled into a ball and savored the smell of line-dried cotton sheets and the feel of the soft mattress.

It was her first day in town and she'd endured a trip halfway across the country. Surely no one would deny her a few extra minutes in bed.

"Miss Grimes!" Patrick shouted from the other side of her closed bedroom door.

The brat.

Jessica groaned and pulled the comforter up to her chin. Wasn't it enough he'd ripped her only dress? Did he have to hound her so early in the morning?

Patrick pounded on her door. "Miss Grimes, are you awake?"

When was this nightmare going to end? "Go away."

"You're awake. Good." Without waiting for a response, Patrick opened her door and peeked into her room. "Can I come in?"

"No."

For a moment he didn't answer. "Please?"

"I'm sleeping."

"No, you're not. You're awake."

"I'm just pretending to be awake. I'm really asleep. Now leave me alone."

He hesitated a moment, then walked into the room and sat down on the edge of her bed. He was dressed in a red wool pullover shirt, gray cotton pants and suspenders. "It's time to get up."

Irritated and too tired to care, she ducked back under the covers. "Has anyone ever told you it's impolite to come into a lady's room uninvited?"

"No."

"Don't you have someone else to pester?"

"No."

She waited under the covers, hoping to hear his footsteps leaving her room. She heard only his steady breathing. She peeked out from the covers. "Why are you here?"

His eyes hopeful, he said, "Pa said I couldn't go fishing until I said I'm sorry."

Jessica scooted into a sitting position and drew the sheets up to the lacy neckline of her chemise. "Are you sorry?"

He considered her question before he said, "Sorta."

"What's that supposed to mean?"

"Well, shoving you wasn't nice, but I meant everything I said."

Jessica studied his young face. His jaw was set, defiant, but his eyes betrayed his vulnerability. It was impossible to stay vexed. "Why are you mad at me?"

"Because you're going to leave."

Jessica felt the blood drain from her face. "Who told you I was leaving?"

"You're just like Miss Mamie and Miss Sarah, the other teachers Pa hired. They promised to stay, but they didn't. They found themselves husbands, got married and left town."

Relief washed over Jessica. He had no idea she was an imposter. "I'm not like them, because I'm not making you any promises."

He glanced up at her, alert. "But Pa said you already promised to stay for two years."

"No one knows where they're going to be in two years, myself included."

"But Pa *said.*"

She pushed a curl off her face. "Your father hasn't accepted the fact that I'm not right for the job. Once he does, he'll be glad to see me go."

"Who said you wasn't right?"

She cocked an eyebrow. "Do you really think I am?"

"Well, no. We were kinda expecting someone a little older."

His honesty made her smile. "All the more reason for me to leave. You deserve someone who's more…cuddly."

"Oh, but you're not all that bad, and Prosperity ain't so awful once you get used to it."

"It's too small for me."

"We got a mercantile and a livery, and Pa's considering giving the reverend money for a church.

And we got the best fishing hole in the world just outside of town.''

''It sounds like you want me to stay.''

He shrugged. ''I didn't say that.''

Jessica found herself drawn to the boy. ''Then why talk me into staying?''

''I just said this is a nice place to live.''

''Do you like it here?''

''I didn't like it at first, but it's okay now. I got my own room, and I ain't never had my own room before. Plus I got a few friends, and Pa's...well, I think he's starting to like me.''

''You think he's *starting* to like you?'' How could the child not see the truth? His father adored him.

''When he first brought me here, he didn't talk to me much, and he was angry all the time, like he didn't want me around. But now he even smiles once in a while.''

''Patrick, I think your father's feelings for you run deep. Why else would he build a schoolhouse and hire three teachers?'' Her own father would never have gone to such lengths.

''You think?''

''I know. When he talked about you on the train, his eyes shone with pride.''

''They did?''

''They did.''

She could almost see the wheels turning in his head as he pondered the idea. Despite their shaky beginning, she realized she liked this child.

Jessica cleared her throat, trying to banish whatever tender thoughts she'd had. Unnecessary attachments would make leaving all the harder. She wanted to get along with the boy, not learn to love him. "I propose we call a truce."

"What's a truce mean?"

"It means we'll be friends. It also means you won't be shoving me down anymore."

He considered her words. "Does a truce mean I have to go to school?"

Jessica nodded. "If I have to teach lessons, you've got to learn them."

He cocked his head, confusion etched on his boyish features. "You don't sound like you want to teach."

"I don't."

"But teaching's your job!"

"So?"

Patrick narrowed his eyes. "Pa ain't gonna like that. He hired you to teach me."

"That's between your father and me. Now, do me a favor and fetch me the key to this room. I want to start locking my door."

"There ain't any keys."

"Why ever not?"

"Pa said if you ain't got anything to hide, then there's no reason to lock your door."

"What's wrong with a bit of privacy?"

"Pa says privacy is for rich folks."

"Wonderful." Annoyed, Jessica rubbed the sleep from her eyes. "It's time you ran along. I'll be down in a few hours."

"Pa said to tell you to come downstairs straightaway."

"What's the rush?"

His eyes brightened with surprise. "Heck, it's after eight o'clock. The morning's half gone."

"Then I might as well go ahead and waste the rest." Jessica nestled under the quilt and closed her eyes. "Come and get me at noon." She pretended to be asleep, hoping he'd leave.

Patrick hurried to the side of her bed and bent over until his face was only inches from hers. She could feel his warm breath on her face. "Peg said if you ain't downstairs in fifteen minutes, she's feeding your breakfast to the dogs."

Jessica's stomach rumbled on cue. "She wouldn't dare."

"Yes, she would."

Jessica's eyes flew open. "I'll be down in fifteen minutes, and don't let her feed one bite of my food to anything with four or two legs. Also, tell her I need her upstairs immediately to mend and press my dress."

Patrick's mouth dropped open, then he snapped it closed. "I ain't gonna tell Peg *that!*"

"And why not? She is your father's maid, isn't she?"

"Don't ever call Peg a maid to her face. It makes her spitting mad. She runs things around here. Heck, Pa even takes orders from her sometimes."

"Now that I'd like to see." Jessica started to get out of bed, then remembered she only wore her chemise. "If you don't mind, I'd like to dress in private."

Patrick straightened. "Better not take too long." He left the room and closed the door.

Jessica shivered as her bare feet touched the cold

wood floor. Rubbing her hands together, she hurried toward the fireplace. The embers were dark.

A chill nipped at her heels as she ran around the room gathering up her undergarments. She opened the wardrobe and retrieved her dress. She looked at the ripped hem on the side of her gown. The dress was warm but much too fancy for Prosperity, but with only a few dollars in her pocket, she couldn't afford the luxury of new clothes. She slipped the dress on and buttoned it.

She pulled a comb from her reticule and ran it through her hair until it crackled. She hated wearing her hair down, but without a ribbon to tie it back or time to pin it up properly, she had no choice. Her dark curls made her look young and unsophisticated, and knowing she was going to face McCain today, she wanted every ounce of confidence she could muster. Perhaps Peg had a ribbon, plus a needle and thread she could borrow later.

"I can barely thread a needle, and now I'm going to have to mend my dress," Jessica muttered to herself. "This is just great. The next thing I know, they're going to want me to cook." Resigned, she tossed her purse aside and walked over to the door, yanked it open and hurried down the stairs.

The foyer was bathed in warm sunlight. A vase of freshly picked roses, surely the last of the season, adorned the small table by the front door. She walked over to the table, leaned forward and touched the soft petals with the tip of her nose. Inhaling, she drank in the sweet smell.

All at once McCain's voice rumbled off the walls

of the room at the end of the hallway. "I don't keep liars on my payroll."

Jessica straightened, her cheeks burning with guilt. She pressed her hands to her face and looked around, half expecting to see him staring at her. Thankfully, he was nowhere in sight.

"I ain't no liar," another man shouted.

"I got witnesses," McCain responded.

Jessica cringed at the coldness in her employer's voice. Overcome with worry and curiosity, she tiptoed down the hallway, toward a half-open door. She peeked inside. She saw McCain first. He was standing in front of a crackling fire. Freshly shaved, he wore a blue flannel shirt buttoned up to the base of his throat and a pair of faded denim work pants. His body was tense, ready to fight.

A man with a stocky build, thick black beard and long greasy hair stared back at McCain. His eyes reflected thinly veiled hatred.

Then she noticed the books—hundreds of them filling the tall shelves on the west wall—the heavy but simple mahogany desk, richly woven burgundy carpet and two leather chairs.

"Have you said all you came to say, Zeke?" McCain growled.

Jessica eased closer.

"I ain't leaving till you see I wasn't drinking on the job."

"My foreman said he smelled the whiskey on your breath," McCain countered.

"He's lying, Mr. McCain."

"Sam doesn't lie. That's why he oversees the daily operations at the mine."

Zeke shook his head. "Oh, Sam Jenkins ain't liked me from the day I started work for you."

"None of the other men have had trouble with Sam."

"He's got it in for me, I tell you. He's the cause of all my trouble. If it weren't for him—"

"Enough! Collect your pay and get off my property."

"That ain't fair!" Zeke shouted, raising his fist a fraction as if to strike out.

McCain's eyes burned like those of a predator. "It's my business, my rules. Now get out of here."

Zeke turned his back as if to leave, but instead stopped and pulled a knife from his pocket. He gripped the ivory hilt as the thick blade glistened in the sunlight. Only Jessica saw the blade concealed in his meaty palm.

She didn't stop to think, shouting, "Watch out, he's got a knife!"

McCain reacted instantly, grabbing Zeke's arm and twisting it behind his back until he dropped the knife. "I ought to break you in two."

Zeke shouted. "You act like the big man, telling everybody what to do, but you ain't no better today than the day you drifted into town looking to strike it rich."

"If you ever show your face on McCain property again, I'll see that you spend the next ten years in jail." McCain shoved Zeke out of the library, past Jessica and toward the main entrance. Opening it, he pushed him outside and slammed the door. As he strode back toward the library, the white-hot anger in his eyes took her breath away.

He stopped in front of her, the frown on his face softening. Appreciation replaced anger as he took in the soft curls trailing down her back. She felt warm and giddy as his gaze assessed every detail about her. Then suddenly his frown returned. "What the hell were you doing? Listening at the keyhole?"

Lying, forgery and now eavesdropping. Her list of offenses grew by the hour. Still, she managed a cool smile and said, "If I'd remained quiet and let that man stab you, you'd never have known I was outside the door."

McCain grunted, brushed past her and walked back into the library, picking up the knife. Gently, he touched the tip of the blade with his finger. Blood oozed from a tiny cut on his fingertip. "So, you were listening?"

Jessica ignored the question and drew in a fortifying breath. She ventured into the library. "Who was that man?"

McCain set the knife down on his desk.

"Zeke Hollis worked in the mine," he said finally. "My foreman, Sam Jenkins, caught him drinking on the job and fired him yesterday. Zeke was here today pleading his case."

Miraculously, her voice remained calm. "Of course, you had no choice."

McCain studied her a moment as if measuring the sincerity of her words. His expression revealed nothing of his thoughts.

He walked to the desk, where a tin coffeepot and cups sat on a tray. He poured a cup and handed it to her. "It's about time you woke up. Breakfast is served at seven o'clock in this house." He glanced at a clock on the wall behind her. "Not eight-twenty."

Jessica accepted the cup and changed the subject. "How many books do you have in here?"

"Three hundred and twenty-one."

"Have you read all of them?"

"I've thumbed through them."

"It must be one of the largest collections in the territory."

"It is." He studied a callus on his palm. "I don't want to talk about my books."

"What, then?"

"Patrick. Did he apologize for his behavior last night?"

"Yes."

McCain's gaze pinned her. "How did it go?"

"Fine. In fact, I'd say Patrick and I have come to an understanding."

McCain's eyes held a hopefulness that caught her by surprise. "I'm glad to hear that," he said slowly. "He didn't take to the other teachers."

"I can't say he's actually taken to me."

"He's talking to you. That's progress." McCain walked behind his desk. He hesitated before he spoke again. "Patrick's mother and I separated shortly after we married. Caroline returned to Chicago and never told me she was pregnant."

"Why not?"

"She hated it here and was afraid I'd force her to return." He sighed. "Prosperity was a hard, lawless town then and no place for a lady."

"Rougher than it is now?"

"Worse than Greeley."

"Oh."

"That's why I never went after Caroline to make her return." He grew silent, as if he had returned to the past. Finally, he said, "Only after Caroline died in the spring did her aunt write to me and tell me about Patrick. It seems Caroline had little use for the boy and shuffled him around from relative to relative most of his life."

Her heart went out to both father and son. "I'm sorry."

McCain sighed again. "I tell you this so you'll understand the boy better. Patrick's had no structure or discipline in his life and has grown quite wild. I'm trying to undo eight years of damage. I can put a roof over his head and see that he gets discipline when he deserves it, but he needs more than I can give."

"What are you trying to say, Mr. McCain?"

He chose his words carefully. "Patrick has never really had a stable female influence in his life. I want you to take the boy under your wing. He could use a little mothering."

Patrick could easily steal into her heart if she weren't careful, which was all the more reason to keep her distance. "And what happens in two years when I leave?"

His face darkened. "We'll cross that bridge when we come to it. Today is what concerns me. Will you look after the boy?"

He was backing her into a corner. "What about Peg?"

"Peg is a good woman, but I don't consider her the mothering type. If I wanted Patrick to learn how to roll a cigarette or shoot a gun, I'd send him to Peg.''

"I see your point.''

"So, you'll look after the boy?''

Jessica thought about how alone she'd felt when her own mother died. There'd been no comforting words, no soft shoulder to cry on. Old emotions, long since buried, stirred in her, leaving her feeling defenseless.

Now she had the chance to spare Patrick the same fate.

Saying yes was foolish.

Saying no was cruel.

"Yes,'' she whispered.

Satisfaction glimmered in McCain's green eyes. "You won't be sorry, Miss Grimes.''

"I already am.''

His gaze lingered on her, but he didn't press her for an explanation. He had the answer he wanted.

McCain snatched up his hat. "It's time to buy you some sensible clothes.'' He took her by the elbow and guided her toward the door.

She glanced over her shoulder at her untouched cup of coffee. "What about breakfast?''

"Kitchen's closed.''

"I'm hungry.''

"Lunch is in three hours.''

Jessica fumed as he opened the front door and directed her down the stairs.

"This is a nightmare. A terrible, terrible dream,'' Jessica mumbled.

"Quit your grumbling and hurry up. There'll be plenty of food at the picnic.''

A chilly September breeze blew across the town's only street, bringing with it clumps of sagebrush and the smell of horses, hay and dust. Jessica's skirts whipped gently around her ankles, and her boots clicked against the wooden sidewalk as she and McCain walked toward the mercantile. She heard the sound of a piano playing through the swinging doors of the saloon, and deep snarling voices of two men fighting near the livery.

"The first thing I'm buying you is a pair of sensible shoes," McCain said.

As Jessica hurried to match his pace, she glanced down at her high-heeled boots, made of black kid and straight from the pages of *Harper's Bazaar.* "What's wrong with my boots?"

"If those frilly things last until payday, I'll double your first month's wages."

"The frills are why I bought the boots. If you haven't noticed, I like to dress well."

He shrugged and took her by the arm. "Save the fancy clothes for Sundays."

Her skin prickled with irritation. "Mr. McCain, we have to come to an understanding."

"That so?"

"I know you're used to giving orders, but I am not used to taking them. I propose from this moment forward that we—"

She screeched when the square heel of her shoe caught between the wooden slates of the boardwalk. The sudden interruption in her stride threw her off balance and pitched her forward. Instinctively, her hands shot out in front of her to break the fall. McCain's grip tightened instantly. He held on to her as she dangled in front of him, her face inches from the boardwalk.

He pulled her up until she was standing. "You were saying, Miss Grimes?"

Her face burned with embarrassment. With as much dignity as she could muster, she yanked her arms free, knelt down and tugged on her boot. The soft kid on her heel tore as she pulled it out of the crack. "Somebody should fix that boardwalk. I could have been seriously hurt."

"Sure, princess, anything else?"

She bristled at "princess." "Now that you mention it, some fresh fruit for breakfast would be nice."

McCain muttered an oath as he took her elbow in hand. Silently, he led her toward a two-story wooden building. In fading red letters, Jed's Mercantile was painted on a cracked sign mounted over the front doors, which were propped open by matching milk jugs.

As Jessica stood in front, a curious smell of liquor, tobacco and horse sweat rushed out to greet her. An old man with a long white beard, wearing animal hides and a bear claw necklace, walked out of the store. He paused and stared at her as if he didn't quite believe his eyes. He touched his beaverskin hat. "McCain, who the devil is she?"

Instinctively, Jessica stepped closer to her employer.

McCain placed his hand lightly on her shoulder. "Miss Grimes, I'd like you to meet Wild Jack. He lives up in the mountains and comes into town once or twice a year."

"H-hello," she said.

Wild Jack had a large scar trailing from his left eye down to his chin, leaving the skin on his cheek puckered and uneven. Coupled with the crazed glint in his eyes, it was unnerving.

"Pleasure." Wild Jack looked at McCain and shook his head. "She the new teacher I been hearing about?"

"Yep."

Wild Jack shook his head again. "She ain't gonna last. You need a fat, ugly woman like my Bessie. Nobody's every tried to steal Bessie."

Despite her fear, Jessica found the comment irritating. "Did it ever occur to you I might not want to marry?"

Wild Jack chuckled. "City girl, out here a woman needs a man."

She opened her mouth to speak, but McCain pulled her behind him. "You staying long?" he said.

"I got my gear stowed in a little cabin about an hour's ride outside of town. I'll stay there a few weeks. When you coming up to the mountain? We need to hunt bear, and Bessie has been asking for you."

"Next summer, maybe."

"Don't make it too long. Otherwise, you'll get old and fat and set in your ways."

McCain laughed and pushed his hat back with his index finger. "I can't pick up like I used to do. I've a son now."

"Bring him along. Bessie'd love to meet him." Wild Jack met Jessica's gaze. "But don't bring the city girl. Bessie is liable to skin her alive. She's the jealous kind.''

Jessica's stomach flip-flopped. ''People don't skin people alive, do they?''

''I seen my Bessie take every inch of skin off a rustler with her butcher knife. Only when he was pleading for his Maker did she finally take pity on him and stab the knife into his heart.''

Jessica paled. ''That's nonsense,'' she whispered.

Wild Jack chucked her under the chin and she jumped. ''You got a lot to learn, city girl.'' Suddenly, the old man burst out laughing. ''Don't be a stranger, McCain.''

She watched Wild Jack walk across the street toward the saloon. Miss Madeline's Academy didn't seem like such an awful place now. ''I want to go home.''

''You are home,'' McCain said, as if understanding the full meaning of her words. ''Now let's get inside and get your gear.''

He nudged her forward into the mercantile. Barrels filled with flour, molasses, vinegar and salt lined a center aisle. Crocks of butter, baskets of eggs, tins of coffee and tea and a big glass jar filled with red-striped candy lined the counter. Strings of red peppers and three freshly skinned rabbits hung from the ceiling.

I hope you're getting a good laugh, Father!

Jessica paused in the doorway. ''Don't tell me this is where you plan to buy clothes for me?''

''Sure is.''

Jessica folded her arms. ''I'm not buying any clothes here.''

The store was crowded with a half-dozen people. Two plainly dressed women stood off in one corner, while two men by the front counter bartered with Jed over the price of a gun. A third man carried bags of flour out a side door and loaded them onto a wagon.

Jed peered over the rim of his glasses. "Howdy, Miss Grimes, McCain. What brings you here?"

"Just browsing," Jessica offered.

"The lady needs new clothes," McCain corrected.

The two women stopped talking and stared at her. When she met their curious gazes, they looked away, feigning great interest in a bushel of potatoes.

"You know where everything is, McCain," Jed said. "Help yourself."

McCain took Jessica to a corner of the store stocked with a half-dozen bolts of fabric and a selection of dresses. *Drab colors,* Jessica thought as she fingered the sleeve of a homespun calico dress.

"I don't think any of these dresses are going to do," she said.

"What do you mean?" McCain demanded.

She shrugged. "This fabric is much too coarse. I couldn't possibly wear it."

"Then I'll buy you a bolt of cloth. You can make your own dress."

"I can't sew."

He closed his eyes as if drawing on his reserve of patience. "Damn it, woman, what am I going to do with you?"

"Fire me?" she said hopefully.

He sneered. "No such luck."

Jed cleared his throat. "McCain, can you come over here a minute? These two fools are trying to decide which rifle to buy and they need your advice."

"Be right there, Jed," McCain called back. "Pick out two dresses. I'll be back in a minute."

"There's nothing here for me."

His eyes hardened. "Find something."

As he walked away, she studied the dresses. The calico looked comfortable, but it reminded her of the faded blue muslin she'd been wearing the day she'd arrived at boarding school.

"Did you hear that?" one of the two woman whispered. "She can't sew."

"I never heard such a thing," the other replied with a giggle.

"I've seen her type before. High and mighty. Thinks she too good for the likes of us."

Jessica straightened her shoulders. She might be an outsider, but she wasn't a gawky twelve-year-old child afraid of disapproval. She glanced up at McCain. He'd cracked open a shotgun and was staring down the twin barrels. She was on her own.

Smiling, she walked toward the women. "I don't believe we've met. My name is Emma Grimes. I'm the new teacher."

The woman on the right was short, dumpy, and had a large mole on her upper lip, while her friend had a tall, lean body and birdlike features. In unison, their eyes narrowed.

"Howdy," the shorter woman said. "My name's Harriet Gooden and this here's Iva Kline."

Jessica extended her hand. "It's a pleasure to make your acquaintance."

Harriet thrust out her meaty hand and took hold of Jessica's. Instead of shaking her hand, she turned it over and studied her cuff. "Is those real pearls?"

"I wouldn't know."

"They look real to me."

"Me, too," Iva added, looking over Harriet's shoulder.

Jessica pulled back her hand.

Iva shrugged. "Can't say I want my children learning your fancy city ways."

Jessica swallowed the bitter taste in her mouth. "Will I see you at the picnic?"

"Can't rightly say," Harriet retorted. "We got *real* work to do."

Suddenly, Jessica felt very tired and alone. She retreated a step and bumped into something very hard and very human. The oddly comforting scent of masculine musk told her it was McCain.

He placed his hand gently, protectively on her shoulder, then nodded to Harriet and Iva. "I see you've met our new teacher."

Harriet's and Iva's belligerent stares turned to bright smiles.

"Can't wait to get to know her better at the picnic, Mr. McCain," Harriet hastened to say.

"Can't wait," Iva added.

"Glad to hear it," McCain said. "I expect you two ladies to look out after Miss Grimes and see that she feels welcome."

"Oh, we will," they said.

"Good. Now, if you will excuse us…" His tone

was dismissive and permitted no argument. He waited until the ladies had left the store before he spoke again. "I see you survived your first meeting with Iva and Harriet."

"Just barely, I think."

"Well, hold on, Miss Grimes. It's going to get worse."

Chapter Five

Ross's gaze swept over Miss Grimes's fancy dress as they walked toward the schoolhouse. A man would have to be dead not to notice the way the soft fabric molded to her breasts like a second skin, or how the full skirt emphasized her delicately rounded hips, which swayed just right when she walked.

Inwardly, he groaned.

The dress, like her grace and poise, spoke of money, privilege and society. Firsthand experience had taught him that society types like her were trouble—big trouble. People like her had their own way of thinking and living, and were best avoided altogether.

And still his blood burned hot and his mind ran wild with erotic thoughts. Since he'd first laid eyes on her, he'd been overtaken by a restless energy he'd not experienced in years.

Damn that dress! It was just another reminder that he'd made a mistake in hiring Miss Grimes. Too young, too beautiful and too green, Emma Grimes wasn't cut out for life in Colorado. She belonged in one of those fancy drawing rooms in Chicago or San Francisco and not in a small-town school looking after a dozen children.

Common sense demanded Ross send her back to Sacramento and end it now, before he repeated the mistakes he'd made eight years ago when he'd been younger, brasher and intoxicated by his newfound wealth. Then he'd believed himself unstoppable— life had no boundaries, no limits, and a society miss could be his.

Now, older and much wiser, he knew differently. Work and duty had become the cornerstones of his life. He dealt only in facts, not emotions. And the facts were plain.

Miss Grimes was not Caroline.

And the children needed her.

So, somehow, he would have to put his personal feelings aside and see that she succeeded—come hell or high water.

"Did you pick out a few dresses at Jed's?" McCain asked, breaking the silence between them.

She shrugged indifferently. "I hated them all."

"Too bad."

"Did it ever occur to you to ask me if I wanted a new dress instead of telling me I need one?"

"No."

"You'll get a lot further with me if you ask instead of tell."

He stared at her, convinced she'd lost her mind. "Lady, I don't *ask*. I *order*. That's the way it is in my town."

"Then you and I, sir, are going to have a difficult two years."

The mutinous look in her eyes stoked his temper, so he struck out with the first thought that came to mind. "You deliberately ruffled Iva's and Harriet's feathers, didn't you?"

Though she glared up at him, her shock was clear. "I did not."

His gut told him she was telling the truth, but his pride wouldn't let him back down. "You're hoping the folks in town will hate you so much I'll be forced to fire you, aren't you?"

She smiled. "Actually, that hadn't occurred to me, but now that you mention it, the idea has merit."

"You wouldn't dare."

"If Harriet and Iva represent the kind of people that live in this town, it won't take much to make them all hate me."

Miss Grimes had an uphill battle ahead of her, but he'd never give her the satisfaction of saying so. "It's your job to make them like you."

"Well, then, let's get to that picnic. I'm anxious to make a memorable impression." Her words dripped with sarcasm.

Lord, save him from this woman.

Ross pulled her toward him until they were almost nose-to-nose. "You better not disappoint me, Miss Grimes."

She shrugged as if indifferent. "Oh, stop, you're scaring me."

She matched him glare for glare, giving no quarter. If she didn't make him so blessed mad, he'd have admired her spirit.

He tore his gaze away, tightened his grip on her

arm and started walking again, pulling her along with him.

Soon her gait became uneven, as if her fancy shoes had started to pinch her feet. Served her right for not listening to him.

He picked up the pace. "Everything all right, Miss Grimes?" he asked. "Need to rest a spell?"

"Absolutely not."

He guessed she'd rather eat dirt than admit she was uncomfortable. He made a mental note to order three dresses, shoes and a winter coat for her this afternoon. "Suit yourself."

At the edge of town behind McCain's mining office, the bang of hammers rang through the air as his men straddled the roof of the schoolhouse and repaired shingles loosened by a summer storm. The mountains trailed along the horizon, and Miller's Pond glistened beyond the freshly whitewashed one-room building.

Miss Grimes's flushed cheeks paled a fraction as she surveyed the scene. "Is that the schoolhouse?"

He sensed her reservation. "That building's only temporary. As the town grows, I expect the school to grow with it. One day I see a big school up there on the hill."

"You're ambitious."

He pointed at the town. "I built Prosperity in five years."

Her gaze followed his outstretched arm. "I've never accomplished anything of importance in my life." Her tone was matter-of-fact, with no trace of self-pity.

"I doubt you've ever been given the chance."

"I was raised to produce heirs and be the perfect hostess."

"Is that why you're here now?"

"In part, yes."

A gentle breeze teased the curls framing her face. All traces of mutiny and anger had disappeared.

"Now's your chance to do some good for yourself and this town," Ross stated.

"But what if I'm not up to the task?" she asked with real concern.

"You'll do."

"There's still time to find someone more qualified."

The worry in her eyes told him he had the right woman. Emma Grimes might not have experience, but he sensed she had enough grit to get her past, through or around any obstacle. "I've got the teacher I want."

He took hold of her elbow and guided her toward the folks gathered directly across from the schoolhouse. A dozen women arranged platters of fried chicken, pies and breads on sawhorse tables as their babies played at their feet. The older children played duck-duck-goose or kicked around a flour sack stuffed with hay.

Miss Grimes's spine stiffened. She drew closer to him, as if seeking his protection. A mysterious sense of satisfaction ignited inside him.

"It's about time you got here!" shouted Sam Jenkins, his foreman.

Sam was a tall, lean man, with wheat-colored hair, a bushy mustache and a peg leg. At his side was his son, Davey, a gangly boy with his father's coloring and a crop of freckles peppering the bridge of his nose.

"Folks was beginning to wonder if you was gonna show," Sam said.

"We got held up." Ross quickly introduced them.

Sam managed to conceal most of his surprise during the introductions; however, Davey's mouth dropped open. "*You're* a teacher? But you're not old and fat."

Sam clamped his hand on his son's shoulder as he tore his own gaze from Miss Grimes. "Davey, now that ain't a polite thing to say."

Davey quickly dropped his gaze to his scuffed shoes. "Meant no disrespect, ma'am."

Miss Grimes smiled. "None taken, Davey."

Sam rubbed the back of his neck with his hand. "So, I hear you come all the way from Sacramento, Miss Grimes. I've been to Sacramento a few times. Whereabouts are you from in the city?"

"My father's home was on Grand Street."

"Fancy. Can't say I ever made it to that part of town." Sam's gaze captured Ross's. "Got a minute, Ross?"

"Sure."

Sam touched the brim of his hat. "Miss Grimes, would you excuse Ross and me?"

"Certainly."

"Davey, look after Miss Grimes for a minute."

"Sure, Pa."

Sam led Ross out of earshot before saying, "I never questioned you during a half-dozen campaigns in Virginia or when you wanted to move west, but

I got to say, I'm not so sure about her. A woman from the fanciest part of Sacramento ain't our kind.''

"*Our kind?* You sound like a snob, Sam."

Sam stabbed his fingers through his hair. "Now, you know I judge a man by the quality of his work, not by his past or the color of his skin."

"Don't you think Miss Grimes deserves the same?"

"'Course she does, it's just that, well…"

"What?"

"She's so beautiful. You're gonna be fighting off every young buck in the territory when word gets out about her."

"Miss Grimes is off-limits to everyone."

Sam glanced over his shoulder at her. "I know the men in town all promised not to court the new teacher, but I doubt they had her in mind when they made the promise. Just take a look at them now. They're all stealing peeks at her."

Ross looked up in time to see Lydia Crumpet, a portly woman with graying hair, smack her husband, Journey, in the back of the head for staring at Miss Grimes.

"I'll personally deal with any man who does more than look at her," Ross said.

"You can't stop the men from dreaming." Grinning like a schoolboy, Sam stared past Ross at Miss Grimes. "Hell, my dreams is gonna be extra special tonight."

Ross's mood soured at the thought. "Don't waste your time dreaming of what can't be."

"You sound as prickly as a bear, Ross. What's

the matter? Have trouble sleeping last night your-self?''

''What's that supposed to mean?''

''Just that I don't believe I could sleep nights knowing Miss Grimes was under my roof.''

''Miss Grimes isn't my type.''

''I remember a time when she was exactly the kind of woman you wanted.''

''I've lost the need to marry a woman with a fancy education to make me feel important.''

Ross watched Miss Grimes as the sun highlighted her ebony hair and the wind blew the dark curls off her face. He grew hard just looking at her.

Miss Grimes, like Caroline, did stir his blood, but he'd spoken honestly to Sam. There was no room in his bed or life for a woman like his late wife. He and his son had yet to recover from her deceptions.

Ross looked past Miss Grimes toward the dessert table, where Patrick stood. The boy glanced from side to side, making sure no one was watching him, then poked his finger into the side of a vanilla cake. He licked the icing from his finger before rejoining the other children.

''How's Patrick doing?'' Sam asked.

''The boy's getting along fine.''

''You spent much time with him lately?''

''I've not had the time.''

''The boy needs more than just a roof over his head. He needs you to be his father.''

''All my time's been eaten up by the expansion of the mining operation. I've barely had time to sleep these past few months.''

''Work's starting to let up.''

"I know." The truth was Ross had allowed work to take over his life. Backbreaking days were easier to bear than admitting his son hated him.

As if reading his thoughts, Sam spat on the ground. "Caroline Sinclair! If Patrick only knew what she did to you—"

"What's done is done. I don't ever want you to speak against Caroline to Patrick. He has a right to enjoy what few good memories he has left of his mother."

"I'll keep my thoughts on Caroline to myself if you do me a favor."

"What's that?"

"Get to know the boy. You've already lost eight years with Patrick. I don't want you to let another year slip by."

"That's easier said than done."

Sam clamped his hand on Ross's shoulder. "Time heals all wounds."

"Does it?"

Before Sam could respond, they both caught sight of Lydia Crumpet. "Brace yourself. Lydia is headed toward Miss Grimes," Ross said.

With her young son, Abraham, on her hip, Mrs. Crumpet ate up the distance between the buffet table and Miss Grimes. Her lips were drawn tight; her face was grim.

Ross stifled a groan. Lydia Crumpet had designated herself leader of the women in the community. She was also one of a few women in town who believed her children didn't need an education. If she didn't like Miss Grimes, there was a good chance more women might follow her lead and keep their children home from school. The success of the school now rested solely on Miss Grimes's shoulders and the impression she made here today.

"Ross," Sam whispered, "this is our cue to leave."

"Stand your ground, man."

"I'd rather fight Indians," he grumbled.

"So would I." Ross nudged Sam back toward Miss Grimes and Davey. "Mrs. Crumpet," Ross said, positioning himself beside Miss Grimes, "come meet our new schoolteacher. Emma Grimes, this is Lydia Crumpet."

Mrs. Crumpet looked at the teacher. Instantly, her frown deepened. "Miss Grimes."

"It's a pleasure, Mrs. Crumpet." Miss Grimes reached out and curled one of the toddler's long ringlets around her finger. "She certainly is cute."

"*His* name is Abraham."

Miss Grimes cheeks paled. "Oh."

Ross thought Miss Grimes would have bolted at that moment if Sissy Nevers hadn't stepped forward. "You sure are looking fine today, Miss Grimes."

A little color returned to Miss Grimes's face. "Thank you, Sissy."

"That dress of hers is a bit too fancy for my tastes," Lydia offered. "I hope your teaching's more practical than your duds."

"I'm sure it is, Mrs. Crumpet," Sissy stated.

"Well, then, what do you aim to teach our children?"

Miss Grimes blinked. "Reading. Writing. Ciphering."

"And what good is ciphering gonna do my boy

Billy when he's one hundred feet below ground mining silver?'' Lydia demanded.

Miss Grimes straightened her shoulders. ''He'll be able to know if he has been cheated out of any wages when payday comes.''

''Everybody in these parts knows Ross McCain don't cheat his men.''

''Perhaps he might want to do something different with his life than mine coal,'' Miss Grimes challenged.

''Mining has been good enough for his father, and it'll be good enough for him.''

''It'll have to do if you don't give him choices.''

Mrs. Crumpet adjusted her baby on her hip. ''Choices is for rich folks.''

Miss Grimes cocked an eyebrow. ''And for people who can read and write.''

''So high and mighty,'' Mrs. Crumpet snorted. ''You don't know anything about us or what our children need.''

Miss Grimes shrugged. ''Perhaps you're right.''

The air crackled with tension as the two women stared at each other.

Sissy broke the silence. ''We started a quilting bee, Miss Grimes. We was just saying how nice it would be for you to join us. We meet every Thursday. Ain't that right, Mrs. Crumpet?''

Mrs. Crumpet snorted. ''Can't see how she'd be interested in spending time with a bunch of miners' wives.''

''Oh, that ain't true, is it, Miss Grimes?'' Sissy asked.

''I am not very handy with a needle.''

Mrs. Crumpet snorted. "Figures."

Sissy's grin belied the growing panic in her eyes. "I'm sure we can learn her how to sew." She turned to Miss Grimes. "Mrs. Crumpet has made some right fancy quilts. I hear she won her share of blue ribbons at the county fairs when she lived back in Virginia."

"They was plain old country quilts. Nothing fancy." Mrs. Crumpet leveled her gaze on Miss Grimes. "You know anything about chopping wood, building fires in a potbellied stove or cooking?"

"I'm a teacher. Why would I need to know that?"

"Honey, those skills is basic," Lydia said. "How you gonna take care of our children if you don't know how to build a fire in the stove?"

Ross smelled disaster. He'd hoped Mrs. Crumpet would accept Miss Grimes; however, now he wasn't so sure that would ever happen. "Ladies, Miss Grimes is the best teacher money can buy. If she's lacking, I'm sure we'll all lend a hand to show her what she needs to know."

"Of course we will," Sissy added.

Ross captured Miss Grimes's elbow in his hand. "Now, if you will excuse us, I'd like to give her a tour of the schoolhouse."

Mrs. Crumpet frowned. "This ain't settled yet."

"Don't worry, Mrs. Crumpet, we'll work it out later," Ross assured her.

He ushered Miss Grimes toward the schoolhouse. She looked up at the plain, one-room building as she climbed the three front steps, then crossed the threshold. Ross removed his hat and followed her.

The room contained six benches, a potbellied stove in the corner, several unopened crates and a desk fashioned from sawhorses and lumber.

Miss Grimes crossed to the desk. She ran her hand over the rough pine and stared at the whiskey barrel that served as a chair. "How could that woman be so ignorant?"

"Don't be too hard on Mrs. Crumpet. Her life's been hard. She only wants what's best for her children."

Jessica whirled around. "How could working in a silver mine be good for her children?"

"It's an honest living."

"I didn't mean to imply it wasn't," she said quickly. "But it's a hard life. I'd hate it if my children had to earn their living digging for coal or silver."

"These folks haven't seen much of the world like you have. But then that's why I hired you—to bring the world to them."

Miss Grimes reached into one of the open crates behind the desk and retrieved a copy of a *McGuffey's Reader*. "I still don't understand why she wouldn't want her children to read and write."

He removed his hat and traced the brim with his thumb. "She might be afraid her children will lose respect for her if they learn to read and write when she can't."

"Education has nothing to do with respecting a parent."

"Doesn't it?"

"Of course not."

"You need to convince her and the others of that."

"I doubt the woman will have anything to do with me."

"Give it time." Ross tossed his hat on the desk, took the reader from her and began to thumb through the pages. "The last teacher made up a list of books for me to order. I had them special delivered from Chicago."

Jessica smoothed her long fingers over a crate of books. "I've never seen anyone so committed to children's education."

Ross handed the reader back to Miss Grimes. "Learning's about the best gift a man could have."

"You make me feel guilty."

"Why's that?"

"I always hated school."

"Then why choose teaching?"

"Let's say teaching chose me."

Ross remembered the fancy script and big words in her letters. "You're nothing like your letters."

She didn't look up from her book. "Oh, really? How so?"

"I got the impression you loved everything about books."

Her cheeks took on a pink hue. "Oh, I do now, but I guess I was like all children. Didn't you duck out on your chores when you were a child?"

"Sure, but I'm not a schoolteacher."

"I'm quite different now," she said quickly. "I read all the time."

Ross rubbed his hand over his chin. "There was

one writer you went on and on about. What was his name?"

"I can't recall. I like so many."

"But there was one in particular you liked a lot."

"Dickens, perhaps?"

"No, that wasn't the name."

"If you showed me my letters I could refresh my memory."

"We'll see."

She smoothed her palms down her skirts. "Mr. McCain, if you don't mind, I've a taste for some of Sissy's pie. Skipping breakfast has left me famished."

He stepped aside and held out his arm. "Lead the way."

Sam poked his head in the schoolhouse door as they reached the threshold. "Sissy says she and the womenfolk have something for Miss Grimes."

"Like what?" Ross asked, suspiciously.

"I don't know, but I think it's a good thing."

"Let's hope so."

Ross ushered Miss Grimes out of the schoolhouse toward the women gathered by the picnic table. The hair on the back of his neck prickled just as it had before the battle of Chancellorsville. He smelled trouble.

Sissy smiled as she approached. "All right, folks, gather around now. I got something to say." She waited until everyone had encircled her before she pulled a leather-bound book wrapped in a yellow ribbon out from her pocket and tucked it under her arm. She faced Miss Grimes. "We wanted to give you something special, seeing as we all got a lot of hopes pinned on you, and we wanted to make you feel welcome.''

Sissy held out the book to Miss Grimes. ''A fella came through town while Mr. McCain was up in Cheyenne fetching you. He had a funny way of talking and said he came from a place called England. He sounded like he was real smart, but he didn't have a bit of money, so he offered to trade me this book for a few nights' room and board.''

Sissy turned to Ross and held out the book. ''Mary Lou Taylor came up with the idea to have him write something in the book for Miss Grimes. Kinda like a special how-do-you-do. Since none of us know how to read, we'd like you to do us the honor of reading it, Mr. McCain.''

Ross hesitated. He took the book, his gut twisting into a dozen knots. ''That was very thoughtful of you, Sissy.''

He felt Miss Grimes's gaze on him as he looked at the townspeople. Patrick stood in the center of the crowd, like the others, staring expectantly at him.

Slowly, Ross untied the ribbon and tucked it in his pocket. He opened the book, taking time to smooth his long fingers over the yellowed pages. The stranger's inscription stared back up at him. The handwriting was bold, handsome—and utterly meaningless to him. He couldn't read a word of it.

He'd always regretted the fact that he couldn't read, even though he'd prospered despite his lack of reading ability. And standing here right now, he realized he'd give a year's worth of the mine's profits to be able to read the few words inscribed on the page before him.

Ross straightened his shoulders and cleared his throat. His heart pounded in his chest, and for the first time in years, he felt sweat trickle down his back.

"Miss Grimes," he said, looking out over the crowd, at the expectant eyes riveted on him, "it is indeed a pleasure to have you here with us today." He glanced down again at the page. Something coiled inside of him. He was trapped.

Then he felt Miss Grimes's cool hands against his hot skin. Their gazes locked, and in that instant, he knew she'd guessed his secret. Yet there was no scorn, no ridicule, only understanding.

"This was so kind of you, Sissy," she said easily. "Emerson's *Essays* is one of my favorite collections. This is a wonderful gift and I thank you. May I impose, Mr. McCain?"

He gave her the book. She leafed through the pages, then flipped to the front of the book and read aloud,

"To Emma Grimes. May your path lead you to your dreams.
Sincerest wishes,

the Women of Prosperity."

Gently, Miss Grimes closed the book and hugged it to her breast. She looked at Sissy. "You have given me more than I could possibly deserve."

Tears glistened in Sissy's eyes, and Ross found it difficult to speak. Again he was struck by how different Emma Grimes was from her letters, which the circuit judge had read to him. And for the hundredth

time, Ross wanted to know more about Emma
Grimes.

The moment was shattered by Lydia Crumpet's
scream. She pushed her way through the crowd,
yelling, "My baby, Abe—he's missing!"

Chapter Six

Ross McCain couldn't read.

As quickly as the thought entered Jessica's mind, it vanished. Her thoughts now were only for Lydia Crumpet and her missing son, Abe.

Lydia Crumpet's face was pinched with worry. "I can't find my baby anywhere!"

McCain placed his hands on her shoulders. "Where'd you last see the boy?"

"Over by the p-pie table," she stammered. "He was playing with a red ball and eating a c-cookie. Oh, Lord, what am I going to do if anything happens to him? He's my baby."

McCain squeezed her shoulder reassuringly. "Calm yourself, Lydia."

Fat tears flowed down the woman's cheeks. "Please find my baby, Mr. McCain."

He touched her cheek. "We'll find him."

When McCain turned to the crowd, the softness vanished from his eyes. Immediately, he fired off orders and organized search parties. His voice was sharp, crisp, as if he commanded an army, and no one questioned him. Within minutes, almost everyone had fanned out to search for the boy.

Jessica, ready and willing to help, stood next to McCain, waiting for her own instructions. "Where do you want me to go?"

McCain didn't acknowledge her as he continued to rattle off orders to Sam. "See that the livery is searched and check the horse troughs. God help the boy, but he may have fallen in one."

Sam nodded. "Anything else?"

"If you don't find him, report back to me. We'll extend the search then."

"Right." Orders received, Sam set off with the others.

Jessica waited patiently as McCain spoke to a few other men. Finally, when he was alone, she stepped forward. "Where do you want me to search?"

"Nowhere. I want you to stay put. You don't know the area so you're no use to us."

His words stung. How many times had she heard those sentiments? Her father, her teachers, William Perry—they'd all reminded her that she wasn't really needed.

But this time was different. She was different. She'd taken more chances in the last fortnight than she had in her whole life, and she wasn't about to stop now. "I can look just as well as the rest of you."

"No."

"Let me help. I *want* to help."

"If I turn you loose, you'll get lost, and I don't want to send a search party out later to find you."

"I won't get lost."

"I don't have time to argue with you. Stay here at the schoolhouse, sit on the steps and let me take care of business."

Jessica stared past him toward the lake. "No one is searching by Miller's Pond. Let me check there."

He looked at her as if she'd lost her mind. "Why would we?"

"The pond sparkles like diamonds," she said. "I could see a child being drawn to it."

McCain's gaze followed hers to the lake's crystal blue waters glistening in the sunlight. "The pond is over five hundred feet away. The boy's only two. He couldn't possibly get that far in so short a time."

"Still, it wouldn't hurt to look."

He grabbed her shoulders. "I don't want you going anywhere, especially to the lake. We've got wild animals roaming around here—plus snakes, Indians, cowboys who've been too long without a woman. I can't do my job if I'm worrying about you."

She folded her arms over her chest but didn't respond. This was so unfair. She wanted to help.

He gave her a hard shake. "Answer me! Will you stay put?"

"All right," she said, hoping she sounded as sour as she felt.

McCain turned to leave her, then paused as if he wanted to say more. But he only cursed softly, then left to join the search.

Jessica kicked at the ground with her foot. Brown tufts of grass and dirt settled on her shoes as she stalked toward the schoolhouse stairs. She flounced down on the wooden steps. Blast his hide. He had no right to tell her what she could or couldn't do.

She sat forgotten as the men, women and children called out Abe's name and searched everywhere, from barrels to haylofts.

Minutes passed and the sun grew hot, but there was no sign of the boy. Jessica tapped her foot, irritated beyond words. More time passed. She wiped the sweat from her forehead with the back of her hand. "I'm a fool for listening to him. I should be doing something."

"Why are you talking to yourself?" Patrick stepped in front of her, blocking out the bright sun. Dirt covered his brown trousers and a stalk of hay stuck out from his hair.

Jessica glanced sharply up at him. "Where've you been?"

"Looking for Abe."

She groaned. "*Everybody* in this town is looking for Abe but me."

"And me. Pa caught me crawling around in the hayloft and said I could break my neck. He told me to get down and check on you."

"As you can see, I'm still here." She patted the spot beside her. "Have a seat."

Patrick sat down next to her on the step. "Pa said if you weren't here, he'd skin you alive."

"Oh, he did, did he? Who does he think he is?"

"The man in charge."

"Well, everybody else in this town may defer to him, but I refuse to." Frustrated, Jessica stood. "Have they found Abe?"

"Nope."

Jessica expelled a breath. "This is insane. *Everyone* should be looking for that child."

She stared ahead at the lake. Its cool waters beckoned her. She unbuttoned her jacket and slipped it off. "Want to walk over to the pond with me? I wouldn't mind putting my feet in the water."

"Pa says to stay put."

"The lake's not far. If anyone called for us, we'd hear them."

"We're going to get in trouble. Pa hates it when you don't do what he says."

"What else is new?"

Patrick looked at her and then the lake. "I dunno."

Defiance pumped through her veins, as it had when she was twelve years old. "He's so busy right now, he'll never notice we're gone. I'm going. Are you coming or not?"

Patrick scratched his head. "Well, it sure beats sitting here doing nothing."

"Exactly."

Jessica held out her hand to him and pulled him to his feet. "We'll only be gone a few minutes."

Jessica slung her jacket over her shoulder, and with Patrick at her side, walked toward the water. "When I was a little girl, my mother and I lived near a lake like this. When I was about your age, my mother taught me how to swim."

"You can swim? I didn't know there were any girls that could swim."

"It's been a long time since I've been in the water, and I may be a little rusty, but I'm sure I could hold my own."

"Could you teach me how to swim?"

Jessica hesitated. Despite her promise to McCain,

her days here in Prosperity were numbered. "I don't know if your father would like that."

"Oh, come on! Please!" He grabbed her hand and jumped up and down, chanting the word *please*.

Despite herself, she laughed. "I'll try. That's all I can promise."

He smiled, satisfied with her answer. "Did you swim a lot when you were little?"

"Every day during the summer until my mother died and I was forced to move in with my father." An old sadness crept into her heart.

"Why'd you stop swimming?"

"My father thought swimming was unseemly for a young lady." Jessica stared ahead at the pond and the large shade tree that drooped lazily over it.

"Was your father a mean man?"

She shook her head. Oddly, she didn't feel anger toward her father, only sadness for the times they could have shared. "He wasn't mean, not really. He just didn't know what to do with a young girl, especially an angry one who'd just lost her mother."

"So what'd you do?"

"I made a lot of trouble for Father."

"Like what?"

"When I moved from the country to Father's city house, I had to leave all my pets behind." In a matter of days, she'd lost her mother, her home and her animal friends. Her throat tightened. It had been years since she'd dredged up these memories.

"While I was in the park one day, I found a stray cat," Jessica added. "He was such a cute little thing, and he looked so hungry that I tucked him under my jacket and took him home. I kept him in my room and fed him milk and cold meats for several days. I named him Sparky.''

''What's so bad about that?''

''I was with my tutor one morning when the upstairs maid noticed an unseemly smell coming from my room. She found the cat and took him directly to the butler, who told my father. Father sent for me immediately. He told me the cat had to go and that I was forbidden to bring another animal into the house.''

''That's pretty mean.''

''You didn't see the mess little Sparky left in my chest, or have to deal with the fleas. A city house is not the place for a cat.''

''If you stay in Prosperity, you can have all the animals you want. Pa wouldn't mind.''

Jessica laughed and draped her arm around his shoulder. ''Somehow, I don't see your father with pets in the house.''

She and Patrick stopped at the edge of the lake. The water lapped gently against the muddy edge. *So peaceful,* she mused as she took note of a wooden flat-bottomed boat floating fifty feet offshore.

''It's a shame the boat has drifted away from shore. We could have rowed out to the middle.''

Patrick cupped his hand over his eyes to shield them from the sun. ''That's Jed's boat. He takes it out fishing sometimes. Usually he ties it up on shore, but sometimes the boys in town turn it loose. He's gonna be mad when he sees it way out there.''

The boat rocked gently from side to side. Jessica began to turn from the lake when suddenly a blond head popped up out of the boat. It was Abe, grinning back at them and holding up his red ball.

Jessica grabbed Patrick's arm. "Do you see him? It's Abe."

Patrick squinted and looked past her outstretched arm. "How did he get out there?"

"He must have been playing in the boat when it got loose. Patrick, go and get your father. Tell him we've found Abe. And hurry!"

"Okay, Miss Grimes." Patrick ran back toward town.

Jessica stood on the edge of the lake. "Abe, now, I want you to sit down, honey. It's not safe to stand in a boat."

Abe giggled and jumped up and down. "Boat! Ball!"

"Yes, that's right. Boat. Now, sit down, please."

He jumped up and down again, but in his excitement he dropped his ball into the water. He leaned over the side of the boat and reached for it.

Jessica's heart thumped wildly in her chest. "Abe, leave the ball in the water. I'll get it for you later. Just sit down!"

The boat tilted dangerously as Abe's chubby fingers grazed the ball. "Ball."

"Abraham Crumpet! Sit down this instant."

Her sharp tone caught the boy's attention for a moment. He drew back, but he did not sit down. "Ball."

"I'll get the ball. Just sit down."

Without taking her eyes off the boy, she sat in the mud and unlaced her shoes, tossed them aside and quickly pulled off her stockings. She glanced over her shoulder. Where the devil was McCain?

Abe leaned over the side of the boat again. "Ball."

"Don't move, Abe." She unfastened the buttons on the side of her skirt and pushed the heavy velvet folds to the ground. Her chemise and pantaloons flapped gently in the breeze as she quickly unbuttoned her blouse and took it off.

"Hold on, honey, I'm coming."

Fearing further delay would mean disaster, she dove into the pond. Her slender arms cut through the cold water, her limbs automatically falling into the old rhythm.

Jessica quickly became winded. Her aching lungs forced her to pause less than ten feet away from the boat to tread water while she caught her breath. A fish jumped and splashed near the boat. Abe giggled and lunged for it. His little body teetered over the edge and he fell headfirst into the water. Within seconds, his head bobbed up as he thrashed his arms wildly, struggling to remain afloat.

"Hold on, Abe. I'm coming." Frantic, Jessica started swimming again.

Abe sank below the surface again as she reached the boat. There was no time to spare. Seconds counted now.

McCain's angry voice and Mrs. Crumpet's frantic cries echoed in the distance as Jessica sucked in a deep breath and dove. She cut through the water with wide strokes until her fingers brushed against the silty bottom. She groped through the muck, searching for Abe, even as her lungs begged for air.

She found nothing.

Forced to retreat, Jessica pushed off the bottom toward the surface. When she broke through, she greedily gulped in air.

"Miss Grimes, wait!" McCain shouted.

She glanced over her shoulder in time to see him pulling off his boots, but she didn't hesitate. Instead, she dove again, swimming even harder. She combed the bottom, more frantic this time. The toddler would die if she didn't reach him soon.

Then suddenly her fingers brushed against an arm. Abe!

Her skin tingled with excitement as she grabbed hold of the boy and swam to the surface. She burst through the water again, expelled the old air and drew in more as she gripped the side of the boat and held Abe's little head out of the water. The boy wasn't breathing.

Tears glistened in her eyes as she glanced back to the shore. "Help!"

Relief washed over her when she saw McCain cutting through the water with long, bold strokes. He reached them in seconds.

"He's not breathing," Jessica sobbed.

Grim faced, he hoisted himself into the boat in one fluid movement, then he reached over the side and pulled Abe into the boat. Laying the boy face-down on the bottom, he straddled the little body and pushed the heels of his hands up the length of his back.

Jessica clung to the side of the boat, shivering, as McCain massaged Abe's back over and over again. "Can you save him?"

Water dripped from McCain's hair. "I don't know."

The bronzed muscles in McCain's back flexed as he continued to work on the boy. Seconds clicked by until, finally, the boy coughed and water trickled from his mouth. Immediately, McCain picked him up, angling his head toward the bottom of the boat. Water gushed from his mouth and nose.

Abe began to cry.

Jessica reached into the boat and touched Abe's foot. She closed her eyes. "You go ahead and cry, Abe. Fill your lungs with air and wail as loud as you can."

McCain hugged the boy against his chest and looked toward shore. Almost the entire town was there now, waiting and watching. In the center of the crowd were Lydia and Journey Crumpet. They held each other, waiting.

McCain waved to them. "The boy's fine."

Mrs. Crumpet dissolved into tears as Journey hugged her against him and everyone cheered.

McCain brushed a damp curl from Abe's face. "How did you know he was here?"

"I noticed the boat drifting out into the lake, then Abe stood up. He went over the side as I was swimming toward him."

McCain grinned. A lock of black hair hung recklessly over his forehead, giving his features a boyish quality. "You must have good eyesight to have seen him all the way from the steps of the schoolhouse."

She smiled. They both knew she'd disobeyed him, and neither cared. "My eyesight is quite excellent."

"Let's get you into the boat," he said gruffly.

McCain set Abe down in the bow of the boat. "Now don't move an inch. You got that, pardner?"

Abe nodded, then popped his thumb in his mouth.

Satisfied the boy was going nowhere, McCain turned his attention to Jessica. On his knees, he moved to the center of the boat, reached over the side and grabbed her by the arms. The gunnel of the boat nearly touched the waterline as he lifted her out of the pond and over the side.

Jessica's limbs felt heavy and tired as she pulled herself up onto her knees. Her chemise and pantaloons stuck to her like a second skin, accentuating every curve of her body. Her soft, damp ringlets draped her shoulders past the tops of her breasts. To her chagrin, her attire now left nothing to the imagination.

McCain realized it, too. His boyish grin vanished and his eyes darkened with a primitive emotion that set her heart to thumping faster in her chest. "You are full of surprises, Miss Grimes," he said quietly.

She blinked, picked Abe up and put him in her lap, grateful his little body offered some protection from McCain's eyes. Her skin glowed with embarrassment.

McCain chuckled and reached for the oars hooked to the side of the boat, driving them through the water. The boat glided easily toward shore.

Jessica had never seen a man without a shirt before and she found her gaze drawn to McCain. He sat tall, with his bare feet braced against the wooden bottom of the boat. A long, jagged scar cut across his right shoulder. Black curling hair covered his broad chest and tapered down over his flat stomach, which rippled with muscles.

There was no other way to describe his body but beautiful.

Jessica's mouth grew dry as she hugged the baby closer to her. His skin was cold and he'd begun to shiver. Neither spoke as McCain navigated the boat toward shore. Abe sucked his thumb and nestled against her body.

Her heart softened as she gently combed his damp hair back with her fingers. In the few moments before they reached the shore, Jessica felt more content than she had in years.

When they'd almost reached land, Mrs. Crumpet ran into the water to meet the boat. She scooped up her son and cradled his wet, wriggly body against her.

"Thank the Lord." Mrs. Crumpet chanted the words over and over again as she rocked back and forth, kissing the boy. Tears streamed down her face. Her husband hovered behind her.

Patrick ran to the boat, carrying McCain's shirt. "You ain't mad at Miss Grimes, are you?"

McCain jumped out of the boat and took the shirt. "No, I'm not mad."

Jessica sat huddled in the boat, her arms wrapped across her chest. If she moved, she'd certainly compromise her modesty. Several of the men were already staring boldly at her.

McCain wrapped his shirt around her shoulders and blocked everyone's view of her as she shoved her arms into the sleeves. The shirt hung past her knees. Only after McCain had fastened the top four buttons did he help her from the boat.

Her muscles ached and her limbs felt as if they were forged from iron. Tired, she staggered against McCain. He tightened his hold and drew her against him.

The entire town had gathered, forming a semicircle around them. "It's over now, folks," McCain shouted. "Everybody get on back to the picnic. Abe's gonna be fine."

Excited murmurs raced through the crowd and everyone turned back toward town.

Only Lydia Crumpet remained still. "Wait! I want everybody to hear this." The crowd halted. With Abe in her arms, she turned to Jessica. "I know I was a mite hard on you today."

"It's not important," Jessica said.

"No, it is. I can't say I'm sold on the idea of my young'uns learning to read and write, but I owe you a debt."

Jessica shook her head. "You don't owe me anything."

"Yes, I do, and a Crumpet always settles his debts. When you open the school, my brood will be there."

"Thank you."

Lydia stared at her with red-rimmed eyes. "No, Miss Grimes, you're the one that deserves the thanks."

Jessica touched Abe's damp curls. "You're most welcome."

"Mr. McCain," Lydia said, loudly enough for all

to hear, "you make sure you take good care of Miss Grimes. We don't want to lose her."

McCain's arm tightened around Jessica's waist. "Don't worry, Lydia, she's not going anywhere."

It was nearing midnight. The lobby of Sacramento's Concord Hotel was quiet. Simon Clooney lowered his ample bottom onto the stool located behind the front desk and eased his weight off his numb feet. He'd welcomed a record number of guests today. Ninety-three times he'd climbed the main staircase carrying luggage for the hotel guests. The added weight of coins in his pocket from tips did nothing to soothe his feet, but it lightened his spirits.

Closing his eyes, he slumped against the wall. Less than thirty minutes remained on his shift, and as he sighed and drifted off to sleep, he prayed they would be quiet ones.

Ding! Ding! Ding!

Clooney's eyes snapped open to the ringing of the front desk bell. He jumped to his feet and straightened his fading red jacket. "May I help you, sir…er, miss…madam?"

A plump woman with rosy cheeks and radiant blue eyes laid her parasol on the front desk. Wisps of gray hair stuck out from the chignon pinned loosely at the nape of her neck. She smiled broadly and smelled of peppermints. "Are you the manager?" she said brightly.

"No, ma'am. Mr. Shackleford is the manager, but he ain't here right now."

"*Isn't* here," she said automatically.

"Ma'am?"

"The manager *isn't* here, dear. The contraction is short for *is not. Ain't* stands for nothing and is not a word."

"Yes, ma'am."

"Where is the manager?"

"Mr. Shackleford is gone home for the evening. He ain't expected back until morning."

"Isn't," she corrected. Her brows knitted and she tapped a meaty finger against her cheek. "I need a place to stay for the night, and I was hoping the manager could tell me about the train schedules, since the station has closed."

"Like I said, the manager won't be here until morning."

"What is your name, good sir?"

"Simon Clooney, at your service. I'm the night bellman."

"Since I must wait the night, I would like to rent a room."

Mr. Clooney opened the register and turned it to face her. He dipped the pen in the inkwell and handed it to her. "Yes, madam."

She leaned over the register, and as the pen scratched the paper, Mr. Clooney pulled the last key out from a tiny cubbyhole in the wall behind the front desk.

The woman laid down the pen. "I have never had such a string of bad luck as I've had in the last fortnight. It's a wonder I made it at all."

Mr. Clooney stifled a yawn. "Yes, ma'am."

"I must also send a telegram first thing in the

morning to let my employer know I'm running late.''

Squinting, Mr. Clooney turned the book around and looked down at her signature. He couldn't decipher the chicken scratch. ''I'm sure Mr. Shackleford will be happy to see you, Mrs....''

''It's Miss. Miss Emma Grimes.''

Chapter Seven

A full day and night had passed and still Ross's blood ran cold each time he thought about Miss Grimes diving into the pond.

He sat at his desk at the mine office, staring out the window toward the schoolhouse. The sun hung high in the sky, shining down on the one-room building's cedar roof and whitewashed exterior.

Emma Grimes was part fool, part guardian angel.

Why else would she have braved the depths to save Abe Crumpet? Ross remembered how her arms had sliced through the waters toward the child and how she'd dived down and pulled the boy to the surface.

Caroline wouldn't have ventured into that lake. Certainly, she would have run for help, but she'd never have risked her own life. Miss Grimes had more courage than he'd ever guessed.

Thanks to her, Abe Crumpet had been toddling down Main Street this morning with a peppermint stick in his hand, as his mother recounted the story of his rescue to the few folks in town who'd missed it. With one single heroic act, Emma Grimes had completely won over Lydia Crumpet, along with everyone else in town, and had assured the success of the school.

He removed Emma Grimes's letters from his desk drawer and held an envelope to his nose. Peppermints. He remembered she liked peppermints.

The circuit judge had secretly read Emma Grimes's letters to him when he'd passed through town three months ago, but now Ross could only remember bits of what the judge had read to him. He could have asked Reverend Summers or Sam to read the letters to him, but his pride wouldn't allow it.

McCain pulled one letter out of the envelope and smoothed the paper flat on his desk. The long fluid letters on the parchment were perfectly formed and slanted delicately to the right. He traced several words with his finger, wishing he could unlock their secrets.

They were just as much a mystery to him as the inscription in Miss Grimes's book.

He thought back to the moment yesterday when Miss Grimes had taken the book from him and read the message. Had she discovered his secret or merely wanted to read the words for herself? He didn't know. She'd not spoken a word about the incident, and he wasn't about to ask her.

His illiteracy embarrassed him. He'd overcome poverty, the war and the Colorado mines by using wits, strong will and sometimes raw strength. By any man's standards, he'd prevailed in all areas except one—reading. It was the demon he'd never been able to conquer.

As a boy in Virginia, he'd attended school for nearly a year. It had been a frustrating and humiliating time. Unlike his schoolmates, he'd been unable to grasp the meaning of the jumble of letters and words quickly, and when the teacher had pronounced him stupid, he'd walked out of the classroom and never returned.

But the yearning to read had never left him.

"Ross, we've got trouble." Sam's voice broke the silence.

Ross folded up the letter and stuck it in the top desk drawer. "What's wrong?"

Sam swung his hip forward, favoring his bad leg, and limped to the chair. He sat down and took off his hat. "You're not going to be happy about it."

Ross didn't like his friend's solemn face. "Spit it out."

"The single men have walked off the job and have gone over to the saloon."

Ross leaned forward. "What's gotten into them? This isn't a holiday."

"They're fixing to take a vote."

The men had always talked to him when they had a problem. They'd never gone behind his back. He prided himself that there'd never been a strike at a McCain mine. "What are they voting on?"

"Miss Grimes. The men decided they want to court her and are fixing to repeal their promise to you."

Ross's fingers curled into fists. "That so?"

Sam drew in a deep breath. "I tried to talk them out of it, but there's no stopping 'em."

Ross stood and scooped up his hat. "Every one of those men gave their word to keep their distance from Miss Grimes, and I aim to see that they keep it."

Sam pushed himself out of his chair. "She's a damn fine-looking woman, Ross, and there are so few women in the territory. Hell, she's the only single woman in town."

Ross put on his hat. "They made a promise to stay clear. A man who can't keep his word isn't any use to me."

"I'm not arguing, but you can't fault the boys. She's a damn fine-looking woman."

Frustration and anger boiled inside of Ross. "I'll fire any man who comes near her." He strode out the front door of the mine office toward the sidewalk.

Sam followed him. "Then McCain Mines might just shut down. And she's a damn fine-looking woman."

"That's the third time you've said that!"

Sam shrugged. "It is a shame to keep her on the shelf."

"Tough. She's not available."

The shouts of the men ricocheted off the saloon walls as Ross shoved open the doors and paused in the doorway. Jed McManus stood behind the bar, pounding the bottom of a whiskey bottle on the bar and calling for silence. All twenty of Prosperity's single men were crowded around the bar, shouting out their opinions. The air was thick with smoke and the room reeked with the heavy scent of rotgut whiskey.

The fools must have swallowed a hell of a lot of liquor, Ross realized. Otherwise they wouldn't have challenged him.

Jed thumped his bottle against the bar again. "All those in favor of lifting the ban, say aye."

All the men shouted, "Aye."

"Then the motion is carried," Jed said. "Miss Grimes ain't off-limits no more!"

The men cheered.

Ross rested his hand on his gun belt. "Mind telling me what's going on?" His voice sliced through the room.

The men turned together, watching him with a mixture of fear and anger etched on their faces. They stepped aside as he walked toward the bar. Jed froze, his makeshift gavel suspended in the air. When Ross reached the bar, the old man lowered the bottle and backed away.

Ross faced the crowd, mentally taking note of every individual there. The men lowered their gazes, pretending great interest in the floor. "Nobody seems to have an answer for me. Jed, looks like you're running this show. Why don't you tell me what's going on?" His voice was deadly calm.

Jed cleared his throat and tugged on his store-bought collar. "The men just took a vote."

"That so?" Ross pulled the whiskey bottle toward him.

"Yeah. We men want to…court Miss Grimes."

Ross wrapped his fingers around the neck of the whiskey bottle and tightened his grip. "We all agreed we'd stay away from the new teacher for two years."

"Th-that was before we all got a look at her. We were all smitten the instant she stepped off the train."

"Jed, you're sixty-two years old," Ross stated.

"There's still fire in my hearth."

Nervous chuckles echoed through the crowd. Ross's frown deepened, and the men grew quiet again. "We already lost the last two teachers to marriage, and I don't want to lose a third."

Larry Sanders, a tall, lean man dressed in coveralls, stroked his long black beard and cleared his throat. "She's a hard woman to ignore, Mr. McCain. When she swam out into the lake to save little Abe, every man realized she had grit and spunk to go with her looks. That's a hard combination to beat."

Jim Smith, a white-haired man with a round stomach and warm brown eyes, hooked his thumbs in his suspenders. "And the winters are mighty long and cold in these parts."

Ross grunted. "Throw another log on the fire."

Larry puffed out his chest. "Miss Grimes has brought more life to this town in two days than any of us have seen in three years."

Ross jabbed his finger at Larry. "She's *not* in the marriage market."

Jed shook his head. "You can't stop the course of nature, Mr. McCain."

He slammed his fist against the bar. "Like hell I can't."

"What are you gonna do?" Jed countered. "Fire every man who courts her?"

"I just might."

Zeke Hollis staggered through the crowd waving a half-full bottle of whiskey. His shirt was smeared with dirt and his hair slick with sweat. "You might be able to take my job away, but you sure as hell ain't gonna say whether or not I can see that pretty little schoolteacher."

A vein pulsed in Ross's temple. "Come near her and I'll kill you."

Zeke sniggered. "I don't think you're the type to shoot a man in cold blood."

Ross rested his hand on his gun. "Care to test me?"

Zeke's smile faltered and he stumbled backward. "Watch your back, McCain, and keep an eye on the little lady. I just might steal her away from you."

A low growl rumbled in Ross's chest as he stared at the man. Zeke scrambled through the crowd and out the door.

Ross followed him to the door and would have gone after him, but Sam caught him by the arm. "Zeke and all these men are full of whiskey. Once they sober up, they'll wise up."

The skin on the back of McCain's neck tightened. "I'm not going to let these men get the upper hand. Ever! This was *my* town and Miss Grimes is *my* teacher. I found her and I'm going to keep her."

"Ross, you need to cool off. These men live a hard, lonely life, and you can't blame them for wanting a woman to warm their beds."

"They can have any woman they want, *except* Miss Grimes."

"There's nothing you can do to stop them unless you marry her yourself."

Ross looked at Sam. His anger eased as an idea took root in his mind. "What'd you say?"

Sam shrugged. "Nothing. It was a bad joke."

"No, it is the answer to my problem. If I marry Miss Grimes, I'm solving two problems. The men will realize they can't cross me, and the town gets to keep its teacher."

"You're not serious."

Ross smacked Sam on the back. "I am. And the sooner I marry Miss Grimes, the sooner we can all get back to our lives."

"Now, wait just a minute."

"I don't have a minute to waste. Luck's on my side. Reverend Summers is in town this week. Go get him and bring him back here. I'll get Miss Grimes."

"Ross, have you considered that she may not want to marry you?"

"No."

"You can't just drag the woman down the street and marry her in the saloon."

"Sure I can. Besides, it's not a real marriage. When her contract expires, we'll annul it." Ross smiled. "The more I think about the idea, the more I like it. It's the perfect solution."

Sam stabbed his fingers through his hair. "What about you?"

"What about me?"

"I remember you swearing you'd never marry again."

"I'm not a young man crazy in love. This is business."

"You sure?"

"Of course. Now go get Reverend Summers and have him back here in five minutes. He's got a wedding to perform."

Jessica smoothed her dirty hands over her work apron, which was covering her new, yellow calico dress. The color of the dress did nothing for her, and the fabric scratched her skin, but it was practical, and her own dress had been ruined when she'd discarded it by the pond yesterday.

She, along with a half-dozen other women, had spent this morning scrubbing the schoolhouse windows, wiping away the last of the grime. With a bit more work, the little room would be sparkling.

Her muscles and fingers ached, but for the first time since her mother's death, she felt at peace and wonderfully needed. She closed her eyes and savored the unfamiliar yet pleasant sensation.

"We're gonna have this place spruced up in no time," Lydia Crumpet said. She stood by another window hanging a set of blue curtains.

Harriet Gooden peered over her glasses as she unpacked a crate of books. "Lydia's right. It might take another day or two, but if we keep working shifts, we'll have this place ready for school on Monday."

Jessica climbed down off the stool, dipped her rag in the bucket of water and wrung it out. "I couldn't have done this if you ladies hadn't been here to help."

"Ain't nothing we wouldn't do for you, Miss Grimes," Lydia said.

"I appreciate it, but I think we should stop work for today. The sun will be setting soon and I know you ladies have families to tend to."

"I believe I'd rather clean windows than face that wild brood of mine," Harriet said.

Mrs. Crumpet laughed. "The evening hour can try a woman's soul."

Jessica laughed, too, and turned toward the door. To her surprise McCain stood there. His broad shoulders blocked out the dimming sunlight. His eyes sparkled a brilliant green and possessed a wild, barely restrained energy.

His grave look frightened her and squashed whatever sense of peace she'd enjoyed. She dropped her rag in the bucket. Had he discovered her secret? "What brings you here, Mr. McCain?"

"I need for you to come over to the saloon."

Jessica glanced at Mrs. Crumpet and Harriet. They'd stopped working. Their glances darted between Mr. McCain and her. "Whatever for?" she asked.

"There's been a bit of trouble, and I need you to help me sort it out."

"We'll be finishing up here soon. I'll come by once we're done."

Mrs. Crumpet wiped her hands on her apron. "Miss Grimes, you go on ahead with Mr. McCain. Harriet and I will finish up."

McCain took hold of her arm. His fingers banded around her flesh like iron. "Let's go."

Jessica straightened her shoulders. "Would you mind telling me what this is about?"

"I'll explain when we get to the saloon."

McCain guided her out the door and across the street. Jessica nearly had to run to keep pace with his long strides. They brushed past Sissy and Mrs. Miller, but McCain didn't slow his pace.

Sissy raised her hand. "Where're you two headed in such a rush?"

Jessica glanced over her shoulder. "The saloon."

"Whatever for?" Sissy asked.

"I don't know."

Sissy and Mrs. Miller stared at each other as Mrs. Crumpet and Harriet walked up to them. The four followed Jessica and McCain to the saloon. The small parade caught the attention of other people, and by the time they reached the saloon, a half-dozen other folks had joined the procession.

McCain ignored them all. He didn't stop until he reached the saloon doors.

Jessica's breathing grew ragged. "Mr. McCain, what is going on?"

"We're getting married."

She shook her head. "What are you talking about?"

McCain stared down at her and placed his hands on her shoulders. "Don't look so worried. This isn't going to be a real marriage. It will only be a formality—a way of keeping any unwanted suitors away. It'll just be easier if you're Mrs. Ross McCain while you're here."

"Easier for who?"

"You, of course."

McCain was serious. "I'm not marrying you," she stated bluntly.

He ignored her as he stared out across the street toward the barbershop. "Good, Sam's found Reverend Summers now."

Jessica looked over her shoulder. Next to Sam was a medium-sized man in his middle years. The man's face was covered in shaving cream and he wore a barber's smock.

Panic swelled inside her. "You are insane," she insisted.

Sissy rushed forward. "Are you two getting married?"

"No," Jessica answered.

"I just sprung the idea on her," McCain said calmly. "But she'll get used to it."

"How can I get used to a stupid idea?" Jessica demanded.

"It's a great idea," McCain said easily. "I don't know why I didn't think of it sooner."

Sissy folded her arms. "Is she gonna keep teaching school?"

"Of course," McCain said.

Sissy shrugged, "Well, he is a good catch, Miss Grimes."

McCain smiled. "See?"

"I wouldn't have you if you were the last man in the territory."

McCain winked. "That's no way to speak to your intended. Here comes the reverend now."

When Sam and the minister reached them, the latter was huffing. "What's this I hear about an emergency wedding, Mr. McCain?"

"I need for you to marry Miss Grimes and me."

Reverend Summers's jaw dropped. "What? Now? Here?"

McCain nodded. "Inside the saloon in front of the men."

The minister peered through the swinging double doors. The men were laughing and drinking. A few were singing. "This is highly unusual," he said.

Relief washed over Jessica. "Thank goodness. Someone here has some common sense. Reverend, would you please explain to Mr. McCain that you are not going to marry us?"

"Reverend," McCain explained patiently, "I hear you're looking to build a church. I also hear you'd like to have a bell and bell tower on that church."

Reverend Summers shrugged. "Sadly, there aren't enough funds for either."

"There will be, right after you marry us."

"That's bribery!" Jessica shouted.

McCain ignored her. "What's it going to be, Reverend? It sure would be nice to have your own church."

The minister's skin reddened under the white cream. "Does the lady want to marry you?"

"No!" Jessica exclaimed.

McCain pulled her against his side. "Yes, she does. She's just a little angry with me right now. Once we're married, she'll settle down. Now, let's get inside."

Jessica stumbled as McCain dragged her into the saloon. Sissy and the others followed. The music and laughter stopped. Every man in the room turned to face McCain and Jessica.

Jed lowered his beer from his lips. "What is this all about?"

"Miss Grimes and I are getting married," McCain said evenly.

"What?" Jed roared.

Jessica tried to jerk her arm free but couldn't. "We are not getting married. I just told Mr. McCain I have no interest in marrying anyone."

McCain smiled. "Reverend, would you do the honors?"

Reverend Summers stepped forward. "I don't have my Bible. And I'm not dressed. Just give me a moment to clean up—"

"You look fine, and I'll bet you know the vows by heart."

"Well, yes, but—"

"Do you want that church or not?"

Jessica's desperation grew. "I am not going to marry you!"

"I would like a church," Reverend Summers hedged.

"I'll even throw in one of those fancy-colored windows," McCain added. "What are they called?"

Reverend Summers's eyes brightened. "Stained glass. That's most generous."

"Then you're ready?"

"I suppose."

"Good." McCain hauled Jessica to his side. The harder she tried to push him away, the tighter he held on to her. He took off his hat. "Get on with it, Reverend."

The minister cleared his throat. "Dearly beloved, we are gathered here in the sight of God to join this man and woman in holy matrimony."

Jessica stamped her foot. "Stop this! I am not going to marry him."

Sissy raised the tip of her apron to the corner of her eye. "This is kinda romantic."

Mrs. Crumpet nodded. "It's beautiful."

Reverend Summers shifted uncomfortably. "Do you, Ross McCain, take this woman to be your lawfully wedded wife?"

"Yes," McCain said clearly.

"Do you, Emma Grimes, take Ross McCain to be your lawfully wedded husband?"

"No!" she yelled.

Reverend Summers stared at McCain. "She said no."

"She said yes," McCain corrected.

"I did not," Jessica said.

McCain raised an eyebrow. "I heard a yes." He turned and stared at the silent gathering. "Whoever didn't hear a yes can collect his pay and get out of town now." His body tensed as if he were ready to fight every man who disagreed with him.

Larry shrugged. "I heard yes."

"Me, too," Jim said.

All the men nodded.

Sissy touched Jessica's shoulder. "He'll make you a good husband."

McCain smiled. "Reverend, you can continue."

"No, he cannot," Jessica insisted. "I will not have you railroad me into this! It's not right. It's not fair."

"He's really a fine man," Reverend Summers whispered to her.

"He's the devil," she countered.

The minister dropped his gaze. "You've just got jitters, like all new brides." He then added quickly, "I now pronounce you man and wife. You may kiss the bride."

In shock, Jessica looked up into McCain's green eyes, which were filled with triumph. "Don't you dare."

McCain took her by the shoulders, then gathered her up in his arms. For all to see, he pressed his lips against hers. The kiss held no emotion, no tenderness. It was his way of branding her in front of the other men. They all understood she belonged to him now.

But slowly the kiss changed. It softened and drew her into a sensuous web of sensations she'd never experienced before. Her body relaxed against his, and she curled her arms around his neck, savoring the way his touch made her tingle. She heard the hoots and hollers of the men around her, but their voices seemed distant and unreal.

Then, without warning, the kiss ended. When McCain drew back, she could see that his eyes sparkled with arrogant pride. Slowly, he unwrapped her arms from around his neck.

Humiliation replaced desire. The knowing leers of the men around her made her cringe.

McCain put his hat on. "Ready to go home, Mrs. McCain?"

Jessica stumbled backward and wiped her lips with the back of her hand. "How could you?"

"You didn't seem to mind."

Her cheeks burned with shame. He'd stirred feelings inside her she'd never experienced before, and now he was playing her for a fool in front of the whole town. Suddenly, she wanted to wipe the smirk from his face.

So she did the first thing that came to mind.

She slapped him.

Chapter Eight

A hush fell over the crowd as Jessica and McCain faced each other. The imprint of her hand blazed red on his cheek. His expression grew taut.

McCain reached up and rubbed his face. "We'll talk about this at home."

She planted her hands on her hips. "Home? I'm not going anywhere with you! If you want to talk, we'll do it here."

Nervous chuckles drifted through the crowd as McCain took her by the arm and pulled her against his chest. "Lower your voice."

Jessica tried to twist free. "You've gone mad if you think I'll lower my voice after what you just did."

McCain's lips brushed her ear. "I'm very sane, and we are going home."

Jed smacked his hand against the bar. "Drinks on the house. I think we owe a toast to the new Mrs. McCain."

McCain raised his head and smiled. "Pour one for me."

The men cheered and bellied up to the bar. Jed lined up two dozen glasses and filled each with whiskey. The men pushed and shoved each other as they reached for a glass.

McCain pushed Jessica through the crowd toward the bar, then picked up a whiskey. He held up his glass. "To the new Mrs. McCain."

Jed raised his glass. "I wish you all the luck in the world, Mrs. McCain. You're gonna need it."

Jessica shook her head. "I don't need your luck, Mr. McManus, because Mr. McCain and I are not married."

McCain swallowed his whiskey in one gulp. "Yes, we are."

Jed winked at her. "McCain's right. As far as this town is concerned, you two are married right and proper."

She tried to yank her elbow free. "Anyone with an ounce of sense knows this marriage isn't legal."

McCain set his glass down on the bar. "We've given everyone enough to talk about. Time to go."

As he pulled her through the crowd again, men and women stepped aside to make room for them. McCain shoved her through the swinging doors onto the boardwalk.

The people in the saloon had moved to the window to watch them. Several of the men held up their glasses to her before they downed their whiskey, while a couple of women wiped tears from their eyes.

Jessica looked away. "They'll never have respect for me."

"Yes, they will," McCain said.

Wagon harnesses jangled and clattered as Mr. Miller drove his wagon by the saloon. He touched the brim of his hat. "Afternoon, Mr. McCain. Miss Grimes."

McCain pulled his own hat down over his eyes. "Good day to you, Mr. Miller, and the lady's name is McCain now, not Grimes."

Mr. Miller's smile vanished and his mouth gaped open. He pulled his wagon to a stop. "Say that again."

"The lady is my wife."

Mr. Miller rubbed the back of his neck with his hand. "Kinda sudden, ain't it?"

"No time like the present," McCain said as he resumed a fast pace.

"You've ruined everything," Jessica huffed.

McCain sighed. "You're easily upset, aren't you?"

She tripped and would have fallen if he'd not held her arm firmly. "I have a tendency to get upset when a man forces me into marriage."

He raised an eyebrow. "Does this happen often?"

"More often than I'd like."

His eyes darkened. Without warning, he stopped in the middle of the street. Unmindful of the crowd gathering on the boardwalk, he grabbed her by the shoulders and turned her to face him. "Is that why you left Sacramento? Are you already married?"

"That's none of your business."

He stared down at her. "You're my wife. Your business is my business now."

"*If* I recognized that farce of a ceremony as real and considered us married—which I don't—then I suppose my past might be your business. But I do not, so it isn't.''

His expression turned ominous. He stared down at her, his gaze searing. Stubbornly, she stared back. If he was trying to intimidate her, it was working, but too much had happened for her to back down.

"I asked you a question. Why did you leave Sacramento?''

"To live *my* life as *I* chose.''

He frowned. "Answer my question!''

She glared at him. "Has anybody ever told you that you are overbearing and insensitive?''

"Only when they're trying to get on my good side.''

"Let go of me.''

"Answer my question.''

"Give her hell, McCain,'' Larry called from the boardwalk. He tossed back another glass of whiskey. "She's your wife now. Show her who is boss.''

"Miss Grimes, set your man straight,'' Mrs. Crumpet shouted. "A woman rules the house, and don't you ever forget it.''

Laughter rumbled through the crowd. Half the town had gathered on the boardwalk still watching them. The women smiled, and a few waved at Jessica as if this were some grand romantic adventure. The bachelors scowled.

"I bet a dollar he has her in bed by sundown,'' Jed declared.

"I'll take that bet,'' Larry answered. He dug a silver dollar out of his denim pants and tossed it in the air.

"Hey, McCain,'' Larry shouted as he stumbled

into the street after them. "Your bride doesn't look very happy."

Jim Smith hooked his thumbs in his overalls and sauntered to the front of the crowd. "You boys ever hear the story about the schoolteacher and the farmer?" His voice trailed off as he told his joke. When he'd finished, men and women alike howled with laughter.

A wave of embarrassment washed over Jessica. She'd been raised never to show emotion in public, yet she was shouting at McCain in front of her neighbors. She'd been a respected teacher this morning. Now she was the butt of jokes.

"Let me go," she demanded.

He tightened his grip. "As soon as we get home."

They marched toward his white house, the towns-people trailing behind them. She struggled with a rush of panic. What if he decided he wanted more than just a marriage in name only?

Jessica moistened her lips. "I don't have time to go home now. There's work to be done at the schoolhouse."

"The work will wait."

"I can't possibly teach on Monday if I don't fin-ish my work."

"Then classes will be delayed. After all, this is your honeymoon."

They reached the steps to his house. Without warning, McCain swept her up into his arms and turned toward the crowd. Her fingertips pressed against his chest and she felt the slow, steady beat of his heart. How could he be so calm when her own heart hammered in her chest?

McCain smiled, but his eyes held no trace of humor. "Jed, are bets still open?"

Jed waved a fistful of dollar bills. "Yes, sir, they are."

"Good. Put me down for a dollar."

Jed laughed. "Sorry, you can't get in on this one, McCain. It wouldn't be fair, seeing as you have an inside track."

Jessica felt the color drain from her face. "Put me down this instant."

"In a minute, dear," McCain said, still grinning. "Show's over, folks. Time my bride and I had some privacy."

Laughter rippled through the crowd. With a nod of satisfaction, McCain carried Jessica over the threshold into the house, kicked the front door closed with his foot and put her down.

She scrambled backward, anxious to put distance between them. "How dare you humiliate me like that!"

"Calm down." He tossed his hat toward a ladder-back chair.

She started for the door. "I'm leaving immediately. I'll send for my things later."

McCain blocked her path. "My wife lives *with me*."

The foyer seemed to shrink. A chill crawled down her spine. This moment reminded her of the last one she'd shared with William Perry. But this time she wasn't afraid—she was angry. "I'm not your wife and we don't have a *real* marriage."

He shrugged. "Beautiful wives are more trouble

than they are worth. All I want is a schoolteacher, so your virtue is safe, Mrs. McCain.''

Before she could respond, the back door banged open, then closed. Peg stood at the end of the hallway, holding a basket of freshly gathered eggs. Wisps of gray hair framed her flushed face. ''What the blazes is going on? I got half the town trampling my black-eyed Susans.''

''Miss Grimes and I got married a few minutes ago.''

She stalked down the hallway toward them. ''You want to say that again?''

''We got married,'' he said mildly. ''The boys voted to court Miss Grimes. Marriage seemed the best way to put a stop to it.''

Jessica stepped forward, hoping to find an ally in Peg. ''Don't listen to him. I never once agreed to love, honor, let alone cherish this man.''

Peg met McCain's stare. ''But you got a half-dozen witnesses who say she did?''

McCain nodded. ''Yep.''

Jessica reached out to Peg. ''But it's not legal. It's not binding.''

Peg sighed. ''Honey, in these parts, McCain's word is law. If he says you're married, you're married.''

Jessica smacked her fists against her thighs. ''But it's not right.''

The back door opened and shut again. Patrick stood at the end of the hallway. His shirttail was out, his face was smudged with dirt and a drop of blood trickled from his nose.

McCain went to Patrick. "Boy, what happened to you?"

"Billy Crumpet and I got into a fight."

"Over what?"

"Billy Crumpet says you married Miss Grimes, but I said he was a dirty liar."

"Billy's right, boy. Miss Grimes and I are married."

Patrick looked Jessica up and down. "Well, she don't look like she's gonna have a baby."

Jessica buried her face in her hands. Less than fifteen minutes had passed since they'd left the saloon and already rumors were circulating about her.

McCain cleared his throat. "Miss Grimes isn't going to have a baby."

"Billy heard it straight from his ma."

"There's no baby," Jessica insisted.

Worry lines creased the boy's face. "Well, if she does, can I still stay here?"

McCain laid his hand on his son's shoulder. "You are my son, Patrick. Nothing is going to change that. Nothing."

Patrick rubbed his nose. "You sure?"

"I'm positive. Now why don't you ask Peg to give you a slice of pie? Miss Grimes and I have some things to talk about."

"Okay!"

McCain pressed his hand into the small of Jessica's back and pushed her toward the study. "Let's finish this in the library."

Jessica didn't want to upset Patrick, so she allowed McCain to guide her down the hallway. Only when he had closed the door behind them did she speak. "I never stopped to think about Patrick and how this would affect him."

McCain leaned against the door. "Our marriage changes nothing. The boy will always have me, no matter what happens between us."

Her throat tightened. "I'd never hurt that child."

"That's yet to be proved." He nodded toward the chair. "I didn't bring you here to discuss my son. Sit down."

"I'd rather stand."

"Suit yourself." He walked over to a cabinet, removed a whiskey bottle and two glasses. He set the glasses on his desk and filled each to the halfway mark. He handed her a glass, his fingers brushing against hers, and then sat in a chair next to the cold fireplace. He took a sip of whiskey.

She watched him warily. For an instant she imagined his eyes softened. But that was impossible. If he had any shred of decency, he would not have dragged her down to the saloon for that mock wedding.

"You may not like the idea of being married to me now, but you'll be glad in the long run. As Miss Grimes you'd have been overwhelmed with suitors. As Mrs. McCain you can do what you came here to do—teach school. In two years, when your contract expires, I'll give you a divorce if you want it."

"And I will be a divorced woman. You will have ruined my reputation."

"No one need know we were ever married."

"And I'm supposed to trust you?"

"I never break my word."

"So we just continue on as if nothing had happened today?"

"Exactly."

She couldn't resist baiting him. "And if a suitor does come calling, you wouldn't mind if I encourage his attentions. I'd like to have a few suitors. I've never had one before."

McCain frowned. "My wife won't entertain suitors."

"But you just said nothing's changed."

"Don't play games with me, *Mrs. McCain*."

She cringed at the name but chose to ignore it. "Isn't that what this is—a game? Some game of deception designed to fool everyone in town?"

He set his glass on the table beside his chair. "We may not have a marriage in the truest sense, but nevertheless, when we are in public you will treat me with the respect a wife gives a husband."

Outrage welled inside her. "As your *employee,* I owe you a fair day's work, but beyond that I don't owe you anything." She started for the door.

"We aren't finished."

"Yes, we are."

"Why did you leave Sacramento? Or do I have to send a telegram to my attorney there and find out?"

Suddenly, her knees felt weak. If McCain sent a telegram to Sacramento, he'd find out she wasn't Emma Grimes. Would he send her back to William Perry if he knew the truth?

The truth—or at least part of it—was her only option now. "My father wanted me to marry. I wanted to teach school. So I left town."

"Just like that?"

She stared at the brown liquid in her glass. "Yes."

"Can't say most women would have that kind of gumption."

Jessica rubbed her fingertips over her eyes. "I've spent the last ten years of my life being told what to wear, what to read, what to think. I wanted more."

"So you accepted a job in the wilds of Colorado teaching children."

Jessica hesitated. "Yes."

McCain studied her as he swirled the whiskey in his glass. She wondered if he could tell she was lying.

Without thinking, she sat down in the chair and gulped down the contents of her glass. Liquid fire burned her throat. Tears filled her eyes as she coughed and sputtered. She gasped for air.

Strong fingers took the glass from her and thrust a cup of water into her hand. Gratefully, she gulped the water down. "We are not married," she croaked finally.

McCain squatted in front of Jessica and rested his hands on the arms of the chair. He brushed a curl from her face. "We are married," he said quietly. "So let's make the best of it."

She pushed past him and stood. "That's out of the question."

He straightened. "Why?"

"Because you are a selfish man and I've had my fill of men like you." She stalked toward the door.

"Where are you going?"

She paused, her hand on the doorknob. Where could she go? She had no friends to speak of and there wasn't a hotel in town. For an instant, she was speechless, then the answer came to her. There was only one place in town where she felt truly comfortable. "To the schoolhouse."

"You'll make me look like a fool. I won't allow it."

"Go to the devil." She slammed the door.

The clock chimed as Ross traced the rim of his coffee cup and stared at his wife's empty place at the dinner table. Patrick sat to his right and Peg to his left. Dinner had been quiet and solemn. Hours had passed since his new wife had stormed out of his library. She'd not returned.

Dishes clattered as Peg stood and started to pile dishes on a wooden tray. "Hell's bells, I still can't believe you married her."

"It was the right thing to do."

Peg cocked an eyebrow. "For who?"

"For everybody."

Patrick stared into his mug of milk. "Should I call her Ma?"

Ross's gut tightened. During the last six hours he'd been forced to secretly admit that he'd married Emma rashly. He'd not stopped to consider Patrick's feelings or the fact that his son had not had a stable home during his short life. And he owed the boy a decent home. So, for Patrick's sake, he'd accepted the fact that his marriage had to work.

Ross wiped the milk off of Patrick's upper lip with his napkin. "Yes. Call her Ma."

Patrick nodded. "Okay. Can I have another piece of cake, Pa?" The boy had accepted the marriage as easily as that.

"Have as much as you can stomach tonight. It isn't every day I get married."

"Thanks!"

Ross tossed his napkin on the table. It was time to bring his wife home. "I'm going over to the schoolhouse. Likely, Emma was so busy working she forgot her dinner."

Peg snorted. "Hope she didn't run away."

"She didn't."

Peg looked as if she wanted to say something more, but instead she said, "Tell her I'll keep a plate warm for her."

His mood darkened. "Don't wait up for me."

Ross stopped at the front door and picked his gun belt off a side table, strapped it on and walked outside. The night air was cool and the sky clear. Moonlight shimmered on the wood frame buildings and cast long gray shadows into the street. Lanterns burned from many of the buildings, and piano music and laughter drifted from the saloon's open windows.

As he strode toward the schoolhouse, Ross saw Emma pass in front of a lighted window. Unexpectedly, he breathed a sigh of relief. At least she hadn't run away.

Since the moment he'd met Emma he'd been attracted to her. He'd dreamed about touching her soft hair and caressing her smooth skin. Even now his body hardened at the thought of her lying naked under him.

But he'd given his word he wouldn't touch her. If they came together, she'd have to invite him into her bed. And that wasn't likely to happen right now.

Ross sighed. Hate him or not, it was time for her to come home.

He marched up to the schoolhouse and pushed open the door. Twin lanterns sat on her desk, burning brightly. The light danced on the walls, five open crates of books near the door and half a dozen benches pushed against the wall. His wife knelt on the floor in the corner behind her desk. She was spreading out a blanket.

McCain drew in a steadying breath as he stared at the delicate shape of her rump. Fighting with her was the last thing on his mind. "It's time to go home."

She started at the sound of his voice and looked up at him. Her face was pale and her hair a tangled mass of curls. A smudge of dirt on her cheek marred her otherwise flawless skin.

She rose. "I am home. I'll be by tomorrow to pick up my belongings."

Ross forced himself to remain calm as he walked over to her. Something about her reached into him and for an instant touched a part of him he thought had died long ago.

Before he could speak, the sound of footsteps outside diverted McCain's gaze to the open door. Zeke staggered into the schoolhouse. He held a whiskey bottle in one hand and a gun in the other.

"Well, ain't this a cozy scene." Zeke raised the bottle to his lips, swigged the remains from the bottom and tossed it to the floor.

Ross put himself between Emma and Zeke. His feet braced shoulder width apart, he slid his hand to his gun. "I told you to get out of town."

"Guess I didn't feel like it, *Mr.* McCain. Besides, I got just as much right as any other man to live in this town."

He wiped his mouth with the back of his hand, his lips curving into a gap-toothed grin. "Your new wife sure is a pretty little thing."

"Stay away from her."

"I don't work for you anymore, so I don't have to listen to you."

"Then take a piece of advice. Get out of town while you still can."

Zeke waved his gun. "I'll move along as soon as I've talked to the lady—alone."

"I don't want you talking to my wife."

She glanced at Zeke, then back at him. "Stop insisting we are married when we're not."

Zeke jabbed the tip of his gun at McCain. The barrel glistened in the lantern light. "Tell *your wife* to shut up."

Emma pushed past Ross and poked her finger at Zeke. "I am not his wife. And would you kindly get out of my schoolhouse?"

Ross yanked her back behind him. "Woman, stay out of this."

"I will not," she countered. "I've had it with men telling me what to do. This is *my* schoolhouse and I say who stays and who goes. Both of you leave."

Zeke cocked his revolver. "Lady, do as your husband says."

"If you think—"

"Shut up, Emma," McCain ordered.

She folded her arms and pursed her lips, staring mutinously at both men.

Zeke nodded. "That's more like it. Now, if you don't mind, I think I'd like to take that walk with Miss Grimes—er, I mean, Mrs. McCain—now. I've a need for some companionship this evening."

Emma cringed and drew closer to McCain. "I don't want to go with him," she whispered.

Emma needed him. A mysterious satisfaction burned inside of Ross. At this moment he knew he'd do anything to protect her.

He kept his expression blank and shrugged. "You're welcome to her. She's been more trouble than she's worth."

"McCain!" she gasped. "That's an awful thing to say."

Zeke stole a glance at her and licked his lips. "She sure is a spirited little thing."

"She's all yours," Ross said.

Her face paled with anger and fear. "How dare you just toss me away? I'm *your* wife."

Ross raised an eyebrow. "You're the first to tell everybody we aren't married."

She shot a glance at Zeke. He winked at her. "Well, I was wrong. We are married."

"Sorry, too late."

"But—"

"Go on outside," Ross said slowly, as if speaking to a child.

She hesitated.

"Go!" he urged.

Her back rigid, she walked past him and Zeke toward the door. She turned. "If we get out of this, Mr. McCain, you'll have me to reckon with."

Damn, he admired her spirit. "Gladly."

"Stop talking," Zeke ordered. "It's making me kinda crazy. McCain, toss her your wallet. I know you always carry a good bit of cash on you."

Ross reached inside his coat and drew out a worn wallet. He threw it on the floor next to a stack of primers. "If you want it, get it yourself."

Zeke shook his head. "Yeah, right, and have you jump me. No, let the lady get the money. Mrs. McCain, pick it up."

Slowly, she walked toward the wallet. She paused an instant, but instead of picking it up, she grabbed a primer and hurled it at Zeke. She hit him squarely in the face.

The distraction was all Ross needed. He drew his gun, but the sudden movement caught Zeke's eye and he raised his own gun. Both men fired at the same time.

Deafening explosions sliced through the night air. The acrid smell of gunpowder filled Ross's nostrils. And then he felt the hot, searing pain in his shoulder.

Zeke fell to the floor. Ross walked forward, the smoking tip of his gun still pointed toward his rival, who lay curled in a ball on the floor, moaning. Ross kicked Zeke's gun out of his reach, then slipped his own into its holster. "Are you all right?" he asked Emma. His shoulder burned like the fires of hell.

"Yes."

"Good." He drew in a deep breath. "Do me a favor. The next time a man's got a gun pointed at me and I ask you to do something, do it, don't argue.''

She planted her hands on her hips, as if she'd remembered she was angry. ''You told me to go with him.''

Ross winced. ''I never would have let him take you. You've got to learn to trust me.''

Her retort died on her lips as she stared at his shoulder. ''You're bleeding,'' she whispered.

''Yes.''

He groaned when she lifted his jacket. Blood stained her hand.

''My God, why didn't you tell me you'd been shot?'' she asked.

''You were too busy yelling at me,'' he retorted through clenched teeth.

She touched his side and he flinched. ''I wasn't yelling.''

His entire right side, damp with blood, throbbed. ''How does it look?''

''I can't tell.''

''You're as white as a ghost.''

''I've never seen so much blood before.''

''You're not going to faint on me, are you?''

She wrapped his good arm around her shoulder. ''No,'' she said firmly. ''You're going to be fine,'' she said more loudly, ''but we've got to stop the bleeding. Let's get you home.''

He leaned against her. ''Did I hear right? Did you admit you were my wife a few minutes ago?''

She looked up at him. ''You can't hold me to that. I was scared. Desperate.''

He grinned. ''Yes, I can.''

Chapter Nine

McCain's shirt, soaked with sweat and blood, clung to his chest. He groaned painfully and leaned heavily on her, giving her more of his weight. She wrapped her arm protectively around his waist. She reminded herself McCain was a strong man and that he'd be all right.

McCain glanced down at her. His eyes seemed to bore right into her as if reading her thoughts. The idea was unsettling. "You look worried," he said.

"I'm still mad enough to shoot you myself."

He raised an eyebrow. "I've a bloodthirsty wife."

Jessica's tart reply died on her lips when a half-dozen men ran out of the saloon toward the schoolhouse. Each had his gun drawn.

Jed, with a six-shooter in one hand and a lantern in the other, led the pack. "What in tarnation happened?" he barked. "We heard gunshots coming from the schoolhouse."

Jessica and McCain stopped in the middle of the street as the men encircled them. "There was trouble."

Jed's lantern cast a searing glow on McCain's bloodstained shirt. "What the hell happened? Did the schoolteacher shoot you?"

"No!" Jessica gasped, horrified.

McCain chuckled, then grabbed his side as if it hurt. "She didn't shoot me. Zeke did. He came by the schoolhouse looking for a fight."

"Where's he now?" Jed asked.

"Back at the schoolhouse."

"He dead?"

"Nope, but he's got a bullet in him," McCain said. "Send for the sheriff. I want him locked up."

"We'll take care of it," Jed said. "Let me get the boys to help you home."

McCain shook his head. "My wife has everything under control."

Jed walked up to McCain, his lantern held high, and inspected his wound. "A lot of blood. But it looks like a flesh wound. I'd say you'll be fit as a—"

McCain groaned, drowning out Jed's voice, and leaned more heavily on Jessica. She staggered under the extra weight and prayed she could get him back to the house. He tightened his hold around her waist. For an injured man, he was surprisingly strong.

"Believe me, Jed," McCain said, "it's worse than it looks."

Larry grinned. "Getting shot on your honeymoon ain't the best of timing."

Heat rose in Jessica's cheeks.

"You underestimate me, Larry," McCain said. "Now, if you'll excuse me, my shoulder is on fire, and I've a taste for some strong whiskey."

The men's laughter rekindled Jessica's anger. "Gentlemen, if you'll pardon us."

Jed nodded and put away his gun. "Make sure Peg does the doctoring. I don't know if I'd let your wife get too close to you with a knife, McCain. She's got fire in her eyes."

McCain shrugged. "She's already threatened to shoot me."

"But Zeke beat me to it," Jessica said flippantly. Hoots of laughter followed as she led McCain home.

Peg stood on the front porch of McCain's house, a shotgun in one hand and a box of shells in the other. She wore rag curlers, and black boots peeked out from beneath her thick blue robe. "What in the hell is going on? I heard gunshots."

"Mr. McCain has been shot," Jessica said.

Peg frowned. "You shoot him?"

"Why does everyone think I shot him?" Jessica guided McCain up the stairs.

Peg shrugged. "Maybe because you got reason to."

McCain scowled. "What's that supposed to mean?"

Peg picked up the lantern. "Quiet! My patients ain't allowed to ask questions." She opened the front door and waited as they walked inside, then closed the door. She set her gun and shells on the side table. "Mrs. McCain, get your man up the stairs to his room and strip off his shirt. I'll get my doctor bag and be right up."

"He's not my man."

"Right now he is. Now get him upstairs before he drips blood on my clean floor."

Jessica and McCain climbed the stairs slowly. When they reached his room, she nudged the door open with her foot.

McCain's bedroom was sparsely furnished with a simply constructed four-poster bed, nightstand, dresser and stiff-backed chair. The smells of beeswax and tobacco filled the air. Like the man, the room was Spartan, practical and somewhat unapproachable.

McCain groaned as he sat down on the bed and lay back. He closed his eyes.

Jessica laid her palm on his forehead. It was cool. "Peg will be here soon."

"Your hand feels so soft."

Jessica drew back. "Let me get you a compress."

He captured her wrist with his strong fingers. "You handled yourself real well back there. You didn't back down and you didn't run. I'm proud of you."

His praise warmed her heart. "Thank you."

He tugged her arm gently, coaxing her toward the bed. The gesture wasn't a demand. Oddly, it felt natural to sit down beside him.

He stroked the side of her cheek with his hand and traced her rounded lips with his thumb. Her anger and frustration melted away as she savored his touch. He cupped the back of her neck with his hand.

She drew away. "Your shoulder."

"Don't worry about my shoulder." He guided her face toward his. She closed her eyes, sensing he would kiss her. Lord help her, she wanted to feel the touch of his lips.

When he pressed his mouth to hers, moist, tantalizing sensations jolted through her body. She leaned into the kiss and savored the softness of his lips, the roughness of his cheek and his heady masculine scent. She was completely ensnared and oblivious to the fact they had an audience.

"You call that taking care of your patient?" Peg grumbled.

Shocked and humiliated, Jessica pulled back and stood up. "It's not what you think."

Peg cocked an eyebrow. "My eyes are old, but they still can see you was kissing him on the lips."

"Yes, b-but…" she stammered.

"A man's allowed to kiss his wife, isn't he?" McCain drawled.

Jessica clenched her fists at her side. "I'm not your wife."

Peg set her bag on the bed. "Save it for the judge, honey. I got work to do." She snapped open the bag. "Mrs. McCain, or whatever your name is, there's water in the pitcher on the table beside the dresser. Pour some into the basin and bring it over here."

Grateful for a job, Jessica hurried to the small table. As she poured the water into the basin, the glint of silver on the dresser caught her attention. Her silver comb, freshly shined, sparkled in the soft lantern light.

She glanced around the room. Her cape was draped over a chair and her reticule and hat sat atop the small table by the chair. McCain had moved her belongings into his room.

Fear. Anger. Frustration. Thanks to Ross McCain,

each emotion raged inside of Jessica. The man had turned her life upside down.

"Mrs. McCain, get over here with that water," Peg ordered.

Automatically, Jessica picked up the basin and a towel. The cool liquid sloshed from side to side as she walked to the side of McCain's bed. Peg stood at the foot, inspecting the contents of her black bag and muttering to herself.

McCain's eyes were closed, his lips curled slightly into an arrogant smile. Jessica gnashed her teeth. Why shouldn't he smile? The town had a teacher and he had a willing wife. Like a fool, she'd just kissed him, ready to surrender herself to him. Stupid, stupid, stupid.

Outraged at her own folly and his arrogance, she stood over him with the bowl of water. A good dousing would serve him right. She hesitated.

Training. Etiquette. Miss Madeline.

Damn them all.

Jessica dumped the water on McCain's head.

His eyes popped opened and he sucked in air through his clenched teeth. "Are you trying to drown me, woman?"

"Drowning would be too quick a death for you," Jessica snapped.

Water dripped from his chest and seeped into the sheets. "What the hell has gotten into you? Just a moment ago—"

"I was acting like a complete fool. How dare you move my things into your room?"

"What the devil are you talking about?"

"My comb. My reticule. Everything I own is in this room."

"I didn't have anything to do with moving your things in here."

"Oh, and I'm supposed to believe that?"

"I moved your belongings in here," Peg said evenly.

Jessica's bluster faltered. "Why would you do such a thing?"

"A wife's place is in her husband's bed."

"I'm not his wife."

Peg took the bowl from Jessica. "After what I just saw, it's only a matter of time."

McCain chuckled.

Jessica's eyes narrowed. "Don't say a word, Ross McCain. Or I will finish what Zeke started."

Peg cleared her throat. "If you two are done, I'd like to patch him up."

"I'm finished," Jessica said. "I'm going to collect my belongings and move over to the schoolhouse."

McCain swung his legs over the side of the bed, then winced in pain. "Now wait just a damn minute. If you think I'm going to let you leave this house and sleep in the schoolhouse, then you've lost your mind."

Jessica opened the door. "Try and stop me."

"All right." He started to push himself off the bed, she caught the raw determination in his eyes.

McCain halted when Patrick stumbled into the room, rubbing his eyes. Barefoot, he wore his night-shirt. He walked up to the bed. When he saw his father, his eyes grew alert, then frightened. "Is that blood, Pa?"

McCain sat straighter, all traces of pain gone from his face. "It's not as bad as it looks."

Patrick's face became pinched with worry, and Jessica knew there'd be no grand exit tonight. She put her arm around Patrick's shoulders. "He's going to be fine."

McCain winked. "Of course I am. Don't worry, boy, it's not the first time I've been shot. I'll be just fine."

Patrick studied his face. "You were shot before?"

"Chancellorsville. Back in '63. And that one was much worse. Don't you worry yourself."

Peg handed the empty pitcher to the boy. "Patrick, if you want to help, go outside and draw some water from the pump. We're running low."

"Okay." Patrick touched McCain's hand. "You can count on me, Pa." He ran out of the room.

McCain's eyes softened. "That's the first time he's shown any concern for me."

"The boy adores you," Jessica said softly. "It's just he's intimidated by you."

"Why?" McCain asked, sounding surprised.

"You have a tendency to bully people, Mr. McCain."

He cleared his throat. "What do you suggest I do?"

"Soften up a little. Compliment him. Hug him. I guarantee you'll be pleased with his response."

He seemed to consider her words, then nodded.

Peg opened her black bag. "In case you'd forgotten, Ross, I got some doctoring to do."

"I haven't forgotten."

Jessica stepped back, ready to give Peg room to work.

"Where do you think you're going, missy?" Peg demanded. "I need your help."

Jessica swallowed. "My help? I don't know anything about injuries like this."

"Ain't no better time to learn than the present, is there?"

McCain raised an eyebrow. "You're looking a little pale now, Mrs. McCain."

Jessica folded her arms. "I'm fine."

Peg grabbed Jessica's hand and slapped the handle of a knife into it. "Use this to cut the shirt off, and be quick about it."

Peg ladled the remains of the water from the basin into a cup, opened her sack and dumped a green powder into the cup.

Jessica shook her head. "Peg, let me mix those herbs for you while you take his shirt off."

"Take it off, Mrs. McCain," Peg ordered.

McCain's eyes sparkled with laughter and challenge. "Well?"

With trembling hands, Jessica reached for the buttons on McCain's shirt. The thick coarse hair of his chest brushed her fingertips, setting her senses afire.

"You look flustered," McCain said.

Jessica's mouth went dry. "I'm fine." She took the knife, sliced his shirt open and quickly peeled it off.

Jessica dreaded what was to come. Drawing in a deep breath, she set the knife aside and looked at his blood-caked chest. The sight left her feeling light-headed. "I really don't think I can do this."

Peg gave her a fresh cloth. "Yes, you can. Now put that on the bullet hole."

Jessica closed her eyes. She felt the color drain from her face.

"You look faint," McCain said.

"I am." Jessica pressed the clean fabric against McCain's shoulder.

After several minutes, Peg pushed Jessica aside and inspected the wound. "The bullet just grazed your shoulder. It ain't nearly as bad as it looks, but cleaning it is gonna hurt like the devil." She dipped a cloth into the water and rung it out. With a heavy hand, she scrubbed the dried blood from McCain's skin.

He grabbed Jessica's hand and squeezed tight until her fingers ached, but she didn't pull away. Peg dumped a green paste from the cup into the palm of her hands, then rubbed it into his wound. By the time she had finished, McCain was as pale as her chemise.

"You've got the touch of an iron-mill worker," he said to Peg.

"I could say the same for you," Jessica grumbled as he squeezed her hand harder.

"Both of you, quit your bellyaching. I'm finished." Peg laid a fresh cloth over McCain's wound, then handed Jessica some bandages. "Bind him up. There are clean sheets in the chest over there. I'll look in on him in the morning."

Jessica stared at the white cloths in her hand. "I don't know how to wrap a bandage or make a bed."

"You'll figure it out."

"Where are you going?" Jessica demanded.

"Back to bed." Peg snapped her bag closed. "Ross, you're gonna favor that arm for a few days, but you'll be good as new by next week."

"Thanks, Peg," McCain said. "What would I do without you?"

"You'd be in jail or dead." She cackled. "Now, I best go find Patrick and make sure he gets that water up here."

Peg slammed the door behind her. Light from the lantern flickered on the walls, casting long gray shadows. Jessica looked at the bandages in her hand and then at McCain. He regarded her with a mixture of surprise and admiration.

McCain eased himself into a sitting position. She wrapped the bandage around his shoulder and across his chest like a swordsman's sash. Helping him to a chair, she quickly stripped off the wet sheets and remade the bed. Fluffing the down pillows, she helped him into it again.

He eased back against the pillows. "For a first-time nurse, you're not too bad."

"You need to rest." She started to leave.

"Don't go. Talk to me."

"About what? All of my experiences centered around Miss Madeline's."

"What's that, a whorehouse?" His eyes sparkled with laughter.

Jessica laughed. "Miss Madeline would absolutely die if she heard you say that. She runs one of the most respected schools for young ladies in the East."

"What does a woman learn in a school like that?"

Jessica brushed back a curl from her forehead. "Witty dinner conversation and proper etiquette."

"We don't get much of a call for that out here."

"No, I suppose not."

"Tell me more about Miss Madeline's. Where was it?"

She sat on the side of the bed. "New York City."

He yawned. "How'd you end up so far away from home?"

She was too tired to make up another lie. "Father wanted me as far away from him as possible."

He touched the side of her face. "I'd never send you away," he said.

A comforting warmth spread through her body.

"Close your eyes. I'll stay until you've fallen asleep."

"I'm counting on it."

He closed his eyes and within minutes, his breathing deepened. Even in sleep, his features were hard and utterly masculine.

This time when she stood, he said nothing. She tucked the blanket under his chin. "Good night, Mr. McCain."

Morning light streamed through the windows when Ross woke. He tried to sit up but immediately regretted the action. His shoulder burned and his head pounded like a cannon. Gingerly, he touched the cloth bandages that encircled his chest and shoulder.

What the hell had happened?

He lay back on the pillows, rubbing his eyes. He'd been shot. Miss Grimes...Mrs. McCain. Zeke. It all came back to him.

The images thundered in his brain, reigniting the primal anger that had overtaken him last night. He'd have done anything to keep that bastard's hands off his wife. Anything. He clenched and unclenched his fingers.

Nine years had passed since he'd felt anything other than lust for a woman. Living in a self-imposed exile, he'd been content to keep women at arm's length. Life had been easier without a woman in it, until now.

Bit by bit, Emma Grimes McCain was thawing the ice inside him. He didn't know whether to be glad or scared that his emotional purgatory was ending.

He swung his legs over the side of the bed.

Ross nearly stepped on his wife.

Emma slept on the floor. Using his wool jacket as her pillow, she was curled up like a babe, still dressed in the bloodstained clothes she'd worn last night. His mouth went dry as he watched the rise and fall of her breasts against her bodice. Her wind-tossed hair and flushed cheeks gave her a wild, exotic air he found pleasing. Too pleasing, he thought.

He drew up his legs and lay back on the pillow. "Mrs. McCain!"

She didn't move. Instead, she turned on her side away from him.

"Miss Grimes!"

She rubbed her nose and curled into a tighter ball,

pushing her delicate rump closer to him. For a moment, Ross forgot to breathe.

With his good arm, he grabbed a pillow and swatted it against her rear end. "Miss Grimes! Wake up!"

She sat up in an instant, searching wildly around the room as if lost in the dark. "What's going on?"

Ross stifled a groan. "Up here."

When she looked up at him, her eyes were vacant and blank. Only as the haze of sleep passed did she seem to recognize him. Her eyes widened. "Mr. McCain, what are you doing in my room?"

"That's supposed to be my question."

Emma looked around, then closed her eyes. "Oh…you're right."

Despite the discomfort in his arm, he wanted to smile. "Why are you sleeping on my floor?"

"You were shot last night."

"I know."

She scrambled to her feet and pressed her hand against his forehead. "Peg told me to watch for a fever."

"I'll live."

Even disheveled she was beautiful.

She shifted uncomfortably. "I'll tell Peg to bring up your breakfast."

Ross wasn't ready to let her go yet. "I need help shaving and getting dressed."

She blushed. "That's a job for Peg."

"Peg's got enough to do around here without having to nursemaid me. The razor's in the bureau over there."

Fire sparked in her eyes. "I really don't think—"

"I don't want to argue. I just need a shave."

Emma frowned.

He bit back a grin as he saw indecision on her face.

She rolled her eyes. "Where did you say the razor was?"

"The top drawer of the bureau."

Emma crossed the room, opened the drawer and retrieved the soap cup, brush, towel and razor. From the pitcher on top of the bureau, she poured water into the basin. Crossing the room in three stiff strides, she set her supplies down on the nightstand.

He ran a hand through his hair, then swung his legs over the side of the bed. "Have you ever done this before?"

She set a hard-backed chair next to the bed. "No."

He let her help him to the chair. Already he was feeling better, more like himself. "Remember, I've already lost a lot of blood."

The shaving brush clicked against the bowl as she stirred the cream. "How difficult can it be?"

The unrestricted view of her face revealed details he'd not noticed before, such as the soft sprinkling of freckles on the bridge of her nose and the delicate arch of her eyebrow.

He stiffened when she raised the blade to his cheek.

"Relax."

"I've never been able to relax with a blade at my neck."

"I've never lost a patient yet."

He watched her as she made the first pass across

his jawline. On the third pass she nicked his chin. He flinched and she drew back instantly.

"I am so sorry." She raised the edge of the towel from around his chest, moistened the cloth with the tip of her tongue and then dabbed away the fresh blood.

Her touch drove him to the edge of sanity. "Just finish the job."

Quickly, she dipped the blade in the basin and wiped it on the towel. With greater care, she tilted his head to the side again and slid the blade down his cheek. She walked around to his other side and repeated the process.

His skin tingled wherever she touched him. He couldn't take his eyes off her lips, so full and sensual. He wanted to taste them again.

She pushed his nose to the left and made three even strokes above his lip. When she stepped back, he lifted the towel from his chest and wiped his face clean. "That does it," she said.

Already missing her touch, he rubbed his hand over his smooth chin. "Feels like a professional job."

Emma blushed at the compliment. Quickly, she crossed the room and retrieved a shirt from the bureau. "Perhaps you'd better put this on."

She threaded her hands through the garment, then pulled the thick cotton over his head, helping him ease his injured arm into one shirtsleeve and then the other. She smoothed the fabric over his coarse chest hair and flat belly, then she reached to fasten the few buttons.

When she stared at his untucked shirttail, his gaze

followed hers. He thought about her long fingers sliding into his pants, and instantly the blood drained from his head. Disconcerted, he cleared his throat, shoving himself to his feet. "I can manage."

She backed away, her relief evident.

As he tucked in his shirt, he watched her clean up. Even in the wrinkled calico dress smeared with his blood, she had the poise and bearing of a duchess. A week ago he'd have laughed at the idea of taking another wife. Now the idea grew on him more every minute.

As if sensing his appraisal, she blushed. His stomach flip-flopped.

"You must be hungry," she said.

"Starving," he said gruffly.

"I'll go and tell Peg to cook breakfast for you." Without a backward glance, she left the room.

When the door closed behind her, the emptiness overwhelmed him. Inhaling deeply, he drank in the lingering aroma of her scent—wildflowers.

"I'm not hungry for food," he whispered. "I'm hungry for you."

Chapter Ten

"Sissy, is there supposed to be this much smoke coming out of the potbellied stove?" Jessica asked, coughing. She stood in front of the schoolhouse stove watching puffs of gray smoke seep out of the joints around the metal door.

Sissy and her older sons, Dan and Owen, looked up from the floor they were washing by the front door. Sissy dropped her rag in the wash bucket and hurried up the aisle dividing the rows of desks toward Jessica. "Oh, Mrs. McCain, I told you not to light it until I'd checked your kindling."

Owen started jumping up and down. "Fire! Fire! Do you want me to go get Pa or Mr. McCain?"

"No!" Jessica shouted. "Let your ma and me handle this."

Sissy wrapped her apron around her hand and opened the metal door. Smoke billowed out. "There's no need for alarm. Dan, take Owen and go over to Mrs. Crumpet's and tell her I'll be by shortly to pick up Elizabeth."

"Can't we stay and watch the fire?" Dan asked, disappointed.

"There's no fire to see," Sissy said. "Now you two *get*."

Sissy's sharp response silenced the boys' protests. Dan took Owen by the hand and the two scurried out.

"I thought this was *one* thing I could do," Jessica said.

Sissy grabbed an empty wash bucket in the corner, picked up a long piece of kindling, then scraped the smoldering wood into the bucket. "Too much wood will choke out the flames and make smoke."

"Now you tell me." Jessica reached for another piece of kindling. "Can I help you?"

"No! I got it. Thank you, anyway."

Sissy hurried out the front door, dumped the smoldering logs on the ground and kicked dirt onto them until she was certain the fire was out.

Jessica followed her and leaned against the door-jamb of the schoolhouse. "This is such a mess. I'm hopeless."

She smoothed her hands over the skirt of the yellow calico dress McCain had bought for her. Like the other dresses he'd purchased, it was a size too large, and the color did nothing for her complexion. Lord, she must look as miserable as she felt.

This morning Jessica had been unable to consider the ramifications of their hasty marriage, so as soon as possible she'd gone to the schoolhouse, where everything felt right and safe. She was determined to put all her energy into it and do the best job she could. The problem was she didn't know the first thing about being a schoolteacher.

Sissy glanced up. "Don't fret so. I know Colorado's mighty different from what you're used to."

"You have no idea."

Sissy kicked more dirt on the charred logs. "You'll catch on."

"Don't count on it. This morning Peg tried to show me how to make biscuits. After I burned three batches, she threw me out of the kitchen and threatened me with bodily harm if I returned."

Sissy chuckled. "We all make mistakes. I've burned more than my share of biscuits."

Jessica propped her chin in her hands. "Mistakes. Later, Patrick tried to show me how to milk the cow." She shook her head. "I squeezed her teats so hard, she nearly kicked a hole in the side of the barn. I doubt the poor thing will ever be the same."

Sissy giggled. "You'll get the hang of things."

Absently, Jessica fingered a loose thread on her sleeve. "I really want to do a good job. I've never been given the chance to prove myself before, and I don't want to mess this up."

"Give it time."

"But I can't do *anything* right."

"What do you mean? You do all the right things right."

"Like what?"

"Like reading and writing. I'd give just about anything to have the learning you got. I was raised in a sod house on the plains. Mama tried to teach me letters from the Bible, but when she died, I had to care for my younger brothers and sisters. No, building fires ain't nothing important. Reading's what counts.''

Jessica stared at her palms, marred with fresh blisters. ''If you only knew why I was out here.''

''We all got our reasons for coming to Prosperity. What counts is you're here and my children are gonna learn things I couldn't even dream of.''

The raw longing in Sissy's eyes made Jessica's heart ache. She'd never had a friend before, yet she sensed she'd found one now. ''I could teach you how to read, Sissy.''

Sissy laughed nervously. ''Oh, I'm too old to be sitting in a classroom.''

''We could have private lessons on Sundays after church.''

''That's kind of you, but on Sunday afternoons I catch up on my mending while Earl takes the children to Miller's Pond to fish.''

''The mending will always be there, Sissy.''

She laughed. ''You're so right about that.''

''Then say yes. Let me teach you how to read.''

Sissy bit her bottom lip. ''I don't know, Mrs. McCain.''

''I think we've gotten past formalities. Call me Jes...er, Emma.''

''Emma,'' Sissy said slowly, as if testing the name. ''I ain't smart like you are.''

''You're every bit as smart as I am. How else could you manage a family and see to a thousand other details every day. I don't know how you do it all.''

''I suppose a couple of hours a week wouldn't

make that big of a difference to Earl and the children.''

''But it could make a big difference to you.''

Sissy nodded her head. ''I surely would like to know how to read. How about you teach me how to read and I'll teach you how to survive out here?''

Jessica extended her hand. ''Deal.''

Tears glistened in Sissy's eyes when she shook it. ''Deal.''

''We'll start this Sunday.''

From the corner of her eye Jessica saw a tall, dark figure approaching. Alert, she turned. It was McCain.

The sun shone on his back, highlighting broad shoulders and windswept hair. He still wore the sling Peg had made for him, but he'd regained most of the color he'd lost, and his eyes sparkled with energy.

An array of emotions swelled inside her. Anger. Respect. Pride. And yes, desire. What was it about this man? He was turning her insides to jelly.

Jessica rose, trying not to think about how her dress hung on her like a sack, or about the dirt caked under her fingernails.

McCain sniffed the air. ''Have you been cooking again, Emma?''

Sissy giggled and stood. ''She was trying to build a fire in the potbellied stove.''

''Just keep her out of the kitchen.''

''It wasn't that bad,'' Jessica protested.

The corner of his mouth kicked up. ''Jed's hound dog, Blue, who's been known to eat buffalo hide and straw, wouldn't have anything to do with her biscuits.''

Sissy patted Jessica on the arm. ''Don't let him rile you. He's just poking fun. Ain't you, Mr. McCain?''

McCain chuckled. ''I'd feel safer on the battle-field than eating my wife's cooking.''

Wife! There was that word again. At first, she'd not taken that mockery of a ceremony seriously, reasoning that McCain was bluffing. Now she wasn't so sure. If she weren't careful, she might end up stuck with him.

Jessica wiped the soot from her hands on her apron. ''If school's going to open day after tomorrow, I'd better get back to work. Thanks for your help, Sissy. I'll see you on Sunday.''

Sissy took Jessica's hands in hers. ''Thank you again, Emma. I promise I'll work hard.''

Jessica squeezed her new friend's hands. ''I know you will.''

McCain cleared his throat. ''Is there more to this conspiracy than teaching Mrs. McCain how to cook?''

Anticipation added sparkle to Sissy's eyes. ''Emma is going to teach me how to read.''

McCain's smile faded. ''That so?''

Sissy nodded. ''Lessons are every Sunday. Won't it be wonderful? I'll be able to read just like you and Mrs. McCain.''

His body tensed. ''You sure you got time for reading lessons, Sissy? You got three little ones and the house.''

Sissy's eyes clouded with doubt. She glanced nervously from Jessica to McCain. "I'll keep up with my work."

"Of course you will," Jessica interjected. She glared at McCain.

"What does Earl think about this?"

"If Earl wants reading lessons, he's going to have to ask me himself," Jessica declared. She laid her hands on Sissy's shoulders, turning her away from McCain. "Lessons start at one o'clock, Sissy. Don't be late."

"Are you sure you have the time for this, Mrs. McCain?" he demanded.

Jessica looked over Sissy's shoulder at him. "I do have Sunday afternoons off, don't I?"

He stiffened. "Yes."

"Emma, I don't want to stir up problems," Sissy murmured.

"You're not," Jessica said. "But Mr. McCain and I have a few things to discuss. Would you excuse us? Oh, and be sure to tell your friends they're welcome to take lessons, too." Silently, she dared him to contradict her.

Sissy glanced quickly at McCain. "Okay."

When Sissy left, McCain glared at Jessica. "I don't want you teaching Sissy how to read."

His reaction shocked Jessica. She'd only known him a few days, but he'd always seemed to treat people fairly. "Why are you doing this?"

"Doing what?"

"Holding Sissy back."

"I'm not holding her back. I'm protecting her."

"I thought you were the great advocate of education."

"I am."

"But not for married women with children?"

"You don't know what you are talking about."

"I *am* teaching Sissy to read. As a matter of fact, if I have my way, by spring the entire town will be reading."

McCain raked his fingers through his hair. "Have you considered some folks can't learn to read?"

Suddenly, the truth of the situation hit her. "This isn't about Sissy or the others. It is about you."

His scowl returned. "What are you talking about?"

"I remember how the color drained from your face when Sissy handed you the book at the dedication ceremony. You can't read."

The look in his eyes signaled danger. He took a step forward. "You don't know what the hell you're talking about."

"Then prove it." She stalked inside and over to her desk, where she picked up a primer. She returned and held it out.

His knuckles tightened around the brim of his hat until they were white. "I don't have time for this."

"Read a page and I will apologize," she said softly.

"We're talking about Sissy, not me."

"We'll get back to Sissy in a minute." She opened the book. "Read something."

"I don't need this."

When he started to leave, Jessica blocked his path. She sensed an edge of desperation and sadness in him.

"You wanted a teacher in Prosperity so badly because you want the children to have what you don't.''

"I didn't come here today to talk about this. I came here to invite you on a tour of the mines. Are you interested in a tour or not?''

"Thanks, but I've got work to do.''

McCain put his hat on his head. "Another day, then.''

"Sure.''

He pushed past her. "Good day.''

"A lot of men can't read,'' she said softly.

He stopped and took a deep breath. "I hate being at the mercy of men who can read. It eats at my gut every day.''

She didn't believe her ears. McCain had admitted he couldn't read.

A heavy silence hung between them. A ray of sunlight sliced across McCain's face. She sensed the confession had struck a blow to his pride, and part of her wanted to comfort him. "You've done more in your life than most university scholars.''

"None of that matters.''

"It matters a great deal.''

He clenched his fist. "Did you ever stop to think that in six months Patrick will be reading and I won't?''

"The boy loves you, Mr. McCain. He doesn't care if you can't read.''

"I care!''

"So what are you going to do about it?''

"What do you mean?''

"Sissy's willing to try to learn. Are you?''

He laughed, shaking his head. "That's out of the question."

"Why?"

"Boys go to school, not men."

"I'll teach you at home."

"No."

"I thought you were an honest man."

"I am."

"Then stop living a lie."

He bore down on her, pinning her against the wall with his body. His breath was hot, his jaw tense as he stared into her eyes. "This is my own damn business."

For just an instant, she saw past the anger and glimpsed the man behind the armor of pride. Ross McCain was afraid.

Instinctively, she reached up and touched his cheek. Despite the early morning shave, his cheek was rough with a fine layer of stubble.

As she stared into his eyes, burning with fire and ice, something primitive and carnal unfurled inside of her. He reached up, his callused thumb touching the tender flesh above her collarbone. Her eyes slid to his lips, and for an insane instant she wanted him to kiss her.

McCain seemed to sense her thoughts. Leaning forward, he touched his lips to hers. It was a bruising kiss, so unlike the gentle kiss they'd shared yesterday. Still, her body ignited. She laced her fingers through his hair and pulled herself into him.

All reasonable thought vanished from her mind. This was insane, and yes, heavenly.

The kiss softened. She sensed McCain's anger melt as passion's fires burned hotter.

"I can't think when you touch me like this," she murmured.

"Emma," McCain breathed against her ear.

Emma. The name hammered in her brain as reality dawned, yanking Jessica from the dewy haze. She pulled back, pressing her fingers to her lips. *Emma.*

She'd just accused him of living a lie, yet here she was pretending to be someone she was not. She was a fool to have pushed him so. "I'm sorry for what I said a moment ago. You are right. Your life is not my business."

He slid his hand down her arm. "Perhaps it should be."

"No, I was wrong."

His fingers wrapped around her wrist. "Let's forget what we just said. I want to begin this afternoon again."

The fire inside her began to cool. She shook her head and forced a wan smile. "We shouldn't be doing this." She looked down at his long tapered fingers gripping her forearm. "I really must be going."

He didn't release her. "What are *you* afraid of?"

She raised her trembling chin. "Nothing."

One corner of his mouth lifted in a faint smile. "Looks like I'm not the only liar."

Chapter Eleven

The sky was a vivid blue and the air crisp and clear. It was a perfect autumn day and the first day of school, Ross thought as he stared out the telegraph office window, watching his wife walk down the boardwalk into the mercantile.

She wore one of the dresses he'd bought for her—the brown one—but the gown no longer hung on her like a sack of flour. Instead, it hugged her curves and accentuated her full bosom and delicately rounded hips. The sight of her aroused him. He'd purposely chosen the ugliest dresses in the mercantile, expecting to hide her lush curves in the homespun fabric.

No doubt the alterations had to be Peg's handiwork. The old bat must have stayed up all night to remake the dress. Likely she was cackling now over a bottle of her own home brew, thinking about how the sight of Emma tied every male in town—including himself—into knots.

Over the past two days, he'd barely seen Emma. She'd spent long hours at the schoolhouse and had taken her meals in her room, expertly staying out of his sight. He didn't have to ask why. She was avoiding him. However, he'd not forced the issue. He'd been shaken by their kiss and he needed time to think.

"You want me to send any other telegrams to Sacramento, Mr. McCain?"

Ross turned away from the window toward Joey Dodd, the telegraph officer. Joey was a burly, bearlike creature with brown hair and a thick mustache.

"No, that'll be it. Let me know as soon as you get a reply."

"I'll do it, sir."

Ross walked to the door. "And do me a favor, Joey? Don't tell anyone I've telegrammed Sacramento for more information about my wife."

"I'll take it to my grave, sir."

"Good."

The bell hanging on the door handle jingled as Ross opened the door and stepped into the bright sun. He rubbed his healing shoulder, working the stiffness out of the wounded muscle.

Part of him felt guilty about the telegram, but another, more battle-weary part demanded he know more about the woman who'd shaken his well-ordered world to the foundation.

Since Caroline had left him, he'd dallied with whores and willing widows. There'd only been lust. No promises. No tender words. No love. His dealings with women had been clean and simple—just the way he liked it.

He had focused on what he did best—making money. Long hours in the mines and shrewd investments in cattle and railroads had made him a very wealthy man.

Then Emma Grimes had come along and ruined everything. In five days she'd managed to tear through his defenses and shine a light into the darkest corners of his soul. If she only knew how much he wanted to take her up on her offer of reading lessons! But he couldn't bring himself to accept.

Ross's eyes narrowed as he watched Jed Mc-Manus escort Emma out of the mercantile toward the schoolhouse. Emma pushed back a curl from her face and laughed. The old man laughed with her. Ross scowled.

"Well, don't you look like a lovesick fool." Sam Jenkins limped forward and pushed his hat back on his head.

"What the hell's that supposed to mean?"

"You're staring at your wife like you're a hungry dog and she's a prime cut of meat."

"I've never liked it when you can see inside my head. It sets my nerves on edge."

Sam clamped his hand on Ross's shoulder. "I remember when I first met my Sarah, God rest her soul. I was sweet on her from the moment I met her. I couldn't have strung two thoughts together if you'd paid me."

"I'm not sweet on her."

Sam raised an eyebrow. "Could have fooled me."

Ross expelled a breath and stabbed his fingers through his hair. He could count the number of people he trusted on one hand and still have three fingers to spare. Sam was one of the two.

"Sam, I haven't felt this reckless since Caroline, and it scares the hell out of me."

"That was ten years ago."

"Maybe, but there are days when it feels like yesterday."

"Some wounds are like that. Caroline treated you mighty bad."

"And she's dead and buried and I have remarried. I need to get on with my life."

"Relax, you've finally started living again."

Ross shook his head. "If this is what living feels like, I'd rather be dead."

Sam slapped his hand on Ross's shoulder. "What I wouldn't give to have your problems. If I had a wife like yours—"

"Watch it."

"I'd treat her like she was a fine piece of porcelain. If you only knew how lucky you are. I'd give anything to have my Sarah back. Life's lonely and downright miserable without her."

"You've got Davey," Ross said softly.

Sam smiled slowly. "I love my boy, don't you doubt it for a minute. But I'd like a woman in my life."

"I've done all right where women are concerned."

"I ain't talking about that kind of need. I'm talking about sharing a life with a woman, not just a bed."

Irritated, Ross studied the tip of his boot. "How am I supposed to do that when my wife resents the hell out of me?"

"Maybe you're going to have to court her."

Ross snorted. "A man doesn't court his wife."

Sam chuckled. "Are you married to her or *married* to her?"

Ross scowled. "That's none of your business."

"I thought so."

"Haven't you got something better to do? Isn't there work to be done at the mine?"

"Nope, everything's right peaceable today. Besides, I kinda like watching you twist in the wind."

Ross shook his head. "How am I supposed to court Emma?"

Sam smacked him on the back. "That, my friend, is for you to decide."

Ross shook his head. "I've had enough of this foolishness. It's time I go get Patrick and take him to school."

I can do this.
I am a teacher.
I can do this.

Butterflies fluttered in Jessica's stomach as she stared out one of the schoolhouse windows. Sunlight streamed across the land, lighting the plains in a buttery yellow glow and touching the snowcapped mountains on the horizon.

She prayed the beautiful day was a good omen.

Eaten up with worry about the first day of school, she'd barely slept a full two hours last night. This was her classroom and she intended to give her best to the children. During the past two days, she'd polished the pine floorboards with beeswax and shoveled every last ash from the potbellied stove. Her muscles ached from the hard physical labor, but it didn't matter.

For reasons she could not begin to explain, she wanted McCain to be proud of her work.

She hadn't seen him since their meeting in the schoolhouse two days ago, but her mind had been filled with thoughts of his rugged features and the memory of his soft lips touching hers.

McCain had awakened desires she'd never known existed. Desire made her knees weak when she remembered their last meeting.

But as much as her heart yearned to explore her newfound desires, her mind refused to surrender her hard-won independence. She'd escaped William Perry, and she wasn't about to turn her life over to a man who promised to be just as dominating.

Jessica stepped back from the window and stared at her reflection in the glass. She tucked a curl behind her ear and pinched her cheeks. She'd taken extra care to twist her unruly curls into a tight chignon this morning and had said a prayer of thanks when she realized Peg had taken in her dresses.

Turning, Jessica studied the benches and small tables arranged in a circle. She picked up a piece of chalk and crossed the room to the blackboard. In bold script she wrote "Welcome." Then below it, "Miss Tierney."

Jessica froze, her gaze riveted on her name. Still holding the chalk, she remained poised in front of the board. How could she make such a foolish mistake? Quickly, she picked up a rag and erased the board. Her heart beating wildly, she reluctantly spelled out "Mrs. McCain."

"Mrs. McCain! Mrs. McCain!" The door to the room swung open and banged against the wall.

Jessica turned as Dan and Owen Nevers appeared in the entranceway. Her heart warmed at the sight of them. The boys wore matching white shirts, brown knickers and black boots. A twin set of smiles on freshly scrubbed faces greeted her as each gently swung his gray lunch pail at his side.

"Come in, boys. Welcome to school."

"Thank you." They stepped over the threshold and wiped the dirt from their shoes.

Sissy stood behind the boys with her three-year-old daughter, Elizabeth, nestled on her hip. "Miss Grimes, I know we are a bit early, but the boys were fit to be tied this morning. Both would've been up here an hour ago if I hadn't stopped them."

"It's all right, I'm happy to have them. Welcome to school, Dan, Owen."

Sissy set Elizabeth down beside her, then knelt in front of Owen to fasten the top button of his shirt. She licked the tip of her thumb and rubbed a smudge from his chin. "You listen to Miss Grimes now, you hear? Ain't many boys your age who get the chance to better themselves like you. So you listen."

Jessica patted the boy on the shoulder. "I'm sure they'll both be fine."

Sissy wiped a tear from her cheek. "They're good boys and they're smart. Earl and I are so grateful you and Mr. McCain are giving them this chance."

"Mr. McCain is very dedicated to the children's education," Jessica said.

Sissy lowered her voice. "He didn't seem too happy that you were teaching me."

"Sometimes he just comes across as mad, but he's not really," Jessica lied.

"Well, he is your husband, so I guess you know him best."

"He's not my…" Jessica paused. "Never mind."

Lydia Crumpet stepped through the front door. She had Abe on one hip and her older children, Billy and Susie, beside her. "And you're lucky to have him. I never met a better man."

Jessica ignored the comment. She helped Billy and Susie off with their coats. "Why don't you two go find seats. I'll be with you in a moment."

Mrs. Crumpet sniffed. "The best thing he ever did for you was marry you."

Jessica blinked. "What?"

Sissy glanced at Mrs. Crumpet before she spoke. "We women held a little meeting. We didn't mean to stick our nose in your business, but—"

"Stop pussyfooting around, Sissy," Lydia barked. "The schoolteacher's business is our business. If you'd married anyone other than Ross McCain, we would have lost another teacher."

Jessica didn't know whether to be flattered or angry. "It's a shame Mr. McCain didn't stop to ask me if I wanted to be married or not."

"He's a man who takes the bull by the horns," Lydia said. "You gotta respect that."

Jessica straightened. "I doubt it."

Lydia snorted. "No disrespect, Mrs. McCain, but there will come a day when you'll be glad you've made a home with Mr. McCain." She shifted Abe to her other hip.

"Even Peg agrees you and Mr. McCain are a

good match," Sissy added. "Since you ain't got no ma to teach you the ways of being a wife, the ladies in town are gonna help you."

"The children's education is more important to me than keeping Mr. McCain happy," Jessica said.

Mrs. Crumpet chuckled. "Honey, you're gonna find a man's a lot easier to handle if he has a hot meal in his belly and a willing wife to warm his bed."

"And don't forget to throw a few flowery words his way once in a while. Men eat that up," Sissy exclaimed.

Jessica stared at the two women. It was clear they had her best interests at heart. "Ladies, I can handle this myself."

Mrs. Crumpet nodded. "Sure you can, dear, but a little help from interested friends can't hurt."

"It's the least we can do," Sissy added.

"Really, ladies, I don't think—"

Mrs. Crumpet waved her hand impatiently. "Enough talk. You got a job to do and I got to get out of here before I start crying like a baby. Can't hardly believe my young'uns have grown so big. Billy, Susie, I'll see you at three o'clock."

Sissy blew a kiss to Owen and Dan. "Be good, boys. You mind Miss Grimes." She and Elizabeth left.

Other children and their parents arrived, and Jessica had no time to ponder what Sissy and Lydia had just told her. Within minutes the room was filled with lively jabbering and laughter.

"All right, children," Jessica called, "let's stop talking."

No one responded. A book crashed against the ground as two children scribbled on the blackboard.

"This sure is a lot more fun than chopping wood!" one child shouted.

"Yeah, this is gonna be fun," another answered.

Jessica's excitement soured into frustration. She clapped her hands. "That's enough, children."

"Is it time to eat lunch?" Owen shouted.

Jessica took his lunch pail away from him. "No, it is not, and Susie, stop writing on the board. I want all of you to sit in your seats."

The giggles grew louder and Jessica feared she'd never get the children under control. Then suddenly the room fell silent. A cold breeze touched the back of Jessica's neck and she turned. McCain stood in the doorway with his hand resting on Patrick's shoulder.

McCain smiled at her. Freshly shaved, he wore a crisp blue work shirt, fawn-colored trousers, an ankle-length gray coat and a wide-brimmed hat. Patrick's overcoat hung open, revealing a red wool pullover shirt, gray cotton trousers and high-topped shoes. Jessica was struck by how handsome they both looked.

McCain pulled off his hat. "Having trouble, Mrs. McCain?"

She turned and glanced around the room. Each child sat silent, stone-faced. "No, I'd say we are ready to begin the day. Patrick, you can hang your coat on a peg by the door and put your lunch pail under your seat."

Patrick shrugged off his coat. "Yes, ma'am."

"You mind the teacher, boy," McCain ordered.

Patrick looked disappointed. He seemed to need a few words of encouragement from his father. "Yes, sir."

McCain squeezed Patrick's shoulder. "I'm real proud of you, Son."

Patrick beamed. "Yes, sir!" he said, and quickly took a seat in the front of the classroom.

McCain stepped closer to Jessica until he was only a breath away. He pulled his hat off and glanced around the room.

Just standing near him made her feel tingly and restless. He could make her so angry, and yet when she was with him, she felt so alive.

"I have to hand it to you," he said, "I didn't think you had the stamina to get this place pulled together so quickly."

Her heart swelled with pride. "You won't be disappointed."

"No, I don't think I will," he said softly.

Her heart thumped in her chest. This was a man who could break her heart, she realized. But she was too smart to love a prideful man like McCain.

The corner of his mouth twitched in a half smile. "I wish you good luck today." He hesitated. "Peg asked me to deliver herbs to a man living outside of town. I thought you might like to come."

As much as she wanted to go, she couldn't trust herself alone with him. "Perhaps another day. The teacher has homework."

His jaw tightened and he drew in a deep breath. "Once winter sets in, we'll be dreaming about warm days like today. It would be a shame to waste it.

Besides, Peg will have my hide if I don't deliver these herbs.''

If Jessica didn't know him better, she'd have guessed he looked nervous. Like a suitor! The idea was preposterous. Ross McCain courting a wife he'd dragged to the altar? Yet there was a part of her that savored the idea.

His eyes burned into hers, silently demanding her to accept. Her resolve melted.

It was a beautiful day, and she had been itching to see the surrounding area.

She glanced over her shoulder at the children. They all watched Jessica and McCain, their mouths gaping.

''All right. I'd love to go for a ride. I'll be finished here at three o'clock.''

He put his finger under her chin and tilted her head back. Her breath caught in her throat, and for one heart-stopping moment she thought he was going to kiss her right in front of the children.

She moistened her lips. Lord help her, but she wanted to taste his lips again.

As if sensing her thoughts, he smiled. ''Good. I'll be here at three o'clock.''

McCain put his hat back on, and in a voice loud enough for all the children to hear, stated, ''If you need me, send one of the older boys to my office. I can be here in five minutes.''

The children blinked, then turned quickly so each faced the blackboard. With McCain backing her up, discipline wouldn't be a problem.

''You're a good man to have around,'' she quipped.

"I'm glad you're finally beginning to realize that."

"That's n-not what I meant," she stammered.

"I know what you meant," he said, chuckling. "I'll see you at three." He left the schoolhouse.

Jessica stood at the doorway, watching him stride toward his office. It was hard not to admire the broad cut of his shoulders and his arrogant swagger.

When they were at odds, the emotional barriers in place, she felt safe. But a kinder, softer McCain could be devastating.

Giggles filtered through the classroom. "Mrs. McCain is sweet on Mr. McCain!" a child shouted.

The entire class erupted in laughter.

Chapter Twelve

The longest day of her life ended at three o'clock.

In the schoolhouse doorway, Jessica stood with her arms folded over her chest, watching the children as they ran down the road, swinging their lunch pails and laughing.

Her head throbbed and her back ached. She'd used a week's worth of lessons and nearly all of her patience. Yet she felt deeply satisfied. She'd completed her first day of work.

Though she'd underestimated what it took to keep twelve active children busy, she couldn't remember a day she'd enjoyed more. Deep down, she believed she might have a talent for teaching and, given a little time and experience, could turn out to be a competent teacher.

She glanced over her shoulder. Patrick was washing slates. "Make sure they're all clean. I don't want to see a speck of chalk."

"Do I have to wash *all* of them?" Patrick protested.

"All of them."

The boy groaned. She smiled. She hated to keep him after class, but he'd forced her to take action when he'd gotten into a scuffle during recess. Independent and strong-minded, he and McCain were cut from the same cloth.

Her heart softened as she watched Patrick wipe the slates. A good boy, he was just a little rambunctious and in need of guidance, but she didn't mind being the one to give it to him. If one of her teachers had taken an interest in her, maybe her years at boarding school wouldn't have been so unbearably lonely.

She wouldn't wish that kind of loneliness on any child, especially Patrick. He deserved better.

Jessica turned back toward the open door. She savored the warm breeze. Everything felt so right and it was hard to worry about the future or the past. There was only now.

"I'm all done," Patrick said, coming up behind her with a half-dozen slates in his hand. "Want to have a look at them?"

"No, I trust you." She raised an eyebrow, and in a stern voice said, "I won't be seeing any more scuffles during recess, will I?"

He shook his head. "No, ma'am."

"Good, because I'd hate to have to mention this to your father."

His face paled. "I don't think he'd like it if he knew I got into trouble on the first day of school."

She nodded. "It will be our secret, if there are no more problems."

"I promise!"

"All right. Go and put the slates away."

As she pulled off her apron and wiped the chalk from her hands, McCain drove his buckboard down Main Street toward the schoolhouse. He'd rolled up his sleeves to just below his elbows and his gray hat sat back on his head.

Jessica moistened her lips as she tossed her apron back in the schoolhouse and smoothed her hand over her hair. It was a shame she didn't have any of her perfumes and powders. She'd have liked to indulge in a little primping.

McCain pulled the wagon to a stop. "Whoa, fellas."

The matching chestnut horses snorted and stomped their feet in the dirt as McCain set the hand brake and tied off the reins. He jumped to the ground, his long, muscular body moving with the ease of a mountain lion.

She realized her mouth hung open as she drank in the sight of him. She snapped it closed as his gaze traveled over her slowly, assessing and cataloging every detail about her. His raw, blatant appraisal left her breathless, frightened and exhilarated at the same time. What on earth was she doing? Ross McCain was more man than she could handle.

Despite her chaotic day, her mind had often drifted to McCain and this excursion. She'd spent almost no time alone with him since they'd married and the prospect left her uneasy.

"You look a little rough for wear, Emma. Tough day?" he said easily.

Pride refused to let her admit how tired she was. "Not at all."

"Good. Are you ready to go?"

"Y-yes. Let me just get my shawl." She nearly ran into the schoolhouse, grateful for a moment of distance between them.

Patrick came out of the school as she returned with her shawl. "Hey, Pa, what are you doing here?"

McCain frowned. "Why haven't you gone home?"

Patrick glanced up at Jessica, then back at his father. "I'm just helping out."

Eyeing Patrick, McCain pulled off his hat. "You didn't get into trouble today did you, boy?"

"Patrick was kind enough to clean all the slates for me this afternoon," Jessica said, slipping an arm around his shoulders.

McCain raised an eyebrow. "That so?"

The worry in Patrick's eyes turned to relief. "They were real dirty."

McCain studied the boy's face, then nodded. "That's what I like to hear," he said to Patrick. He reached in his pocket. "I picked up some peppermints at the mercantile today. Like one?"

Patrick grinned. "Yes, sir!" He took a peppermint stick and popped one end into his mouth.

Amused, McCain tousled his son's hair. "I thought that sweet tooth of yours was getting hungry."

He held out a second stick to Jessica. She took the candy, then tucked it in her pocket. Everyone at boarding school had known how much she hated candy. It had become a joke of sorts. The girls had called her "Sour Puss."

"Aren't you going to eat it?" McCain asked.

Jessica opened her mouth to explain then froze. McCain wasn't offering candy to *her* but to Emma Grimes. "Yes, of course."

She pulled out the candy. She broke a small piece off and popped it in her mouth. The peppermint burned her tongue and the overly sweet taste coated her mouth. Forcing a smile, she crunched the hard candy with her teeth and swallowed the pieces. The candy shards scraped her throat on the way down. "Delicious."

"You look like you just swallowed a handful of dirt."

"Oh, no," she said, swallowing the last bits. "Peppermints are delightful. A real treat."

McCain gave her a long steady look. "Right." He put his hat on and tugged it forward. "Ready to go?"

Jessica's apprehension returned. She wasn't afraid of him as much as she was herself. Her body's reaction to him had surprised her more than once. What if she couldn't control herself when they were alone?

Patrick slurped on his candy stick. "Where you two going?"

"A ride in the country," McCain said.

"Can I come?"

"Yes," Jessica said brightly.

McCain's emerald eyes stared at her. "Doesn't the boy have homework?"

"I didn't give any out today. After all, it is the first day of school."

"I love riding in the buckboard," Patrick said.

The boy's excitement quenched the fire in McCain's expression. "Sure."

"That's great! Are we just gonna ride around?"

"No, we're going to Wild Jack's cabin."

"I've never been there before," Patrick said.

A hint of a smile tugged at the corners of his father's mouth. "I suppose it's time you did. Climb aboard, boy."

"Okay," Patrick shouted as he ran toward the buckboard.

McCain waited until the boy was out of earshot before he spoke. "Nice trick, Emma."

Her heart pounded. "What are you talking about?"

"Bringing the boy along."

"I thought it would be a nice outing for him."

McCain picked up one of the wool tassels of her shawl and rolled it between his index finger and thumb. "What are you afraid of, Emma? Me, perhaps?"

"I'm not afraid of you." *I'm terrified of you.*

"Maybe you should be."

Seconds passed like hours, the air suddenly thick, heavy. Her breathing was slow, shallow. Her limbs felt heavy.

"Hey! Are you two coming or not?" Patrick shouted. His voice shattered the moment and gave Jessica the perfect opportunity to escape.

She clutched the ends of her shawl together. "Here we come."

"Coward."

She glanced over her shoulder. "Maybe I have sense enough to know when I'm in over my head."

McCain laughed as he followed her. "Emma, that bit of news has made my day."

"Pa, how many more minutes until we get to Wild Jack's cabin?"

"About five, son," McCain said. Irritation had crept into his voice. Patrick had asked the same question every five minutes.

They'd been riding for nearly a half hour—McCain in the driver's seat, Jessica at his side and Patrick behind them.

"Why don't you just sit back, Patrick, and relax?" Jessica suggested.

"But there's nothing to do and I think I gotta pee."

"You peed twenty minutes ago," McCain said tersely.

"But I got to go again."

McCain's hands tightened around the reins. "Boy, you must have the bladder the size of a—"

"We'll be there before you know it," Jessica interrupted. "Both of you enjoy the view. I declare I've never seen land so beautiful," she said honestly.

The clear blue sky was the perfect backdrop to endless plains and purple mountains in the distance. "I can see now why you don't like the city, Mr. McCain. The scenery is breathtaking in Colorado."

He nodded, satisfied. "You'll find I'm right about most things."

Jessica tossed back her head and laughed. "I forgot, you have *all* the answers."

His eyes sparkled. "Just about."

His arrogance was charming and irritating. McCain had the backbone and drive to bluff his way through any confrontation, whether it was in a back alley or an exclusive club. He wasn't like the few better-educated boys she'd known. He made his mark with action, not fancy words.

Each day she found fewer reasons why she should ignore the undeniable connection between them.

"I really have to pee," Patrick groaned.

"The ranch is right up ahead, boy."

The wagon rumbled into a gulch blanketed with tall grass and edged with pines. In the center of a clearing stood a crude log house with a sod roof Wild Jack used when he came down from the mountains. In front of the dwelling a chestnut mare fed on grass, and smoke trailed out of the chimney. A deer carcass hung at one end of the cabin. A collie dog barked.

Roused by the dog's growls, Wild Jack came out. As he had days ago, he wore deerskin pants and shirt and a revolver tucked in his boot.

Wild Jack paused and stared at Jessica as if he couldn't quite believe his eyes. She edged a little closer to McCain, who patted her reassuringly on the arm before he tied off the reins and jumped down.

"I brought you some of Peg's herbs," McCain said easily as he strolled toward the man.

"About time. That old bat has been promising me a remedy for my cough for weeks."

"Afraid the fault's mine. She's been after me for days to get up here, but things have been busy in town."

While the men talked, Patrick and Jessica both descended from the wagon. The boy pressed close to her now, and she wrapped her arm around his waist and hugged him.

"Patrick," McCain said easily, "I'd like you to meet Wild Jack. He lives up in the mountains, but he comes down and stays in this cabin twice a year."

"H-hello," Patrick said.

McCain nodded to Jessica. "You remember our schoolteacher?"

Wild Jack whistled through his teeth. "Sure do. Anybody marry her yet?"

"Matter of fact, I did."

Wild Jack hooted with laughter. "I knew it wouldn't take more than a week to see her wed, but, McCain, you're the last one I'd have figured to tie the knot with her."

McCain's body remained relaxed. "Life's full of surprises."

"Well, Mrs. McCain, you have my congratulations and condolences."

Jessica straightened her spine. "Thanks, I think."

Wild Jack turned his sights on Patrick. "My dog's dropped a litter of pups. A damn nuisance if you ask me, but you might like to see 'em. They're out back."

Patrick's eyes brightened. "Can I, Pa?"

"Sure. Just stay close to the cabin."

"Listen to your pa, boy. There's grizzly in these parts, so don't go wandering off in the woods."

"I won't," Patrick shouted over his shoulder as he ran toward the cabin.

Jessica tightened her shawl around her chest. "Grizzly bears? I've read about them."

"I was always too busy hunting or skinning 'em to bother reading about 'em." Wild Jack grinned at McCain.

McCain drew Jessica against him before she could retort. "When are you gonna come to our house for supper?" he asked.

"Soon as you get smart and move out of that damn city."

Jessica scooted away from McCain. "City? You're joking, right?"

Wild Jack leveled his gaze on her. "Any place that's got more than three people standing around is a city in my book."

"You don't like cities."

"The cities is fine. It's the people I can't stand. They make me a little crazy."

"A week ago I might have argued with you," Jessica said. "But after seeing this beautiful countryside, it's hard to remember what I liked about Sacramento or New York."

Wild Jack chuckled. "McCain said the same thing when he came west."

"I'm sure Mr. McCain had no trouble adjusting when he arrived in Colorado," Jessica prompted.

"He was half-starved when I met him."

"That's enough out of you," McCain barked.

"Hey, Pa!" Patrick yelled from behind the cabin. "I want to show you something."

McCain glanced toward the direction of Patrick's voice, then back at Jessica. "You keep your nose out of my business."

Jessica grinned. "Why don't you run along and check on Patrick?"

"I'm warning you, Jack, keep your mouth shut about me." McCain's tone wasn't nearly as menacing as his words.

Wild Jack laughed. "Ain't seen you squirm like this in years, McCain. What is it you don't want the little lady to know?"

"Everything," he grumbled.

Jessica slipped her arm in the crook of Wild Jack's. She couldn't resist teasing McCain. "Let's take a stroll. I've got a hundred questions for you."

"Pa! Come quick!"

McCain started walking toward the cabin. "Remember, Jack, I got a few stories of my own I can tell."

"I'm an open book." Wild Jack waggled his eyebrows. "If I were you, I'd be more worried about your woman falling for my devilish charms than a few lies."

"She's a lot more trouble than she's worth," McCain shouted over his shoulder as he walked around the cabin in search of Patrick.

Wild Jack laughed. "I can count on one hand the number of times that man has smiled in the last ten years. And two of them were in the last few minutes. Hell, I think he's almost happy."

An unexpected surge of warmth shot through her body. "What was Ross McCain like when he first came to Colorado?"

He placed his hand over hers and began to stroll in the direction McCain had taken. "Green as spring grass. Didn't know how to trap or skin. He could shoot like the devil, but that was about it. Back then all he was interested in was getting away from people. I reckon the war did that to him.''

Jessica tried to imagine a younger McCain—a man untouched by betrayal or war. She couldn't.

''But he was a quick learner,'' Wild Jack continued. ''You only had to show him once—whether it was setting a trap or skinning a lynx—and he had it. Ask him sometime about the first grizzly he killed.''

As they rounded the corner of the cabin, Jessica stopped in her tracks. Both she and Wild Jack stood staring.

McCain sat on the ground, cross-legged, with two black-and-white puppies in his lap. Patrick was beside him with another puppy jumping up and licking his ear. Deep masculine laughter mingled with puppy barks and Patrick's giggles.

Nothing prepared her for the sight of Patrick and his father playing with the dogs. For the sight of McCain, respected by his men, feared by his enemies, being mauled by puppies.

A pleasant glow eased through her body, chasing away all the anger and resentment she still harbored about their marriage. In its place was something gentle and soft.

''Cute little devils, aren't they?'' Wild Jack said.

McCain chuckled as one of the puppies chewed on his thumb. ''How old are they?''

''Six weeks, give or take.''

Patrick giggled as his puppy burrowed his nose into the crook of his neck. ''Pa, can we keep one?''

McCain shook his head. ''Peg'll skin us alive.''

"Oh, Pa, please! They're so cute."

"Sorry, boy. Besides, Wild Jack might have plans for them himself."

Wild Jack shrugged. "Not me. I'm leaving in a day or two. When I go, I'm taking their ma, but not them."

"You're leaving the puppies behind?" Jessica asked. "But they can't survive."

"They won't survive the climb into the mountains."

Patrick's face paled. "Pa, we can't leave the puppies here to die. We just can't."

"Boy, we don't have a place for three dogs."

"Maybe we could find homes for them in town," Jessica offered.

McCain shot her a warning look.

She raised an eyebrow. "We can't leave them here."

"They'll be fine."

"They'll die," she countered.

"Wild Jack, tell my wife these puppies are going to be fine."

"They're going to be fine," he parroted.

"Is that really true?" she asked.

"No."

One of McCain's puppies ran to her and started tugging on the hem of her skirt. She knelt down and picked it up. "Mr. McCain, we can't leave them."

McCain sighed. "Peg's going to have a fit."

"No, she won't, Pa," Patrick said. "I'll talk to her."

"You say that now, but—"

"I'll take responsibility for the animals," Jessica

offered. The puppy licked her cheek and she laughed.

McCain rose with his puppy tucked in the crook of his arm. "I'll bet you don't know the first thing about caring for an animal."

"Patrick will help."

"Yeah! I'll help."

"The blind leading the blind." McCain studied Patrick's hopeful face, then groaned. "I'm going to regret this."

Patrick jumped to his feet. "No, you won't. This is gonna be great! I've never had a dog before. Pa, did you ever have a dog?"

"Once, when I was a boy." He cleared his throat.

"What was its name?" Jessica asked.

"Jake." A hint of a smile touched his lips. "He was a damn fine dog. I had him for fifteen years."

"We could name one of the puppies Jake, Junior," Patrick said. "J.J. for short."

McCain looked into the brown, moist eyes of the puppy. He cleared his throat. "We'll see."

"Does that mean we get to keep them?"

"It means we'll see. Now get these little bundles of trouble loaded in the wagon before I change my mind."

Five minutes later, they were all in the buckboard. Patrick was in the back holding two yapping puppies and Jessica was next to McCain with a dog in her arms.

McCain grunted. "If Peg takes a hunk out of my hide, I'm coming after you."

Wild Jack tossed back his head and laughed. "That old woman has a softer heart than you."

McCain pushed his hat back with his index finger. "I'll remember that when she throws me out of the house."

Wild Jack pulled off his rawhide necklace with the bear claw dangling from the end, and pressed it into Jessica's hand. "Better keep this for good luck. Something tells me you're gonna need it with a husband like McCain."

She studied the bear claw. She was torn between tossing the wretched thing on the ground and thanking him. "I don't know what to say."

"No thanks needed, ma'am. It's the least I can do. It makes powerful magic and wards off evil spirits."

"Thanks and give my regards to Bessie," McCain said.

Wild Jack nodded and walked back into his cabin and slammed the door.

"He's a little strange, but nice," she stated.

"In these parts, you're the strange one," McCain amended.

The puppy licked Jessica's face and she laughed. "Maybe so."

The puppy nestled in her lap. McCain reached down and scratched it between the ears. "I think Wild Jack conned me into taking these pups."

"I believe you are right, Mr. McCain."

His eyes darkened and he reached out and touched her face. "Don't you think it's time you started calling me Ross?"

Jessica glanced back nervously at Patrick, who was wrestling with the other puppies. "We are not alone."

"All I'm asking you to do is say my name."

Saying his name was a small concession, yet she'd carefully maintained the formality because it served as a barrier of sorts. She didn't want to give it up.

"Say it," he urged. The earnest, almost raw tone of his voice touched her heart.

She moistened her lips. "Ross," she whispered. Part of the imaginary wall crumbled and suddenly she feared and anticipated the day there'd be nothing keeping them apart.

"Louder."

She drew in a deep breath. "Ross."

"I like the sound of that." He seemed pleased with himself as he snapped the reins and the wagon jerked forward. "From now on there'll be no more formalities between us, Emma."

Chapter Thirteen

In the predawn hours of Saturday morning, the air was crisp, the bed warm and sunrise a good two hours away. Jessica could have savored the extra time in bed, except for three puppies, sitting on the edge of her bed, whimpering softly.

She rolled on her stomach and pulled her pillow over her head. It had been a long, hard week and she desperately wanted to rest. "Just another half hour. That's all I'm asking."

In response they scurried to the head of the bed and nuzzled wet noses under her pillow.

"I already took you out twice last night. Isn't that enough?"

They yapped and thumped their tails on the bed as if chanting, "No."

The puppies had been in her charge all week and they'd bonded to her. If they lost sight of her, they yapped. If they were hungry, thirsty or needed to go outside, they came to her.

Peg had begrudgingly fixed the three a bed in the kitchen, but they'd whined and cried despite Patrick's loving hugs. The trio wanted only Jessica. Finally, she'd ignored common sense and Peg's warnings and let them sleep with her.

Jessica rubbed her burning eyes and sat up. Three black-and-white, furry faces stared at her. The puppies waggled their rumps with excitement. Begrudgingly, she smiled. How could she resist them?

"All right, fellows, let's go outside."

She tossed back the covers, slid her legs over the side of the bed and shoved her feet into her unlaced boots. She reached over to the nightstand and lit a candle. Wrapping a quilt around her shoulders, she picked up the candle and steeled herself for the chilly trip outside.

The puppies jumped off the bed. Their claws scraped against the bare wood floor as they scrambled around her feet. "Shh. Would you three be quiet?" she whispered. "You're going to wake the entire house."

She opened the door, and with the puppies on her heels, descended the stairs and hurried toward the kitchen at the back of the house. The kitchen door was ajar, letting light and heat out into the hallway. Jessica caught a warm and inviting whiff of coffee and freshly baked bread. Peg's handiwork, no doubt. She promised herself a cup of the hot brew once she returned with the puppies.

The wind whipped up her nightdress and the rocks on the path crunched under the soles of her boots as she followed the dogs into the field behind the house. She stamped her feet, warding off the cold as the puppies relieved themselves.

Minutes later, the puppies tumbled through the

open kitchen door with Jessica on their heels. She savored the rush of heat from the cast-iron stove and the smell of biscuits cooking. Copper pots and a freshly skinned rabbit hung from the ceiling, giving the room an inviting, homey appeal. Dried herbs draped a large screen that partitioned off a corner of the kitchen off near the stove.

A large bowl filled with meat scraps and another filled with fresh water sat on the floor by the stove. The puppies rushed toward them.

Jessica chuckled. ''Looks like Peg is looking after you as well.''

One of the puppies, in a rush to get to his food, stuck his oversize paw into the water bowl and spilled it. Jessica scooped him out of the puddle and repositioned him in front of the food. ''I don't know what I'm going to do with you three,'' she said, kneeling beside them.

She scratched one puppy on the head and was rewarded with a few overeager licks on her hand before he returned to his breakfast. ''I think I'm starting to like all the changes in my life.''

Three little tails waggled.

In her wildest dreams she'd never imagined herself in a town like Prosperity. Hopefully, William Perry hadn't, either. Just the thought of him set her nerves on edge. She knew nine days remained before the marriage offer in her father's will expired and she was truly safe.

She glanced around the room. For an instant, she had the distinct feeling she wasn't alone. She drew in a steadying breath but saw no one.

"My nerves must be on edge. William will never find me here."

She stood and poured herself a cup of coffee. She raised the cup to her nose and enjoyed the delectable smell.

"Mind pouring me a cup?" McCain's deep, masculine voice echoed from behind the partition.

Jessica jumped, spilling hot coffee on her hands. She whirled around. "McCain?"

"Yes."

"Where the devil are you?" She heard water splashing.

"Over here."

She followed the sound of his voice and peered around the screen. She froze. McCain was taking a bath!

A large brass tub dominated the corner behind the screen. McCain leaned against the back end of the tub with his legs stretched out in front of him and his elbows resting on the sides.

Water droplets glistened from his black hair, slicked back from his sharp features. Steam rose from the water, hovering like mist in the morning over his long body. She stared at the thick mat of chest hair that trailed down his abdomen to the soapy surface of the water.

Her gaze shot up and met his. For a long second they stared at each other.

Laughter sparkled in his eyes as he drew his legs slowly up to his chest and leaned forward in the tub. "How about that coffee?"

Shock paralyzed her. "What are you doing in here?"

"You're the teacher, you tell me," he said easily.

"I know what you're *doing*. It's just that I didn't expect you *here*."

"I could say the same for you. You're never up this early."

"The puppies needed to use the... And then I saw the lights burning in the kitchen so I thought Peg..."

His lips curled with amusement. "Are you going to stand there gawking at me or are you going to turn around so I can dress?"

Heat rose in her cheeks. "Ladies don't gawk."

"You were doing a fair imitation."

She whirled around. "It never occurred to me you'd be in here...bathing."

"Where else am I supposed to bathe?"

"In your room, of course."

"We common folk don't take baths in our rooms."

"I have!"

"I was wondering when you'd get tired of hauling that water upstairs."

"My privacy is worth the extra trouble."

She heard water slosh as he climbed out of the tub. She imagined him rising from the water, his limbs slick and warm. Her heart hammered in her chest. She heard his bare feet pad across the floor. "Why don't I leave you so you can return to your bath?"

"Stay. While I finish dressing, you can pour me that cup of coffee."

Grateful for the task, Jessica hurried to the stove and picked up the coffeepot. The spout clanged against the stoneware cup. Mercy, her hands were shaking. Drawing in a deep breath, she filled the two cups.

"Are you decent?" she said. She didn't dare look around the screen until he answered.

"Depends on your definition."

Her cheeks burned anew. "Are you dressed?"

"Just about."

She stared into the black depths of the coffee cups. "I thought I'd be the only one up this early."

"If you'd risen an hour ago, that might have been true."

She heard him slide one leg into his pants, then the other. She stared at her boots. "Where's Peg?"

"She's milking the cow."

"Oh."

"How are the puppies doing?"

As if they sensed they'd become the topic of conversation, the puppies stopped wrestling and perked up their ears. They ran to Jessica's feet, sat down and looked up at her. She relaxed enough to smile. "Up bright and early and into everything."

"They've taken a liking to you."

"Yes."

"They're not alone. Seems most folks in town have taken a liking to you."

"I suppose."

"Last I heard there were nearly a dozen folks planning to attend your Sunday afternoon reading lesson."

"What?"

"Sissy spent the better part of the week getting folks excited about reading."

Jessica sensed he had more to say. "I'll take as many students as I can get."

Ross cleared his throat. "I was thinking about your offer to teach me how to read. I've changed my mind. I accept."

"You do?" Jessica turned in her excitement. She got an eyeful of bare chest and a thick mat of chest hair that trailed down into the V of his unbuttoned pants. She turned back and cleared her throat. "You do. That's wonderful."

"You're right. It's high time I learned how to read."

"When would you like to begin lessons?"

"No special lessons for me. I'll join your Sunday afternoon class."

Shocked, she realized he'd made a large concession. "No one knows you can't read."

"I'm tired of living a lie."

She moistened her lips. "I'm sure you had a good reason for keeping your secret."

"There's rarely a good reason to lie."

Not necessarily.

"You can turn around now."

She turned. He had buttoned his simple work shirt up to the base of his neck and tucked it into his denim pants. His feet were bare, and he'd combed his fingers through his damp hair.

He smiled. "Fact is, I'm growing to trust you."

"You hardly know me."

He walked up to her and traced her jawline with his thumb. "I've decided to make it real hard for you to leave Prosperity."

"I have a two-year contract. I have to stay."

"I'm talking about after the contract expires. Two years isn't long enough, Emma."

"Two years is a lifetime." She edged backward. *I'm tired of living a lie.*

He brushed a curl from her forehead. "You've got to start trusting me, Emma."

Emma. God, how many lies had she told him?

"I do," she croaked.

"Who's William?" He fired the question like a bullet.

Surprise shot through her. "Who?"

"You mentioned him a few minutes ago."

"William?"

Ross folded his arms as if he had all the time in the world. "Uh-huh."

"Oh, *William.* He's an acquaintance of my father's. Nobody important, really."

"Then why are you hiding from him?"

Her stomach tightened a notch. "I'm not hiding from him."

McCain laid his hands on her shoulders. "I can always tell when you're lying."

Her heart slammed in her chest. She was so tired of lying. "How?"

"Never mind. Just know I can tell." He traced her collarbone with his thumb. "I'm giving you my trust and I want you to give me yours."

She wanted to confess all her lies. She wanted him to take her in his arms and forgive her. She wanted to begin again with Ross. The words begged to be spoken. They were on the tip of her tongue, until a dark thought occurred to her. What if Ross didn't forgive her? What if he sent her away? Suddenly, the threat of William Perry paled compared to the idea of losing Ross.

His green eyes turned to steel. "You are *my* wife. And your problems are now *my* problems. If this William is after you, I want to know about it so I can protect you."

"William's not a problem. I'm fine."

"Liar."

"There's nothing to say." She glanced over her shoulder at the door, ten feet away. God, how she wanted to bolt.

"Emma."

Only the acrid smell of smoke stopped her. "Do you smell something burning?"

They turned and looked at the stove. Black smoke seeped out from the edges of the oven door.

McCain's intensity gave way to horror. "Oh, no. I forgot about the biscuits. Peg's going to have my hide."

Relief washed over Jessica. She'd never been more grateful for burned biscuits in all her life. "Don't worry, Peg's going to assume this is my doing."

"I'll be sure to tell her that," he said, hurrying to the stove.

"Traitor."

Jessica and McCain grabbed for a cotton towel at the same time. When he yanked on the towel, she stumbled toward him. Still gripping the towel, she stared up into his eyes. "Let go," she ordered.

He tugged on the cloth until she was inches from his chest. "No, you let go," he whispered.

He jerked the cloth again and their bodies

touched. She held tight. The sudden desire that appeared in his eyes took her breath away.

"The biscuits," she whispered.

"Right." Reluctantly, he took the cloth from her and opened the oven door. Black smoke tumbled out.

"Damn it all." Ross coughed. He pulled out a pan filled with black, smoking biscuits. He kicked the cast-iron door closed with his knee, hurried to the back door and tossed the whole mess outside. "Peg told me to keep an eye on them."

"What's she going to do? Take you to the woodshed or put you over her knee?"

He threw back his head and laughed. The deep resonant sound vibrated off the walls, lightening her soul. But as quickly as the laughter came, it faded. "You've managed to brighten all our lives," he murmured.

The room stilled. Ross's eyes darkened with desire.

He picked up one of her curls, caressed it between his fingers and held it to his nose. "You're the most beautiful woman I've ever seen." He leaned close to whisper against her ear. "And you smell like roses. Roses in September."

Her fingers itched to reach out and touch the curly mat of hair she knew was under his shirt.

His arm came around her. "I've wanted to hold you in my arms since the first day I saw you standing on the train."

"Ross…"

"I like it when you say my name." His voice was

like raw silk. He leaned a fraction of an inch closer and pressed his chest against hers.

"We shouldn't be doing this," she whispered. Jessica's mind screamed for her to put distance between them, but her heart and body demanded more.

He smiled. "Our bodies fit well together." He gathered her closer. "I think you were made for my arms. This feels so right."

Yes, it did feel right.

He lowered his lips and she closed her eyes in anticipation. He rubbed his unshaved cheek against hers and weaved his fingers into her untamed hair.

His breath caressed her skin. "I promised myself I'd take it slow with you, but that's impossible. My body aches for you."

"We shouldn't do this," she breathed again.

But she didn't move away. She wanted to believe her past didn't matter after all, that what she saw in his eyes—the energy, the flash of longing—were there for her, Jessica.

"You want this as much as I do. Admit it."

"Yes."

He pressed his lips against hers. His touch was gentle at first, but as she slipped her arms around his neck, the kiss deepened. His masculine scent made her blood boil with desire.

A soft moan rumbled in her throat and gave him all the encouragement he needed. His next kiss was longer, more insistent. She melted into his arms and her doubts faded.

Jessica tilted back her head, her cascade of dark curls tumbling down her back. Her heart thumped wildly in her chest, her mouth suddenly dry.

"I will always be there for you, Emma," he breathed.

Emma.

Cold reality splashed her in the face. He was making promises to a woman he only thought he knew. Her lies stood between them and would eventually destroy what they had.

Her eyes filled with tears. She had to get out of here and away from him until her blood cooled. "I've got to go."

His eyes narrowed. "Why do you keep running from me?"

"I can't do this."

His grip tightened. "Do you think I'm not good enough for you?"

"No," she choked out. "It's not you."

"Then why aren't you giving us a chance?"

She pressed her cheek against his soft cotton shirt. "There is no us, Ross. We were not fated to be together."

"We could be. There's no love between us now, but in time there could be. We could build a good life together—you, me, Patrick and the children we'll have."

The image was unbearably beautiful and impossible. "I've made no promises beyond teaching school."

"But you want this. I can feel it. Sense it."

"It doesn't matter what I want."

"Emma."

"Stop!" She ripped free of his grip and cupped her hands over her ears. Before he could respond, she ran out of the kitchen.

Cheyenne, Wyoming

Emma Grimes sighed. She watched William Perry pace past the conductor standing on the lonely stretch of track in the early morning hours. The air was cold and a light snow had begun to fall.

"When the devil are we going to get out of this backwater town?" William Perry gingerly touched the large yellowing bruise on the side of his face.

The conductor shoved his hands in his pockets. "The engineer said ten minutes. We will be in Prosperity in a few hours."

"Let's hope so. Time is running out."

"Time, sir?"

"Nine days to find a needle in a haystack," William said absently.

The conductor shifted uncomfortably. "I'm sure you'll find whatever it is you're looking for."

"Let's hope you're right. My future depends on it."

As she always did when she was nervous, Emma Grimes reached into her pocket and pulled out a peppermint stick, broke off a piece and popped it in her mouth. She settled back in her seat and hugged her wool coat tighter around her chin.

She'd spent only eleven days in Mr. Perry's company, but she had serious doubts about him. They'd met in the Sacramento train station. Emma had been trying to convince the conductor she was the real Emma Grimes, while Mr. Perry had been standing behind her. Apparently, he'd been looking for a young woman named Jessica Tierney. Based on the bits of information she'd supplied and the conductor's description of the other Emma Grimes, Perry had deduced Jessica Tierney had taken her name and job.

When Mr. Perry had stepped forward and explained his theory, Emma had been tremendously grateful someone finally believed her. And when the man offered to rent a private car for her and agreed to accompany her to Prosperity, she'd felt as if her luck had changed for the good.

In Sacramento, Mr. Perry had been so considerate, so thoughtful, Emma had wondered why Jessica Tierney had run away from him.

But now, eleven days later, she understood why Miss Tierney had left.

It wasn't anything the man said or did, but something she sensed. He wasn't the savior he claimed to be, but a hunter. And Jessica Tierney was his prey.

The train whistle blew, shattering her thoughts. Her traveling companions climbed aboard the train and entered the private train car. Mr. Perry stamped his feet and poured himself a brandy. It was his fourth this morning.

"Well, Miss Grimes," Mr. Perry said, "I know you are anxious to get to Prosperity."

"I'd say you are the one who is truly anxious, sir."

He had snake eyes.

"You are very perceptive." He raised his brandy glass. "I have been under a great deal of strain. I've been terribly worried about Miss Tierney."

"I can see that," she said slowly. "Tell me, why is finding Jessica Tierney so important?"

A slow smile curled his lips. "Miss Tierney is my fiancée. Two and a half weeks ago, we had a lovers' spat. It was a petty fight, really, but she was very upset."

"Did she give you that nasty black eye?"

Mr. Perry touched his blackened eye with his fingertips. "She struck out blindly and accidentally hit me."

"It must have been a terrible fight for her to leave."

"Jessica can be very impulsive. She obviously wanted to punish me by disappearing for a while." Mr. Perry walked across the car and sat down across from Emma. "You see, my fiancée is not entirely…stable. She has bouts of depression and sometimes gets confused."

"How sad."

"Her family has spent years protecting her," he added before he gulped down the remains of his brandy then refilled his glass. "My only fear now is that she's gotten in over her head," Mr. Perry added. "She's run to some very wild and untamed country, and what started out as a hasty prank could very well put her in harm's way."

"Well, then, it's best we get to her as quickly as possible. I wouldn't want anything to happen to the poor dear."

Emma had developed a keen eye for liars in her years of teaching. She knew one sat before her now. The question was—what was she going to do?

Chapter Fourteen

Jessica ran out of the kitchen and up the stairs. She didn't stop running until she reached her room. She slammed the door and slumped against it, closing her eyes. Her palms were sweating.

She was in love with Ross McCain.

Elated and sick at the idea, she squeezed her fists to her temples. What was she going to do?

During the last ten years at boarding school she'd taught herself to embrace loneliness, to accept it as an unchangeable fact of life. She'd always wanted someone to love—dreamed of it—but in her heart, she'd never really thought it would happen. Yet in less than a fortnight, Ross had stolen her heart. Her dream was so painfully close and so out of reach.

She lit a candle, walked to her nightstand and looked in the mirror. ''I'm a mess.''

''You look like you've seen Lucifer himself,'' Peg said.

Startled, Jessica glanced up in time to see the housekeeper push herself out of the chair in the corner and walk slowly toward her. Candlelight flickered over the old woman's wrinkled features. Her face revealed nothing of her thoughts.

"I thought you were milking the cow," Jessica said.

"Just finished. We need to talk."

"Peg, please, just leave me alone."

"I will as soon as you tell me who you are."

Jessica's mouth dropped open before she snapped it closed. "I don't understand."

Peg pulled a pipe from her pocket. "Don't play dumb with me, Miss Grimes, or whoever you are. I've hustled the best in my time."

A dozen different lies sprang to Jessica's mind, but lying to Peg now seemed pointless. She sat down on the edge of her bed. Strangely, she welcomed the truth. "My name is Jessica Tierney."

Peg pressed a wad of tobacco into her pipe bowl, then struck a match against the sole of her boot. She held the flame to the pipe and puffed until smoke curled around her head like a cloud. "And you ain't no teacher, are you?"

Jessica sighed. "No."

"Why are you here?"

"You have to believe me, I never meant for the lie to go so far. I was sure Ross would let me go once I explained I wasn't right for the job. But he wouldn't let me out of my contract."

"Once you make a promise to Ross McCain, he expects you to keep it."

Jessica looked up at her. "I never expected to fall in love with him or come to care so much for Patrick, you and everyone else." Tears streamed down her face.

"I'm supposed to believe that?"

Jessica's shoulders slumped. "No, but it's the truth."

Peg studied Jessica for a moment. She clamped her pipe between her teeth and dug a piece of paper out of her apron pocket. She handed it to Jessica. "Read this."

"What is this?" Jessica stared at the paper, trying to shake a deep sense of foreboding.

Peg stared into the bowl of her pipe. "You tell me."

Jessica smoothed her hand over the wrinkled paper and read:

Sheriff:

The schoolteacher who calls herself Emma Grimes is a fraud. I suspect Jessica Tierney has taken her place. Miss Tierney is criminally insane and dangerous. Detain her until I arrive in Prosperity on Thursday.

William Perry

She glanced up at Peg. Words did not come. She could barely think. Barely breathe.

William had found her! Her first thought wasn't for her reputation or her own safety. She worried about Ross and what he would think when William reached town and told his lies.

Peg cleared her throat. "The telegram came in late last night. The sheriff can't read so he asked me to read the telegram to him."

"Is he going to arrest me?"

"If I had read the telegram to him, he would have."

"I don't understand."

"I told Sam some of the words was too big for me and that I'd have to get you to read it to me. He's waiting on my answer."

"Why are you protecting me?"

"Can't rightly say. My gut's telling me you ain't so bad. Unless you're a better liar than I suppose— and I don't think you are—that telegram don't ring true."

Jessica shook her head. "William Perry is an evil man."

"Why is he after you?"

"He wants to marry me so he can take control of my father's inheritance. There was no one I could turn to so I ran."

"How the devil did you end up here?"

"After I hit him, I was desperate to get out of Sacramento. I have no friends or family, so I ran to the train station. I was ready to buy a ticket to anywhere, but when I got to the station, they were holding the train for Emma Grimes. I was frantic. I knew time was precious, so I told the conductor I was Emma Grimes. I meant to tell Ross the truth as soon as I met him, but I was so scared I signed the contract he had ready."

"And later?"

Jessica crushed the telegram in her hand. "The lie just got bigger and bigger. As the days went by, it got harder and harder to tell the truth."

"You're in one hell of a mess, girl."

"I know."

"There's only one thing you can do."

Jessica knew she'd violated everyone's trust. How could she honestly expect anything from anyone in Prosperity? "You want me to leave town."

Peg snorted. "Hell, no. I want you to go talk to Ross. It's time to be straight with him. He is gonna be madder than hell, but he'll get over this. He's got strong feelings for you. He'll stand by you and protect you from this Perry fellow."

Jessica shook her head. Her chest ached. "He'll never forgive me."

"Don't underestimate the man. I'll grant you he can be stubborn as a mule, but he can take a lot, and he's got a forgiving heart. Talk to him."

"I couldn't bear it if he sent me away."

"Girl, the way I see it, the truth is your only chance with Ross. Don't sell him or yourself short."

Jessica stood. Peg was right, of course; she had to own up to her lies. "You're not going to tell Ross?"

"Honey, I got more than my share of secrets, so I ain't one to judge." Peg walked over to the door and opened it. "You got any other skeletons in your closet?"

"I've told you everything…I swear." Tears ran down her face.

The housekeeper nodded. "Wash your face and go find Ross."

When Peg closed the door behind her, Jessica sank back down on the bed. She clenched the telegram in trembling hands. The thought of facing Ross scared her witless, but the alternative—running away and leaving him and Prosperity behind—was too painful to consider. She had to chance the truth.

"Don't make me leave!" Patrick's voice rang out.

Jessica wiped the tears from her face. Patrick? What was he doing up so early? Her own problems forgotten, she hurried into the boy's room.

Patrick had thrown off his quilt. Drenched in sweat, his body thrashed back and forth as he whimpered. Jessica went to him, knelt down by his bed and stroked his hand gently. She hummed softly as she brushed his soft skin. "Don't you worry, honey. You're just having a bad dream. It's all right."

He stopped crying. His eyes fluttered open. He smiled up at her. "You came."

"Of course I did."

His small brows knotted. "I dreamed you'd left."

His words hit her hard. "I haven't left."

"I don't ever want you to leave me."

Whatever happened with Ross, she knew her feelings for the boy wouldn't change. But she couldn't make false promises to him, not when his father could easily send her away.

"I'm here now and that's all that counts. Close your eyes again, Patrick."

She picked up his hand and studied the small fingers. He was so young, so innocent. Minutes passed. His breathing deepened. She studied every detail about him—the light peppering of freckles across the bridge of his nose, his pink cheeks, the cleft in his chin.

She pulled the quilt up and gently pressed her lips

against his cheek. He smiled and rolled onto his side.

"Sleep well, Patrick. I love you." Slowly, she rose to her feet.

When she turned, she saw Ross standing in the doorway. He leaned against the doorjamb, his arms folded over his chest. His hair, still unbound, hung recklessly around his shoulders.

How long had he been watching and listening?

His gaze fixed on her. "Is everything all right?"

"Patrick had a nightmare," she whispered. She stood and walked toward the door. Her insides tightened with each step that took her closer to him. "But he's fine now."

"You've a mother's touch when it comes to the boy. He's lucky to have you."

"He's a good boy."

"The best."

Jessica glanced over her shoulder at Patrick. He was sleeping peacefully. Her heart twisted with sadness as she turned and walked past Ross into the hallway.

McCain closed Patrick's door, then, taking her by the elbow, led her down the hall. He stopped and turned her toward him. He reached up and traced her cheekbone with his knuckle. "You've helped me realize what a wonderful son I have."

"I think you always knew that."

"Yes, I suppose I did."

McCain's eyes softened. Guilt ate at Jessica as the image of the crumpled telegram on her bed sprang to mind.

Tell him the truth.

The truth begged to be spoken, yet she couldn't speak it. It broke her heart to think McCain could end up hating her once she confessed. "If you'll excuse me, I've got a full day ahead of me."

McCain grabbed her wrist, halting her retreat. "Why did you run out of the kitchen?"

She knew she wasn't going anywhere until she answered his question. "You frightened me," she said honestly.

"You know I'd never hurt you."

"Yes."

He nodded, satisfied. "Then explain why you ran."

"It's complicated."

"I've got the time."

She clenched her fists. "This is harder than I thought it would be."

"Best just to spit it out."

"If I didn't love you so much, I would."

"What did you say?" he said quietly.

Jessica pressed her fingertips to her lips and raised her gaze to his. She couldn't deny her feelings any longer. "I love you."

Ross cupped her face in his hands, then he kissed her. When the kiss ended she was breathless. Disoriented.

"I will be a good husband to you," he said.

Jessica shook her head. Breathing was difficult.

She reached up and touched his cheek. The rough stubble on his chin sent a wave of emotions through her. "I don't deserve you."

"You deserve more than I could ever give." Ross

wrapped his arms around her waist, drawing her to him. He pressed his lips against hers.

Enveloped by his strength and warmth, she wrapped her arms around his neck. One kiss. She wanted only one kiss.

He hugged her tighter against him. A soft moan escaped her as his touch became more insistent.

This was their moment—their chance to be together—and she couldn't let it slip by. She wanted to know what it felt like to make love to Ross McCain. It would be a memory she would treasure forever. Her reckoning would come soon enough.

She kissed him fully, matching his passion. He groaned and tightened his hold around her body. He slid his hand up her thigh, smoothing it over the curves of her hip. She gasped at the surge of desire.

A few hours of uncompromised love wasn't too selfish, was it? She kissed his neck and nuzzled her nose against his ear.

A low groan rumbled in his chest. "I want you."

Jessica's hunger matched his. "Make love to me."

He scooped her up in his arms. She wrapped her own arms around his neck. He strode down the hallway toward his room, stepped over the threshold and kicked the door closed with his bare foot. He crossed the room and set her down in the center of his large bed. He pulled off his shirt and slid out of his pants, letting them both fall in a pile at his feet.

For an instant, her eyes widened at the sight of him. She swallowed. "My mother died when I was a young girl and no one has ever explained... things...to me. Ross, I've never..."

The mattress sagged under his weight as he lay beside her. "Shh, I know. It's all right."

"What I mean is, well, Ross, are you sure...I mean, that you'll fit...it'll fit inside me?"

"We'll fit together just fine."

She sucked in a deep breath when his hand slid up her ribs and cupped one of her full breasts. His fingers skimmed her nipples.

"So sweet, so beautiful." His hand moved down her back, then over her buttock, cupping the soft mound with his long fingers. He dropped another searing kiss on her lips.

She felt dizzy. "I'm not sure what you're doing to me, but I like it."

Ross chuckled, nibbling her ear with his teeth. "Good."

He stared down at her. He ran his fingers over the worn lace of her nightgown collar. "You're so beautiful."

He gathered twin handfuls of her nightgown, pulled it over her head and tossed it in a heap in the corner. A single candle burned by his bed, sending a flickering light over her white skin and the contoured lines of his face. Unable to ignore a stab of modesty, she raised her hands to cover her naked breasts.

He ran his hands over hers and pulled them away. "Don't hide from me. Let me take in every detail of you."

His softly spoken words coaxed Jessica toward boldness. "I love touching you," she said.

"Not nearly as much as I love seeing and touching you. Your skin is as smooth as china."

Her hands trembled with want as she smoothed her hands over the coarse hair of his chest and his finely honed muscles. He was perfect.

"Only in my wildest dreams did I dare believe you could be mine." He drank in every detail of her.

Ebony curls cascaded over her creamy shoulders and full breasts. She moistened her lips as she stared up at him, waiting, willing.

She leaned forward to blow out the candle on the nightstand.

He stopped her. "Don't. I want to remember everything about this moment." His gaze skimmed over her naked flesh.

She trailed a single finger over his backside.

"Be careful what you touch. This might be over before it begins. I've not shared a bed with a woman in a long time."

"I don't understand. Don't you like it when I touch you?"

He groaned. "Like it? I love it, but it's hard keeping a tight rein on my desire with you so close. I want our first time to be perfect, so when you look back, you'll smile."

"That I can promise."

He drew a callused hand up her smooth leg, over her hip. She sucked in a breath when his hand cupped her breast again. Fear, excitement, sadness—they all shot through her.

Perspiration glistened on her temple as his finger trailed down between her breasts, over her belly to the dark curls between her legs.

She arched her back and hugged him against her. "I feel so strange, so wonderful."

"That's sweet music to my ears."

Gently he pushed her legs apart with his knee. Raising himself on his arms, he poised to enter her. "Ah, Emma. This is what it's supposed to be like between a man and a woman. True and honest love."

She stiffened. Tears welled in her eyes. She was a liar. A coward. Unworthy. "Yes," she whispered.

He reached out with his finger and captured the single tear as it rolled down her face. "You're not afraid, are you?" he murmured against her ear.

"A little."

"I'd never hurt you."

"I know."

"If you want to wait, I will." His face was dark. Tense.

Jessica shook her head from side to side. "I don't want to wait. I want us to be together, now." She cupped his face in her hands and kissed him fully, deeply on the mouth. Boldly, she plunged her tongue into his mouth and arched her back once more, pressing her breasts against him.

A deep groan rumbled in his chest, but still he held back. He began to rub her tender flesh and her body sang with unexpected pleasure. She was hungry for him. Desperate for his touch. "Ross, please, I can't wait any longer."

His smile was arrogant and very male. "Ah, just another moment or two, my sweet wife. I like pleasuring you."

She whimpered slightly when he pulled away.

"The sight of you drives me crazy with want," he said. Then, before she could respond, he slid into her body.

Jessica tensed, bracing herself, as he pressed against the delicate barrier inside her. He kissed her on the lips and entered her. Brief, lightning-sharp pain seared her. She sucked in a breath and gripped his shoulders. At first he didn't move. With his hands planted on either side of her head, he waited for her to grow accustomed to him.

"Emma?" he rasped. "Did I hurt you?"

Oh, how she wanted to hear him speak *her* name. "I'm fine."

He began to move in her. Moments passed. The pain gave way to a delicious tightening that warmed her entire body.

Jessica, relying on instinct, matched his rhythm and surrendered herself up to the erotic dance they shared. She arched her hips, straining to meet his thrusts. Finally, when she thought she'd go mad with wanting, she peaked in an explosion of desire that filled her with awe and amazement. Seconds later, his body, slick with sweat, strained, then jerked before he found his release.

She and Ross were one.

And for an instant, all her fears vanished.

Their bodies spent, Ross collapsed against her. His breathing was ragged; his heart thumped wildly against her chest. He rolled onto his side, drawing her into his arms. She wiggled her backside against him and savored the way his arms tightened around her body.

For the first time in her life, she felt fulfilled, complete and no longer alone.

An hour later, Jessica stood by the window with only a quilt wrapped around her, while Ross slept, his muscular body dominating his bed.

She stared at the mist-covered landscape, longing for the warmth of Ross's arms. The peace she'd felt such a short time ago had vanished. Again she was alone, imprisoned by her lies.

She wanted so desperately to reach beyond the wall of secrets standing between them, but the words wouldn't come. Fear of Ross's rejection kept her silent.

Hot tears burned her eyes when she thought about a future without him.

"The bed's lonely without you." As silent as a cat, Ross had walked up behind her. He wrapped his arms around her and hugged her against his chest.

Jessica turned in his arms. His eyes were misty with sleep. Instinctively, she wrapped her arms around his chest, seeking warmth and solace. She closed her eyes, savoring his masculine scent. "Life would be so lonely without you."

He banded his arms around her and rubbed his chin against her temple. "Fortunately, I'll always be here."

She drew comfort from their embrace. "It wasn't until I came here that I realized how truly lonely I was."

"Lonely is something you'll never be again. Patrick, Peg and I are your family now."

She pressed her cheek against the bare skin of his chest. "Yes."

She released the quilt, letting it pool around her ankles. She wanted to make love to him again. Once hadn't been enough.

Naked in the morning sun, she cupped Ross's face in her hands. Standing on tiptoe, she pressed her breasts against his chest and kissed him on the mouth. The taste of him mingled with the salty flavor of her tears.

Ross drew her hands from his face. "Emma, we don't have to do this now. You might not be ready to do it again."

She shook her head. The ends of her hair brushed her waist. She craved the sweet oblivion they'd shared earlier, her sole source of refuge. Her hands trailed down his back and over his buttocks.

Ross groaned, closing his eyes. "I'm trying to be noble. And you're not making it easy."

Her laugh was husky. "Make love to me again."

He groaned again, surrendering to her touch, and wrapped his arms around her slender body. He lifted her off the floor as his mouth joined hers. The kiss dulled her worries and sparked her hopes for the future. Perhaps she could make him understand and he would forgive her.

He carried her back to the bed. Laying her gently on the sheets, he climbed into bed and pulled the covers over their naked bodies.

She reached for him with an eagerness that shocked her.

"I must be living right for the fates to have given me a woman like you."

Jessica clung to his shoulders, giving herself up to the whirl of sensual feelings. She buried her face in his shoulder, hungrily accepting him when he entered her.

"Always remember that I love you, Ross," she whispered before chaos overtook her.

Chapter Fifteen

Jessica peeked out from under the quilt. Sunlight cascaded onto the bed's rumpled sheets, onto her nightgown puddled on the floor. Fall had turned to winter overnight, and the biting air and the cold embers in the hearth sent her back to the warmth of the covers and Ross. She snuggled her bottom against him.

Ross groaned softly and pulled her nearer. He nuzzled his face in the crook of her neck. "Why don't we spend the winter in bed?"

"If only we could." She wriggled closer to him. Being in his arms felt so right.

She could feel him growing hard and it gave her a sense of satisfaction that she could evoke such a reaction in him. Her own desire grew as she thought of making love to him one more time.

Still, she resisted the urge. The moment for the truth had come. They must talk.

Ross nibbled her earlobe. Shivers danced down her spine. Her body ached for him.

When a moan escaped her lips, he chuckled. "I can't seem to get enough of you."

"I feel the same," she whispered.

He rolled her onto her back and stared down at her. His eyes, like emerald shards, greedily drank in every detail of her. "You are beautiful."

She trailed a finger down his chin. "*You* are beautiful."

His smiled. "I've been called a lot of things, Emma, but never that."

She cupped his face in her hands. "I wouldn't change a thing about you."

His hand ran along her thigh, up and over her stomach to her breast.

Jessica sucked in a breath. He was making this so difficult. "We must talk," she whispered.

"We'll talk all you want. Later."

He kissed the nape of her neck, trailing soft kisses down to her breasts.

"When you touch me like that I can't think clearly."

He kissed her on the lips as he teased her nipple with his thumb. "Good."

They had to talk.

Coherent thought eluded her. What difference could another hour make? She would tell him her story as soon as they'd made love. Just another hour. She arched her back and pressed her breast into his hand.

He needed no other encouragement. "My sweet, wanton wife," he said huskily. He rolled on top of her.

She wrapped her arms around his neck and kissed

him. Within seconds, she was lost, forgetting the words that had been on the tip of her tongue seconds ago.

Into the maelstrom of emotions came the distant sound of knocking. Someone was downstairs at the front door. The thumping grew louder, until it could be denied no longer.

Ross groaned and collapsed against her. "This better be good or I will have to be locked up for murder."

She banded her arms around his chest, refusing to let him go. "Peg'll get it."

"No, I better go. Nobody bangs on my door like that on a Saturday unless there's trouble."

Ross rolled off of her and slid out from underneath the covers. His warmth was replaced by an unreasonable sense of foreboding.

He pulled on his pants, yanked his shirt over his head and shoved his feet into his unlaced boots.

"I'll go with you," Jessica said.

He leaned down and kissed her lips. "No, stay and keep that bed warm for me. I'll be right back." He strode out of the room.

Jessica lay on her back and listened to the sound of his footsteps descending the stairs. Seconds clicked by. She heard him open the front door.

Sam's Virginia drawl was unmistakable. "These folks said they have to see you."

Jessica sat up in bed and clutched the sheet to her naked breasts. An uneasy feeling crept into her bones.

"Can't it wait? I'm busy right now," Ross said.

"I'm sure you are, sir, but I'm afraid my news

won't wait.'' William Perry's voice shattered her sense of peace.

This can't be happening!

Jessica swung her feet over the side of the bed, scooped up her nightgown and slipped it over her head. Grabbing a quilt from the bed, she wrapped it around her shoulders and hurried out of the room to the top of the stairs.

''Mister, unless someone's dead or there's a problem at the mine, it can wait,'' Ross declared.

''It's about Jessica Tierney,'' William said.

''I don't know who you are talking about,'' Ross replied.

It was impossible to see Ross, William or Sam. Halfway down, the stairs turned sharply at a landing before descending to the foyer. Jessica listened, praying for a miracle.

''You must know her,'' William said.

''I don't know any Jessica Tierney,'' Ross retorted.

''But you must!''

''I'm tired of arguing with you, Mr....''

''Perry. William Perry.''

''Sam is my foreman,'' Ross said. ''He'll take you to the sheriff. Make your inquiries with him.''

''I already told him we don't have anybody in these parts by that name,'' Sam said. ''But he ain't listening.''

''Miss Tierney may not be using her real name,'' William said quickly. ''When she left Sacramento she was using the name Emma Grimes.''

''What?'' The shock in Ross's voice made Jessica cringe with guilt.

William's voice grew calmer. "Ah, I can see by the expression on your face you've heard the name before. Jessica is petite, has black curly hair and is quite beautiful."

"That description fits a good number of women." An edge had sharpened Ross's voice.

"There's someone I want you to meet," William insisted.

Jessica heard footsteps, then the front door opened again. A blast of cold air rushed through the front door and up the stairs, chilling her to the bone before it closed.

William cleared his throat. "Let me introduce you to Emma Grimes—the real Emma Grimes."

Emma Grimes!

Jessica hurried down to the landing and peeked around the corner. Next to William and Sam stood a woman she guessed had to be Emma Grimes.

Short and plump, she wore a fawn-colored wool dress with a black cape. Her winter bonnet was tied with a neat bow under her double chin, and her lips were set in a grim line.

"This is some kind of mistake," Ross said. His feet were braced apart and his hair tousled. "I don't know who this woman is, but the *real* Emma Grimes is upstairs."

William smiled, brushing imaginary lint from his black wool overcoat. A diamond tie pin winked in the morning sun. "Miss Grimes, would you tell Mr. McCain how we met?"

Emma Grimes nodded. "I met Mr. Perry at the train station in Sacramento nearly two weeks ago. I was arguing with the ticket master. It seems that several days earlier another woman had taken my place on the private car you'd sent for me.''

"Why should I believe you?" Ross demanded.

Emma Grimes dug into her reticule, pulled out a telegram and held it out to him. "I believe this is the telegram you sent to me, confirming my employment."

Ross made no move to take it. "Telegrams are easily copied."

"In my letters, I mentioned that I like to eat peppermints and love to read John Keats."

Ross's shoulders slumped as if the wind had been knocked out of him. He stepped away from the door and let the three enter.

"Could you ask your Emma Grimes to come downstairs?" William asked.

"Yes," Ross said.

No! No! No! It wasn't supposed to happen like this! Jessica was supposed to be the one to tell Ross the truth. Still, she refused to run. She owed Ross that much.

She clutched the quilt around her, stepped around the corner at the landing and descended the remaining stairs.

Ross turned to her. Worry and confusion etched his proud features. "This man thinks he knows you. Says your name is Jessica Tierney. Would you please do us all a favor and tell him he's got the wrong woman?"

Panic raced through her. "Ross, please, can we talk first? There's something I need to tell you."

"Hello, Jessica," William said. Smug and confident, he puffed his chest out.

Inwardly, Jessica cringed. She ignored William. "Ross, we need some privacy."

Ross searched her eyes. "First tell me, does Perry have the wrong woman?"

William stepped forward. His eyes glittered with victory. "Go ahead. Tell the good man that you really aren't a teacher and that your name isn't Emma Grimes. Tell him how you lied and deceived him. How you used him."

Ross shot a look over his shoulder. "Let her speak. She doesn't need your bullying." He looked back at her with eyes full of hope. "Go ahead, Emma, tell the man he's wrong. Give me an excuse to throw him out on his ear."

Jessica swallowed. "Ross." Her voice was barely a whisper.

"Tell him your name is Emma Grimes," Ross insisted.

She reached up and touched his cheek. "I can't."

Ross jerked his head away from her fingers. "What do you mean, you can't?"

"My real name is Jessica Tierney."

Ross stabbed his fingers through his hair. "This is nonsense. Your name is Emma Grimes. You are my wife."

"My name is Jessica Tierney."

He took a step back. "Is this some kind of game?"

"It's no game. I swear."

"You took over another woman's identity?" he said in disbelief.

Jessica willed the tears not to come. "Yes."

Shock, confusion, pain registered on his face.

William sneered. "Jessica, you had to know your lies would catch up with you sooner or later."

Every muscle in her body twisted. "Have some decency, William. Let me explain myself to Ross."

"While you're at it, my dear, explain how you jilted me, hit me over the head with a marble ashtray and stole my money."

Ross tensed. "Is this true?"

Tears spilled down her face. "It's not what you think. I can explain everything."

"Tread carefully, Mr. McCain," William said. "She's beautiful and quite convincing, but the truth is, she's unstable. Her father knew this and wanted me, his business partner and friend, to marry her and take care of her."

Ross clenched his fingers into fists. "This is impossible."

"I know it sounds fantastic, but I have documents to prove my legal claim to Miss Tierney.

Ross's head shot up. "Your legal claim?"

"I'm not only her fiancé, but also her guardian."

Jessica gasped. "Don't believe him, Ross. He's the liar. He doesn't care about me. He wants control of my father's estate."

William shook his head. "Jessica, when will you accept that I have your best interests at heart?"

For so many years Jessica had been afraid of William. But she was no longer a frightened child. She was a grown woman who stood her ground. "Did you have my best interests at heart when you convinced Father to send me away?"

William straightened his shoulders. "Boarding

school was an appropriate option for a willful young girl.''

She stepped toward him. "Did you care about me when you tried to force me to marry you?"

Ross flexed his fingers. "Enough! I want you out of my house, Perry."

"She's not the woman you think she is. I'm telling you, she's better off with me."

"She's not going anywhere." Ross's voice was low and dangerous.

Emma Grimes stepped forward. "Miss Tierney, I'd like to speak."

Jessica shifted her gaze to the newcomer. "Miss Grimes, I know I have wronged you, but—"

"Yes, you have," she interrupted briskly. "But I think that I've earned the right to speak."

Ross nodded. "Say your piece, Miss Grimes."

"Thank you, Mr. McCain. Traveling with Mr. Perry has given me a taste of his character. Though he pretends to have Miss Tierney's best interests at heart, I doubt he does."

Jessica sighed, relieved. "Thank you."

William shook his head. "Miss Grimes, we did not meet under the best of circumstances. It's unfair for you to judge me so hastily."

Sam stepped forward. "I know I only met Miss Grimes—the real Miss Grimes—less than an hour ago, but she strikes me as a straight shooter."

Emma smiled. "Thank you, Mr. Jenkins."

He winked at her. "Ma'am."

"Mr. McCain," William said, "I know this has been a great shock to you and I sincerely empathize, but there's no point in dragging this on any longer.

We both know Miss Tierney is a liar. Turn her over to me, and I'll see that she never bothers you again.'' He reached out for Jessica.

She balled her fists, ready for a fight. ''No! I am not going with you.''

Ross pulled Jessica behind him. ''For better or worse, Perry, she's my wife.''

''That's right!'' Jessica said. Hope fluttered to life within her. ''Ross and I married five days ago, right here in Prosperity.''

William raised an eyebrow. ''Don't lie to me, Jessica.''

She straightened her shoulders. ''I'm not lying, William.''

''You'd say or do anything to spite me.''

''Perhaps, but that doesn't change the fact that I'm married to Ross.''

''She ain't lying,'' Sam offered. His hat rode back on his head and three days' growth of beard blanketed his jaw. ''Just about the whole town was present.''

Jessica nodded. ''Admit it, William, you've lost.''

William stiffened. ''I haven't lost anything yet.'' He tried to reach around Ross to grab her.

Ross shoved him back. ''She's right. Em—Jessica and I are married. She's not going anywhere with you.''

''You don't even know your wife's name,'' William challenged.

''Her name doesn't matter much at this point. I made a promise to protect her and I intend to keep that promise. Now get out of my house.''

Jessica brushed a curl from her face. "It's over, William."

A smirk curled his lips. "It's not over."

"She's my wife. There's nothing more to say," Ross said.

William pretended to contemplate an idea. "Let me see if I got this right. You married your dear, sweet *Emma* five days ago? Is that right?"

"Yes."

"But she's not Emma," William said, gloating. "She's Jessica. She married you under the wrong name, which makes the wedding invalid."

Jessica sucked in a breath. "We are married. Half the town witnessed it."

"What they witnessed was an illegal union, and if you doubt me, we'll wire Mr. Moore, the Tierney family attorney, for his opinion."

Ross frowned. "You can wire all the people you want, but it doesn't change the fact that the woman is my wife."

"McCain, you should be shouting with joy. I've just given you the perfect reason to rid yourself of a woman who has repeatedly lied to you."

A tremor passed through Jessica's body. William was right. This was Ross's way out of the marriage. "Ross, I know I've a lot to explain, but don't throw away what we've shared."

"We haven't shared that much," he snapped.

The words stung. She didn't want to beg, but false pride was a luxury she couldn't afford now. She would do anything to remain free of William. "Don't let him take me."

For a long moment, Ross didn't speak. Her heart thundered in her chest.

"Be done with the woman, McCain," William coaxed. "I'll marry her today and take her off your hands. You'll never have to worry about her again."

Miss Grimes shook her head. "Don't listen to him, Mr. McCain."

Ross pierced William with a glance. His expression was dark and angry. He nodded to Sam. "Where's the minister?"

"Right across the street at the Millers'."

"Get him."

"What for, Ross?" Sam asked.

"It's time to set things right. He's got a marriage to perform."

Sam glanced at Ross, then at William. "You sure about this?"

"Damn sure."

"All right," Sam said. He left.

The angry set of Ross's jaw frightened Jessica. "What are you going to do?"

"Marry you," Ross said tightly.

"What?" William shouted, stepping forward. "But she lied to you! It's clear she can't be trusted."

"That's my problem, not yours."

"McCain, you won't get a dime from the Tierney estate. The will stipulates that *I* must marry Jessica. If you marry her, the money goes to Saint Bridget's Orphanage."

"Lucky for the orphans," Ross said.

"You obviously don't understand," William said, calmer now. "The estate is worth millions."

"So?"

William forced a smile. "If you let me marry her, I shall see that you are richly rewarded."

"No!" Jessica shouted. "I'd rather die."

"Quiet, woman!" William ordered. "McCain, I'll give you a million dollars if you let me marry her now."

"No deal."

"Thank you, Ross," Jessica whispered.

Emma Grimes clapped her hands together. "Good for you, Mr. McCain. You are a true man of honor."

"A damn fool is more like it," he muttered.

Seconds later, Sam arrived with Reverend Summers in tow. The minister, with a half-eaten biscuit in one hand and a napkin tucked in his collar, stumbled into the room. "Sam said there was an emergency," he said, chewing.

"I need for you to perform a wedding," Ross said.

"Again?"

"That's right."

Swallowing the remains of his biscuit, the reverend glanced at Emma Grimes and William. "Who's the lucky couple?"

"Miss Jessica Tierney," Ross said, pulling her forward, "and me."

Reverend Summers swallowed. "I thought her name was Emma Grimes, and didn't I just marry you two a few days ago?"

Ross's frown deepened. "We'll get into that later. Just marry us."

"You're being a fool, McCain," William stormed. "Why are you turning your back on a million dollars?"

"For better or worse, Perry, she's my wife. If protecting her means I have to marry her again, then I'll do it."

William clenched his fists. "This is an outrage! I'm going to wire Mr. Moore."

Ross pulled Jessica closer to him. "You do that."

Jessica blinked, unable to speak.

Reverend Summers pulled the napkin from his collar and wiped the crumbs from his face. "Mr. McCain, when would you like to get married?"

"Now."

"But it's eight o'clock in the morning. I'm in the middle of breakfast."

"It'll only take a minute."

"But—"

"Do it now!" Ross ordered.

The reverend paled. "Certainly, Mr. McCain. Uh, let me see, we need two witnesses."

"Sam can be a witness and so can Miss Grimes."

The minister looked at Jessica. "Do you want to marry him?"

"Yes."

"Well, that's a step in the right direction." Reverend Summers cleared his throat.

William clenched his fists at his sides. "I won't allow this. She is my fiancée."

"Sam," Ross ordered, "if Perry says another word, shoot him."

Sam drew his gun. "With pleasure."

William's face turned red with anger. He opened his mouth to speak. Sam cocked his pistol. William clamped his mouth shut.

Ross pulled Jessica to his side. "Get on with it, Reverend."

Reverend Summers adjusted his glasses. "Let me see here. Dearly beloved, we are gathered here in the sight of God to join this man and woman. Do you, Miss Grimes—"

"It's Miss Tierney," Jessica interrupted. "Jessica Elizabeth Tierney."

"Oh, that's right. I'm sorry. I keep forgetting you're not Miss Grimes, she is."

"I know this is confusing. I promise to explain later," Jessica said.

"Get on with it," Ross ordered tersely.

"Do you, Miss Jessica Elizabeth Tierney, take Ross McCain to be your lawfully wedded husband?"

"I do."

"And do you, Ross McCain, take Jessica Elizabeth Tierney to be your lawfully wedded wife?"

Ross stared straight ahead. His jaw was tense, his body rigid. "Yes."

"Well, then, by the powers vested in me, I now pronounce you man and wife."

Ross released Jessica's arm. "Thanks, Reverend, you can get back to your breakfast now."

"Oh, thank you. Liza Miller makes the best sweet biscuits I ever did taste, and I'd hate to miss a second helping." Reverend Summers glanced from Jessica to Emma Grimes, then back to Jessica. His eyes sparkled. "I must say, there haven't been too many dull moments since you arrived in town, Mrs. McCain."

When the minister left, Ross turned to Perry.

"You've got one hour to get out of town or Sam is going to shoot you where you stand."

William's eyes widened with shock. "The next train isn't due until tomorrow!"

"That's not my problem."

"I am a respected businessman. You can't treat me like a common criminal."

Sam grabbed Perry by the arm. "I'll point you in the direction of the livery."

"I don't know my way around Colorado," William shrieked.

"Trial and error is the best way to learn," Sam said. He shoved William out the front door, then turned to Miss Grimes. "I'd be proud to escort you to the hotel, ma'am."

Miss Grimes smiled, a faint blush touching her cheeks. "I would appreciate that."

Jessica waited until Sam and Miss Grimes had left before she turned to Ross. She wrapped her arms around his chest, hugging him to her. "Oh, Ross, thank you, thank you. I promise, you won't be sorry. I'll make you a good wife."

Ross stood rigidly, his hands at his side. "Why didn't you tell me the truth?"

She stared up at him. "I wanted to a thousand times, but I was afraid you'd send me away."

"You should have trusted me."

"I know that, but I will never doubt you again."

He pulled away. "But I don't trust you."

She held out her hands to him. "Ross—"

"You've lied to me every step of the way."

"I'll never do it again."

"I would never be sure."

"Ross—"

"Get your things packed. I want you out of my house within the hour."

As if the wind had been knocked out of her, Jessica struggled to breathe. She stepped forward and grasped Ross's arm. "I can explain."

He stared down at her hand as if it were something vile. She cringed and dropped it to her side.

"Ross, I wanted to tell you the truth, but I was afraid you'd put me off the train in Cheyenne, and then you threatened jail."

"What about later? I would have understood."

"There never was a good time, and I wanted to be the teacher you needed and the wife you wanted."

"That doesn't cut it."

Her hands trembled. "I'd planned to tell you this morning."

He shook his head. "Really? As I remember you had plenty of opportunity."

The raw pain in his eyes twisted in her stomach like a knife. "I swear, Ross. I was going to tell you everything."

"Emma…" He stopped and closed his eyes. "Jessica," he amended. "Was last night a lie, too?"

"No, Ross, no. I gave myself to you out of love." Tears streamed down her face. "I'm so sorry."

He shook his head. "You should have told me. You should have trusted me."

Her heart was shattering. "Forgive me. Please."

He jabbed his thumb over his shoulder toward the front door. "Perry mentioned a will. What was he talking about?"

"My father died recently. His will stipulated that if I married William within thirty days and produced a son within two years, his entire estate would go to me. William wanted control of the money. He realized the only way to do that was to marry me. When I refused his proposal, William tried to force me to marry him. He tried to rape me."

"Rape!" Sunlight streamed through the window, accenting the hard planes of Ross's face and the cold fury blazing in his eyes. He struggled for control, then, gaining it, said, "Go on."

"Please, Ross," Jessica begged, reaching out to him. "I had no other choice but to lie my way through everything."

He stared at her. "I might buy that if it wasn't for Patrick."

"Patrick?"

"Why in God's name did you involve the boy? He cares for you like you were his own mother."

Jessica drew in a ragged breath. "And I love him like a son."

"Love? Are you sure you know what the word means?"

"Since I met you and Patrick, I'm very sure."

He flinched. "This is going to destroy him."

"It doesn't have to. We can work this out."

He stepped back as if he needed to put space between them. "The boy's mother lied to him over and over again, until his faith was destroyed. I might not be the most loving father to him, but I've never lied to him. I've always told him the truth."

"But if we explained this to him together—"

"No! I want you to stay away from my son! I

will clean up the mess you've made. Just get out before you make it worse."

"If I could take back all the lies, I would. I love you and Patrick so very much."

He balled his fingers into a fist and rubbed it against his temple. "Stop staying that! I don't even know you!"

"I am the same woman you held in your arms last night."

"That woman wasn't real. She was only a dream."

"I *am* the same woman."

"No, you're not."

Suddenly, she was angry. She had no right to be, but there it was. Pure, white anger. "*Jessica,* not Emma, nursed you when you were ill. *Jessica* opened the schoolhouse. *Jessica* soothed Patrick's nightmares. *Jessica* made love to you. It was never Emma. *It was me!*"

He shot her a hard look. "Save it, *Jessica.* I don't give a damn."

She struggled to keep her voice even. "Now who's the liar? You wouldn't have married me again if you didn't care a little."

"Don't confuse obligation with love. I don't love you, and after today, I never will." He brushed past her and stormed out of the house, slamming the door behind him.

Chapter Sixteen

Jessica stared at the door Ross had just slammed. Unshed tears burned in her eyes as she collapsed on the foyer steps. Never had she felt so alone, so abandoned.

She looked up at the ceiling. She didn't want to cry. She wanted to be as brave as she had been when her mother had died and when her father had sent her away, but somehow she couldn't manage it. Her throat ached and the tears spilled down her cheeks. She buried her face in her hands and began to sob.

She grieved for the man she'd lost, the son she'd never raise and the life that had nearly been hers. How could she have lost so much so quickly?

"That was some show." Peg's voice cut through her noisy crying.

Jessica looked up to see the old woman descending the stairs. She wore a blue homespun dress, white apron and badly scuffed boots. Her tight bun accentuated her piercing brown eyes and wrinkled frown.

Jessica buried her face in her hands. "Please just go away."

Peg pulled a clean handkerchief from her apron pocket and handed it to Jessica. "I supposed you would feel sorry for yourself. You society types are all alike. Life gets a little tough and you crumble. I've seen it more times than I care to admit."

Jessica shook her head as she blew her nose into the handkerchief. "You don't understand! I've lost everything!"

"Have you?"

She wiped the tears from her cheek with the back of her hand. "Ross hates me."

Peg pulled her pipe from her pocket and leaned against the banister. "Life ain't so black and white."

"You're wrong. Ross sees everything in black and white. Good and bad. Truth and lies. With him it's either one or the other."

"Honey, I've been around him a lot longer than you. Trust me, I know when a man cares about a woman."

Jessica shook her head. "Ross cared about me once, but I've destroyed whatever feelings he had."

"The man needs time. Ross is a proud man and you managed to bruise his ego something awful, but he will heal."

"I wish I could believe you."

"Trust me."

A clock ticked softly in the background. Jessica twisted the handkerchief in her hands. "I should leave town."

"Leave Prosperity? Now that is nonsense."

"It's the easiest solution. I couldn't bear to stay here knowing how he feels about me."

"Easy ain't always what's best, girl." Peg narrowed her eyes and pointed the end of her pipe at Jessica. "Do you love him?"

"You know I do."

"You love him, but you're not willing to fight for him?"

Jessica stood suddenly. The quilt fell from her shoulders and pooled around her ankles. "What's there to fight for? He doesn't want to see me again."

Peg stared up at her. "Then why'd he remarry you?"

Jessica sighed. "Obligation. He said so himself."

"A man like Ross McCain doesn't make a lifetime promise to just anyone. He could have walked away from marriage, but he didn't."

She wanted to believe Peg, but Ross's angry words kept playing over and over in her head. She wrapped her arms around her chest to ward off a sudden chill. "You didn't see the anger in his eyes."

"No, but I heard the tone of his voice, and I know the man. He's hurting, bad, but he'll get over it. You just got to give him time to lick his wounds and think a spell. But the most important thing is that you got to be *here* when he comes around."

Jessica reached down, picked up her quilt and wrapped it around her shoulders. She drew no comfort from its warmth. "He told me to get out of his house."

"Since when did you start doing everything Ross McCain said to do?"

"This is different."

"Maybe so, but you can't leave Prosperity," Peg declared.

"I do want to stay."

"Then it's settled. You're not leaving."

"Leaving? You can't leave!" Patrick's voice thundered down from the landing. Wearing only a nightshirt, he ran down the stairs. Worry wrinkled his young face.

Instinctively, Jessica hurried up to meet him. She tried to take his hands in hers, but he jerked back. "You said you'd always love me."

"I will."

"Then why are you leaving?"

"Patrick, let me explain."

He gritted his teeth. "Are you leaving? Yes or no?"

He sounded so much like his father. "I want to stay, but it's complicated."

"Complicated? Grown-ups always say 'complicated' right before they do something that hurts you."

Her insides ached. "That's not true. I'd do anything not to hurt you."

He glared at her. "Then why are you leaving?"

Jessica hesitated, fearing his rejection, too.

"Tell him the truth," Peg said.

Jessica took a deep breath. Peg was right. The boy deserved to hear everything from her. She stared into his green eyes. "I told a lie, Patrick."

Patrick drew in a breath. "What kind of a lie?"

"I told your father and the other folks in town that I was a teacher. I'm not a teacher."

Some of the tension drained from his body. "Is that all?"

"I also said my name was Emma Grimes. It's not. My name is Jessica Tierney."

"It's not good to tell lies. Pa said he'd give me a whipping if he ever caught me telling one."

"I know. I was wrong to tell one."

"Pa's mad at you?"

"He's very mad."

Patrick furrowed his brow. "When you said you loved me, was that a lie?"

She grabbed his hands. "No. I meant every word of that. I love you with all my heart. I swear."

Patrick stared at her a moment. Her insides tightened as she waited for his reaction. Unexpectedly, he grinned. "You scared me for a minute. I thought you had something really terrible to tell me."

Jessica blinked. "What I did was bad. I let your father and the others in town believe I could do things I can't."

Patrick smiled. "As long as you love me and Pa, it'll work itself out."

His innocence made her smile sadly. "I don't know, Patrick. Your father said he doesn't want to see me again."

Patrick shrugged. "Pa gets mad a lot, but if you just kinda stay out of his way for a little while, he gets over it. He'll get over this."

She squeezed his hands. "I want to believe you."

"Just wait and see."

"I love you, Patrick." Jessica hugged the boy against her.

When he drew back, he was frowning. "Seeing

as you ain't really Miss Grimes, what am I supposed to call you now?''

Jessica sat back on her heels. "I don't really know. What do you want to call me?''

"You still married to my pa?''

"Oh, yes.''

He nodded. "Then I'll still call you Ma.''

Jessica's throat tightened. She wanted him to call her Ma but knew it wouldn't be fair to him. His father might still send her away. "I don't think your father would like that right now.''

He stuck out his chin. "I'm calling you Ma. I don't care what anyone else says, even Pa.''

She brushed the bangs off his forehead. Her heart felt close to bursting with happiness. "Patrick, I can't tell you what that means to me.'' She sniffed. "But I won't get between you and your father.''

The set of Patrick's jaw was arrogant. "Don't worry, Ma. Once Pa cools off, he'll be glad.''

She knew now she would never leave this child. For his sake, her own and McCain's, she had to stand her ground, no matter what.

She nodded. "Well, I don't suppose I can leave now. I have a son to raise.''

His face split into a wide grin. "You sure do!''

Peg cleared her throat and climbed the stairs to the landing where they stood. "Now that we got that settled, I'd say the three of us have some work to do.''

Jessica looked over her shoulder at Peg. She could almost swear there were tears in the housekeeper's eyes. "I'm going to need all the help I can get to convince Ross that I love him.''

Patrick puffed out his chest. "What can I do to help?"

Jessica winked at him. "Let me think about that for a minute."

Peg clamped her pipe between her teeth. "The man ain't never gonna know what hit him. Just do me one favor?"

"Anything."

"Stay clear of him for a day or two, otherwise you're sure to find trouble."

Peg's advice went against Jessica's instincts, but she nodded. "Agreed."

Two hours later, Jessica was walking to school. She felt calmer and more hopeful. Given time, everything would be all right. After all, Peg knew Ross better than anyone, and if she said he'd forgive her, then he would—he had to.

Jessica had taken extra care with her toilette this morning. The mundane tasks of washing her face and brushing her hair had helped calm her jitters. With a renewed sense of resolve, she'd put on a fresh dress and pulled back her long hair with a red ribbon. It was important she look her best when she visited her students' homes and confessed her lie.

Jessica paused, pulled a rumpled piece of paper from her pocket and unfolded it. Before she'd left this morning, she had sat at the dining room table and scribbled out the speech she planned to give the parents.

She did not relish the task of telling her neighbors the truth, but it had to be done if she were to make amends. She reminded herself that the folks in Prosperity were good people and likely they'd forgive her once she explained her plight. "I haven't done anything to deliberately hurt them, not really. It's going to be all right."

Drawing in a deep breath, she resisted the urge to think about what she'd do if they rejected her. Now was the time for clear thinking and action, not tears. "Once I've talked to the parents, I'll set things right with Emma Grimes, then I'll find Ross. I can do this. I can. I just need to take it one step at a time."

Jessica folded the paper and tucked it back in her pocket. Oddly, knowing she had a plan calmed her. As she walked toward the school, the sun was warm and the sky crisp and clear. "Just stick to the script, Jessica, and everything will be all right."

When she passed the mercantile, she was surprised to discover the green shades were drawn and a Closed sign hung in the door. She'd heard Jed never shut his store, not even on Christmas Day. Worried, she glanced up and down the street, hoping to ask someone why Jed had closed the mercantile, but there was no one in sight. The boardwalk and streets were deserted. At Thompson's Livery, the horses were hitched outside the corral, but neither Mr. Thompson nor any customers were there.

Instinct told her something was wrong.

Reason told her not to borrow trouble.

Down the street, a commotion near the saloon caught her attention. She clutched her shawl to her throat and started walking in that direction. Something was wrong.

Her nerves tightened as she got closer, and her scalp tingled. Through the saloon's large front window she could see that everyone in town was crowded inside. "Everything's going to be fine. Don't worry. Don't worry," she muttered to herself.

She stepped through the double doors. The room was packed with people. Jed McManus stood just inside the doors on his tiptoes, peering over the shoulders of two large miners. "Get the devil out of my way, you varmints. I can't see or hear a thing."

The miner on the right, a man with burly arms and black hair, turned. "Quiet, Jed, I can barely hear myself. Soon as I know something, I'll pass it along to you."

Jessica moistened her lips. She tugged on Jed's sleeve. "Mr. McManus, what's happening?"

He knotted his brow. "Mrs. McCain, what are you doing out here? I figured you'd be up front with your husband when he makes the big announcement."

She rubbed her damp palms down her skirt. "What big announcement?"

"Ain't got the slightest notion. All I can say is that Ross sent word to everyone in town to meet him here at the saloon at one o'clock sharp."

Panicking, Jessica stood on her tiptoes, trying to catch a glimpse of her husband, but she couldn't see past the miners. "Jed, I need to get up front."

"Unless you can shrink down to the size of a mouse, I don't see how you're gonna do it. Folks are packed tighter than corn on a cob."

The air was thick and hot. Sweat trickled down her face as she stared at the crush of people. Jed was right. She'd never make it to the front of the room.

"Thanks, Jed."

She slid along the back wall until she spotted an opening next to the window and Harriet Gooden. Beside Harriet was a whiskey box.

Harriet's pinched lips curved into a smile. "Now what do you suppose this is all about, Mrs. McCain?"

"I'm not really sure."

"You don't know? I'd have thought your husband would have told you what was going on."

Jessica managed to shrug her shoulders. "He's his own man, Harriet."

"But he is your husband. I'd have thought—"

"Folks!" Ross's voice, clear and deep, boomed inside the room. "I'd like to introduce someone to you."

When Jessica climbed up on the whiskey box, she could see Ross. He had brushed his hair back, buttoned his shirt up to the base of his throat and tucked it in. If not for his tight jaw, he looked composed and calm.

Her heart ached for him. He was so close, yet so very far away. They'd been so blissfully close only hours ago, and now he was furious with her.

He just needs time. It's going to be fine.

Jessica nearly fell off the box when Emma Grimes stepped forward and took her place beside him. Miss Grimes's round face was flushed from the heat and her forehead damp with sweat.

Blood pounded in Jessica's head. Ross was going to tell everyone. No! It wasn't supposed to happen this way. She was the one who needed to tell everyone the truth, not him. The truth was her only chance of redemption.

Ross cleared his throat. "I'd like to introduce you to Emma Grimes," he said clearly.

Jessica sucked in a breath.

Harriet tugged on Jessica's skirt. "Is she a relative of yours?"

"No."

"Ain't that a coincidence! Two women with the exact same name. Can you imagine that? What do you think are the chances?"

Jessica was barely aware of the comments drifting through the crowd. "I have no idea."

Ross held up his hands. "Folks, Miss Grimes is my wife's aunt and her namesake." His lips tightened, as if his mouth tasted bitter.

Jessica cringed. To protect her, a man who valued honesty above all else was lying to a whole community of people who accepted his word as bond.

Ross had lied to everyone! Jessica didn't understand.

He cleared his throat. "She's gonna be taking over the position as schoolteacher in town."

Sissy raised her hand. "No disrespect, Mr. McCain, but we already got us a teacher. And we like her just fine."

"Yeah," Lydia shouted. "I trust Mrs. McCain, but I don't know this woman from Adam. The only teacher I'm sending my babies to is Mrs. McCain."

Miss Grimes reached in her pocket and pulled out a round peppermint. She popped it in her mouth.

Ross held up his hand. "Your children will be well taken care of when they are in Miss Grimes's charge. She has been teaching for many years."

"I'm sure she'd do a fine job," Sissy said. "But

we put our trust in Mrs. McCain and we aim to stick with her.''

Ross frowned. "You don't have a choice in the matter. My wife will not be teaching school."

Dave Thompson hooked his thumbs in his suspenders. "Thought you said you'd honor the contract, McCain, and let your wife teach. It ain't like you to go back on your word."

Ross clenched his fists. "I'm not. I promised you this town would have a teacher and it will."

"Well, we like the other Emma Grimes," Mrs. Crumpet shouted. "The *real* Emma Grimes."

Jessica pressed her hands to her hot cheeks. This wasn't right. Ross was trying to protect her and she didn't deserve it.

"I'm not sending my children to *her* school," Mrs. Crumpet said, shaking her head. "I don't know this woman and I ain't trusting my little ones with her."

Several of the women nodded their accord. "I agree with Lydia," Sissy said. "As much as I want my babies to learn to read and write, I ain't sending my children to her. Emma McCain is my friend and I ain't gonna turn my back on her."

Jessica had never had people stand by her before. Their loyalty warmed her heart and ate at her soul. She didn't deserve any of it.

"Wait!" she shouted.

Ross searched the crowd until his gaze locked on her. His eyes narrowed in silent warning.

Jessica tore her gaze from his, unable to bear it. "I cannot stand here and let you malign this good woman. She deserves your respect."

"I know she's kin to you," Lydia said. "But we like having you as our teacher—that is, unless you don't want to teach our little ones."

Jessica shook her head. "I want it more than anything."

"Then what's the problem?" Sissy asked.

"Ross is trying to do what's best," Jessica said. "He's trying to protect me."

"By taking your job?" Jed said.

"No, by covering up the fact that I lied to everyone in this town."

Ross smacked his hand against his thigh. "That's enough, Mrs. McCain!"

Misery stabbed her heart. "No, Ross. No more lies."

"Go home," he ordered.

"No." Jessica's voice was clear and strong. "I have something to say."

Ross's eyes narrowed. "You've said enough."

Jessica swallowed. It took all her strength not to shrink from him. "It was kind of my husband to try and protect me, but I think all of you are owed the truth."

Ross climbed down from the bar and tried to move forward, but was unable to press through the crowd. The sparks in his eyes ordered her to remain silent.

Jessica ignored the warning. "The truth is I lied to my husband and everyone else in this town."

Ross clenched his fists. "Enough!"

Jessica shook her head. "This woman up there is not my aunt. She is the real Emma Grimes. I'm not. My real name is Jessica Tierney."

After a few angry murmurs, the crowd grew silent. Everyone looked at her.

She swallowed hard. "I lied about my name so I could take Miss Grimes's place in Sacramento."

Their stares bore into her. A myriad of emotions crossed each face. Shock. Disbelief.

"Why'd you lie to us?" Sissy asked.

"I was in trouble. I had to get out of the city, so I told the conductor my name was Emma Grimes so he'd let me on the train."

"I ain't asking why you lied to the conductor in Sacramento, I want to know why you lied to *us*."

The hurt Jessica saw in Sissy's eyes nearly broke her heart. "If I could take it all back, I would."

Sissy's lips thinned into a grim line.

Jessica looked at Ross. "The lie just got bigger and bigger, and I didn't know how to get out of it. I was afraid to tell anyone."

Sissy shook her head. "You could've told me. I would've understood."

Tears pooled in Jessica's eyes. "I'm so sorry."

She wanted to melt into the floorboards. She couldn't stand the faces of her friends and neighbors so filled with shock, disgust and sadness. She glanced up at Ross for support.

His hands were clenched at his sides. For an instant she imagined his eyes softened before he looked away. "I think you've said just about all you need to say. Why don't you leave now?"

She sniffed and wiped the tears away. "I'm willing to stay and be the teacher you all wanted me to be. Perhaps I could teach the adults like I promised."

"I don't think so," Lydia said.

"I may have lied about my name, but I never lied about my commitment to the children."

"How can we believe you?" Sissy asked.

"I don't know. I suppose I'll have to earn your trust all over again."

"Once a liar, always a liar," Harriet said, loudly enough for everyone around her to hear.

"Can't say she'd be the kind of person I want my children to look up to," Dave admitted.

The crowd murmured in agreement. Their anger was so real she could almost taste it.

Miss Grimes cleared her throat. "Once you've all had time to think about this, I'm sure you'll find forgiveness in your hearts. None of us are saints and we've all made mistakes."

"I don't need time to know that what she did was wrong," Harriet shouted.

"That's enough," Ross said. "Everything that needs to be said has been said. Everyone go home. Miss Grimes will reopen the school on Monday."

Jessica pressed her hand into the pit of her stomach, trying to quell the sick feeling. She stepped down from the whiskey box and stood quietly by the wall as the people filed past her and out of the saloon. No one spoke to her or looked at her. She was invisible.

Emma Grimes was one of the last to leave. As she passed, she paused and took Jessica's hand in her own. "It'll be all right, dear. They've all just had a bit of a shock."

Tears spilled down Jessica's face. "I don't know,

Miss Grimes. When I came here today, I was sure I could win their trust again. Now I'm not so sure.''

Delicate creases formed around the corners of her eyes when she smiled. ''Time, dear. Time heals all wounds.''

''I hope you're right.''

Miss Grimes winked. ''We'll talk later, dear.''

When the schoolteacher left, Jessica realized she was alone in the saloon with Ross. He stood by the bar staring at her.

His face was an unreadable mask as he walked behind the bar, picked up a whiskey bottle and poured himself a drink. ''You couldn't keep quiet, could you?''

Jessica straightened her shoulders. ''I had to tell the truth.''

''Since when did the truth become so important?''

She ignored the barb and walked toward the bar. ''I had to tell them.''

''If you'd kept quiet, no one in town would have been the wiser.''

''Why do you care what people think of me?''

''You and I are through, but I thought at least I could save you the public humiliation.''

''You mean that little lie you told was meant to help me?''

Ross scowled and slammed down the drink. ''Yes. I decided you can stay in Prosperity until you can find a family member to live with.''

Her shoulders sagged. ''There is no one else, Ross. Father was my last blood relative, and you already know the terms of his will.''

He stared into the depths of his glass. "I'll give you enough money to see you through."

She managed a shrug. "Charity's not my style."

He slammed the glass against the bar again, sloshing liquid over his hand and the mahogany wood. "Fine! I tried to be the nice guy, take the high road, but if you want to go it alone, I'm not going to stop you."

Her heart ached so badly she could barely breathe. She raised her head high. "I'm not giving up on us."

Ignoring her comment, he raised his glass to her in a toast, then gulped down the remains. "Tell me, *Jessica,* why is it that I'm attracted to beautiful women who can do nothing but lie to me?"

Jessica clenched her fingers. "Don't compare me to Caroline."

"Why not? You two are so much alike."

She whirled around. "I'd never do anything to intentionally hurt you."

"Is that supposed to make me feel better?"

"Caroline and I both may have lied to you, but always remember, she left you. *You* are pushing *me* away."

He swallowed another glassful of whiskey in one gulp. "If I don't, you'll destroy me."

Her heart softened. "I won't destroy you, Ross. I love you."

He squeezed his eyes shut. "Stop it, just stop. I've already told you, I'll give you money."

"I don't want money, I want to stay. Please, can't you forgive me?"

He glared at her.

"What about Patrick?" she said. "The boy loves me."

His eyes shot daggers. "Stay away from Patrick."

"I won't leave that boy."

"I'll break your neck if you hurt my son."

Jessica turned and pushed open the saloon doors. "Patrick's lost one mother, he's not losing another."

"Like hell. You stay away from him."

She stepped outside.

"Where are you going?"

"Home."

"We're not going to live under the same roof."

Her throat ached. "Then you'd better find someplace else to live, because I'm not leaving our home."

She walked away, pausing only briefly when she heard the whiskey glass crash against the wall.

Chapter Seventeen

When Jessica left, Ross went looking for the only company he was fit to keep—a bottle of whiskey. He sat down at one of the back tables in the saloon and began to drink. His plan was to get drunk—good and drunk—and he did.

Ross didn't know how long he sat in the corner of the saloon or how many tumblers of whiskey he tossed back. He was vaguely aware of ordering a second bottle, of hearing the whispers of other patrons, but he ignored it all. The only thing he cared about was making the ache inside him go away, but it never did.

Jessica consumed his thoughts. With each fresh glass of whiskey, he tried to wash her from his mind, but couldn't manage the task. He couldn't erase the image of her smile, the way the light sparkled in her eyes, the softness of her skin. She was in his blood.

A sudden rush of water, as cold as a mountain spring in January, wrenched him from his solitude. He bolted straight up, his heart thundering in his chest. Ready to fight the person who would dare try to sober him up, he reached for his pistol.

Sam stood directly over him, scowling.

His friend picked up the empty whiskey bottle. "I think you've spent enough time with this. I'm tired of watching you feel sorry for yourself."

Ross propped his enormously swelled head in his hands. "Go away."

Sam sat in the opposite chair. "Yep, I'd say you've made a real fool out of yourself. Couldn't have done a better job if I set out to do it myself."

"I'm going to put a bullet in your head if you don't go away."

Sam laughed. "Buddy, you ain't got the strength to lift a gun, let alone shoot straight."

"Try me."

Sam waved to the bartender. "Bring us a pot of hot coffee, the blacker the better, and some fresh bread."

"No food," Ross grumbled.

"You'll eat it even if I have to shove it down your gullet."

"Why the hell are you here? Can't you see I want to be alone?"

"The way you're acting, you're going to get a lifetime of alone."

"Back off."

"The best damn woman ever to come into your life is waiting for you and you couldn't care less."

"If she's the best, then I'm in trouble." His mouth tasted like he'd swallowed a field of cotton.

"You don't mean that and you know it. If you

didn't care, you wouldn't have gotten stinking drunk. I ain't seen you this drunk since Gettysburg.''

Ross lifted his head and sat back in his chair. He'd forgotten just how bad too much liquor could make a man feel.

Sam leaned back in his chair, his arms folded over his chest. He shook his head. "You are a sorry sight.''

Ross grunted. Sam's hair was slicked back and he smelled faintly of bay rum. "You smell bad.''

Sam's smile evaporated. He raised his arm and sniffed. "I took a bath this morning and put on some of Jed's best bay rum.''

"What the hell for?''

"Soon as I get you cleaned up, Miss Grimes and I are going for a stroll down Main Street.'' He sighed. "Never thought there'd be another woman that could make my toes curl like my wife did, but Emma Grimes has got my body humming in places I'd damn near forgotten about.''

Ross grunted. "Take it from me, women aren't worth the trouble.''

Sam grinned. "Oh, they're worth it. You know it as well as I do.''

"Make your point.''

"You love Jessica.''

"Like hell.''

"You love her so bad, your heart feels like it's been split in two with an ax.''

"You're wrong.'' The denial sounded weak even to his ears.

The bartender set a pot of coffee on the table and two cups. "Bread will be here in a minute.''

"Don't bother," Ross croaked.

Sam shook his head. "Bring it. He's gonna need something in his stomach when he goes looking for his wife."

"I'm not going anywhere but home."

"If I was you, I wouldn't show my face around your house unless you're fixing to make things right with Jessica."

"What's that supposed to mean?"

"Peg's gunning for you. She's meaner than a wounded bear and looking to pound your hide. Patrick's not too happy with you, either."

Ross curled his fingers into a fist. "I told that woman not to hurt my boy."

"She ain't hurt him one bit. Fact is, she's been covering for you. She told the boy you were at the mine last night so he wouldn't worry when you didn't come home. He doesn't know his father's been swimming in whiskey for the last twenty-four hours."

"I'll have to thank her," he grumbled.

Sam filled a cup with the hot brew and pushed it toward Ross. "Start drinking. As soon as you've finished a few cups and eaten, I'll walk you home."

Ross accepted the cup of coffee and took a sip. It tasted bitter, thick, but he forced himself to take another gulp. He wasn't about to go looking for Jessica, but he was ready to shake off the groggy, powerless feeling liquor brought with it. After he'd finished the cup of coffee, he refilled it, then tore a slice from the loaf. His stomach flip-flopped when he tasted the first bite. After a third cup of coffee and a few more bites of bread, Ross began to feel human again.

But as the effects of the liquor faded, his emotions roared to life. His chest tightened and his eyes burned with unshed tears. "Sam, how did things turn into such a damn mess?"

"Life ain't clean and neat, Ross. You know that better than anybody. Messes are gonna happen. It's up to us to decide how we're gonna clean them up."

"What if I don't want to clean up this one?"

Sam's eyes narrowed as he stared at Ross. "Can you really say you'd be happier without her?"

"She lied to me."

"Yeah, she did, but have you ever made a mistake you'd do anything to fix?"

Ross stared into the black depths of his cup. "It's not the same."

"Ain't it?"

Ross smacked the palm of his hand against the table. "How can I ever trust her again?"

"I don't know. You're gonna have to figure that one out. But my guess is she'll never give you a reason to doubt her again."

"How can you be so sure?"

"I ain't looking at her with angry eyes. I see how much she's hurting and how much she loves you."

Ross swallowed. "I want her so much it frightens me," he whispered.

"I know."

Suddenly, he felt very tired and alone. "I was watching folks last night in the saloon, laughing and carrying on, and I couldn't understand how they could be so happy. Didn't they understand that the bottom had just fallen out of everything?''

''I felt that way when my Sarah died. Other folks' happiness made me mad.''

''Mad as hell.''

''I couldn't bring my wife back, but you can bring yours back. Stop being a horse's behind and go get her.''

Sam was right. Ross could have a second chance with Jessica if he wanted one. ''I don't know what to say to her.''

''Worry about the words when you see her. They'll come when the time's right.''

''Where is she?''

The saloon doors opened and closed with a whoosh. ''I'm right here.'' Jessica stood in the doorway.

She was so pretty and so fine. He stared into sapphire eyes, ensnared by their beauty. He was torn between anger and happiness.

''What do you want?'' he demanded, his voice rough with emotion.

Her gaze didn't waver from his as she walked toward their table. ''To talk to you. Sam, would you excuse us?''

Sam stood and scooped up his hat. ''Be happy to, ma'am. I got an appointment, anyway.''

Jessica smiled at Sam. ''I just left Miss Grimes at the schoolhouse. She's anxious for that walk.''

Sam puffed his chest out like a peacock. ''Well, that's mighty fine. If you two will excuse me, I got a lady to court.'' He put on his hat and left.

She sat down in Sam's chair. Ross eased back into

his own. Damn but she was a beautiful woman. He wanted to look calm and composed, but he felt as nervous as a schoolboy. The scent of lilacs drifted over to him.

Her foot brushed an empty whiskey bottle on the floor under the table and she pushed it away. As she watched it roll across the floor, she said, "I expected better of you, Ross."

He brushed his fingers though his unwashed hair. Like her, he was disappointed in his actions. Still, it angered him that she'd call him into question. "What the hell is that supposed to mean?"

"A man like you who's accomplished so much shouldn't crumble like a baby at the first sign of trouble."

Who was she to be looking down her nose at him? "If I wanted your opinion, I'd ask for it."

"That's too bad, because you're going to get it."

He moved to stand, but she placed her hand on his. Her soft touch drained the anger and strength from him. "Say your piece," he muttered. He wanted to sound gruff, mean even, but he couldn't quite manage it.

She pulled her hands back and folded them primly on the table in front of her. Damn, but he missed her touch as much as he hated the emotional distance between them. Why was he so weak willed when it came to her?

Jessica cleared her throat. "We don't know very much about each other. I thought maybe we could change that by trading a question for a question."

"Is this some kind of game?"

"No, I just thought if we knew more about one another, we might understand the other better."

"Who says I want to know more about you?"

She flinched but held her head high. "I think you are as curious about me as I am you. That's why I propose that we trade questions. Ask me any question and I'll answer it truthfully. Then I'll ask you a question and you will answer it."

"What if I don't like your question?"

"You must answer it, just as I am obliged to answer yours."

He was quiet as he considered her proposition. Pride told him to dismiss this foolish game of hers and send her away. His heart reminded him that pride had landed him in a saloon with a roaring hangover. And she intrigued him. Hell, what did he have to lose? "I'll play."

Her shoulders relaxed a fraction. He was glad to see he wasn't the only one who was nervous.

She cleared her throat. "You go first. Ask any question."

Thousands of questions about her had plagued him during the past twenty-four hours, but only one came to mind. "How'd you learn how to swim?"

"Swim? Uh, my mother taught me."

Ross shrugged, trying not to look as foolish as he felt. "Always seemed strange to me that a society type would know how to swim."

"Mama wasn't society. She was a maid. My father fell in love with her and they eloped. The marriage was not a success, and when I was three, Pa sent Mama and me to live in the country. Because we lived near a lake, she thought it important I know how to swim.''

The answer wasn't what he expected, but then nothing about her was. ''Tell me about your parents.''

She shook her head. ''It's my turn.''

''What?''

''You asked one question, and now I ask one question.''

''I don't like talking about myself.''

''We agreed on the rules of the game. A question for a question.''

He rubbed his palms over his thighs. ''Ask your question.''

''What's your full name?''

He released the breath he was holding, relieved the question wasn't personal. ''Ross Edward McCain.''

''I like the sound of that.''

''Why'd you ask such an easy question?''

Her eyes sparkled. ''Is that your next question?''

''No!'' He paused and collected his thoughts. ''How much of what you told me about yourself was true?''

''Most of it. Until two days ago I didn't know the first thing about Emma Grimes, and I was afraid if I started lying I'd slip up somehow, so I decided to tell the truth whenever I could.''

''When did—''

''My turn.''

He curled his fingers into a fist. ''Fine.''

She moistened her lips. ''Do you want a divorce?''

"It's a little early to be talking about divorce, especially since there might be a baby on the way."

Her eyes widened with shock and her hands went to her stomach. "With all the commotion, I never stopped to think there'd be a child."

"I did."

"A baby." A blissful look crept into her eyes.

In that moment his anger evaporated and he wanted her more than he ever had. Mentally, he reconsidered his options. He reminded himself he shouldn't open his heart to a woman who'd lied to him. He had to rekindle his anger. "If there is a baby, you might still inherit your father's money."

"There is no inheritance."

"What?"

"I telegrammed my father's attorney yesterday and explained I wouldn't be able to fulfill the terms of the will. I instructed him to give the money to the rightful heir."

"The rightful heir? You don't mean Perry, do you?"

"No, Saint Bridget's Orphanage. It's where father grew up. He wanted them to have the money if I failed to meet his terms."

"So you're penniless."

"Yes." She cleared her throat. "I have one last question."

He barely heard her. He was still mulling over the fact that she'd given away a fortune...for him. "All right."

"Do you love me?"

He shifted uncomfortably. "I'm not too proud to admit I want you."

Her hands were clasped so tightly, her knuckles whitened. "Do you love me?"

He sighed. "I don't know. There was a time when I thought I knew what love was, but now I don't think I will ever know."

She smoothed her palms over the tabletop. Sadness filled her eyes. "At least you've been honest with me." She pushed away from the table and stood.

He stood in turn. He didn't want her to leave. "Where are you going?"

"To the schoolhouse to hold my first adult reading class."

"I thought that wasn't until Sunday."

"Today is Sunday, Ross."

He groaned. "Damn, I was wondering why it was so quiet in the saloon." He reached out for her but stopped short of touching her. He let his arm fall back by his side. "Where do we go from here?"

"I love you, Ross, but I won't beg for your love. You'll have to come to accept me for myself."

When he didn't respond, she turned and left.

Struck by how empty the room felt, Ross strode to the window and watched Jessica walk down the street. As she passed the mercantile, she nodded to Harriet Gooden, who pretended not to notice. Dave Thompson didn't look up from the horse he was brushing, and several women on the corner whispered, stared, pointed as she passed by.

The townsfolk had turned their backs on her even though few of them had the right to cast stones. It seemed Dave had forgotten about his horse-thieving days, and Harriet had pushed aside memories of the two husbands she'd divorced before Bill Gooden had married her.

Damn them all. Fueled by anger, Ross walked outside. Jessica didn't deserve their resentment.

The fools didn't realize how truly amazing she was. None of them had ever stood up to him the way she did, and none of them would have kept quiet about the fact that he couldn't read.

His wife…she had grit, beauty, charm, intelligence, loyalty. If those fools didn't have the sense to forgive her, then—

He stopped cold when he remembered Jessica's last question. Did he love her?

Why had he said he didn't know? In a moment of pure clarity he knew he loved his wife with all his heart and soul. Without her, nothing made sense. He was adrift, a man half living.

She hadn't lied for convenience or pleasure, but to survive. If anything, he should be grateful for her lies. Without them they never would have met.

Ross cursed softly. He'd been a fool for not telling her he loved her when she'd asked him.

He drew in a deep breath as if he breathed fresh air for the first time. His strength and common sense were returning.

It was time to mend the rift he'd created between them. With renewed purpose he set off for his house. He had to bathe quickly if he was going to be ready by one o'clock.

Jessica's knees were shaking by the time she reached the schoolhouse. Despite the whispers and stares, she thought only of Ross. It had taken every ounce of her courage to face him, and he'd all but rejected her.

She walked over to the desk—Emma Grimes's desk now—and noticed the subtle changes—an ink-well, a notepad, a pair of spectacles. With just a few personal items, Emma Grimes had made this desk, this school, her own. It no longer belonged to Jessica. It was no longer her sanctuary. Again she was the interloper, the outcast.

Fighting back tears, Jessica picked up a stack of primers and slates and set one at each of the places. She checked the watch in her pendant. Five minutes past one.

She walked over to the potbellied stove and started shoving twigs in it. Perhaps a fire would drive the chill from the room. She lit a match and tossed it onto the wood. The fire crackled and sparked.

She shoved a larger piece of wood into the stove. "Why do I do this to myself? These people don't want me around. They're never going to forgive me."

She rose slowly and walked over to the window. No one was outside. "Who am I kidding? I'm just wasting my time."

A whiff of smoke caught her attention, and by the time she turned, smoke tumbled out of the stove. "Oh, not again, not now. I don't need this."

She hurried over and picked up a poker, but the more she stabbed at the logs, the thicker the smoke grew. Could this day get any worse?

"By the smell of the smoke, I'd say you're trying your hand at fire building again," Ross said.

Jessica looked up. "Ross!"

He stood in the doorway, his hat in his hand. Since she'd left him thirty minutes ago, he'd bathed, put on a fresh pair of pants and a shirt and combed his hair. The black stubble on his chin was still thick, and dark circles marred the skin under his eyes, but he looked remarkably better. She found herself trapped by the emerald depths of his eyes.

"Open the damper," he said.

"The damper?"

"The lever just above your head. Turn it. It'll release the smoke."

Jessica did as Ross instructed, and to her relief, the smoke snaked up the chimney. She gave a deep sigh. "Thank you."

Ross walked over to the stove and closed the small metal door. "Are you ever going to learn how to build a fire?"

"I seem to be hopeless."

"No, you're not hopeless. Just…just human," he said softly.

Jessica teetered between heaven and hell as she stared at him. "W-what are you doing here?"

"I came to talk."

Hope filled her heart. "I'd like that."

The front door to the schoolhouse banged open. Sissy stood in the doorway. Her cheeks were flustered, her hair wind tossed. "Am I too late for the reading lesson?"

Jessica turned. "No, I was just about to get started."

Sissy sighed. She nodded to Ross, then directed her full attention to Jessica. "I meant to be early today, but getting away from the house was near impossible.''

Jessica smiled. "It's all right.''

"No, it ain't. It's important to me I get something off my chest.'' She paused and looked at Ross. "It's just as well you hear what I've got to say.'' She took a deep breath. "I had no business judging you or looking down at you. I've done my share of sinning, and I ain't got the right to cast stones.''

Jessica's throat tightened. She could feel Ross's gaze on her. "The past is the past. Let's get started with that reading lesson.''

"I'd like nothing better,'' Sissy said.

"Sissy Nevers, what in tarnation are you doing in here with her?'' Lydia Crumpet scolded. The older woman stood on the threshold of the schoolhouse as if she were afraid to come inside.

Jessica squared her shoulders. "We're having our first reading lesson. You're welcome to join us if you like.''

"I don't think so.''

"Mrs. Crumpet, you don't have the sense God gave a mule,'' Sissy interjected. "Otherwise you'd be taking a seat next to me right now.'' Sissy turned to Jessica. "Three days ago taking reading lessons was all she could talk about.''

Mrs. Crumpet's face blanched. "That was before...well, you know, before we found out she wasn't a teacher.''

"I may not be a teacher,'' Jessica responded, "but I know how to read, and I'm willing to share what I know with anyone who wants to learn.''

Sissy cocked an eyebrow. "Lydia ain't got the guts to go against the folks in this town."

"I do, too," she said. She stepped inside the schoolhouse. "I do as I please." Her jaw dropped open when she saw Ross.

"Then sit down," Sissy ordered. "And close your mouth before you catch a fly."

Jessica offered a smile. "We've plenty of seats."

Mrs. Crumpet was silent for a moment. "There are a few other folks out there. They're real curious about what you're gonna teach, but they didn't have the nerve to ask."

Ross stood silently by, watching. His eyes gleamed with satisfaction.

Jessica would have given anything to have a few minutes alone with him. "Have them all come in and take a seat."

Mrs. Crumpet nodded and turned. "Get on in here. She's having class and I aim to see what she's gonna teach." She didn't wait for a response, but marched into the classroom and took a seat beside Sissy.

Within seconds, Jed, Dave and a half-dozen other townsfolk filed into the classroom like naughty children.

Jessica passed out chalk to each person. Silently, she reveled in this success.

Jed cleared his throat and glanced nervously at Ross, who still remained standing by the stove. "There are other folks who wanted to be here but couldn't make it for all the chores they had."

"Perhaps I could offer a lesson on another day," Jessica suggested.

Jed nodded. "I'll pass the word along." He cleared his throat. "Mrs. McCain, I for one am sorry for the way I acted the other day."

Everyone else nodded.

"We've all made mistakes. I'm ready to start afresh, if you're willing."

Everyone murmured their approval.

Jessica walked up to the board. She picked up a piece of chalk and wrote the name Jessica McCain. "Since we're starting fresh, let me introduce myself. My name is Jessica McCain."

"Pleased to meet you, Mrs. McCain," Jed said. The class chuckled. "Mr. McCain, if you don't mind my asking, what are you doing here?"

A shadow of a smile tugged at the corner of his lips. "I'm here to learn how to read."

Sissy dismissed his comment with a wave. "Mr. McCain, you can read as well as the best of them. Really, why are you here?"

He met Sissy's gaze, all traces of humor gone. "I can't read the first word."

Overcome with pride, Jessica beamed. She knew how hard the confession was for Ross.

"But that's nonsense," Jed said. "You own the mine, you built this town…"

Ross scanned the crowd. "I can't read."

"Well, I'll be darned," Mrs. Crumpet said.

Ross clenched the brim of his hat in a white-knuckled grip. "It's been a secret I've been hiding since I was a boy. I have a hunger to read, just like you folks, but pride wouldn't allow me to admit that I needed help."

Ross's gaze locked onto Jessica. "We've all had secrets and told lies."

Jessica pressed her palms to her flushed cheeks. "Oh, Ross."

"Can you ever forgive me, Jessica, for not standing by you when you needed me most?"

Jessica rushed to him and wrapped her arms around him. "I love you, Ross McCain, with all my heart and soul."

He crushed her against his chest as if she were his lifeline. Finally, he drew back, his expression serious. "I love *you*, Jessica McCain, and I want everyone in this town to know it."

Ross leaned down and kissed her, taking her breath away with a slow, smoldering kiss.

She'd forgotten the class until Jed cleared his throat. "I don't know about you folks, but I know how to kiss just fine, so how about we move on to the reading lesson?"

Epilogue

Summer was Jessica's favorite time of year. She stood on the steps of the schoolhouse watching the children as they headed home. She rubbed her hand over her rounded belly as the baby inside her kicked.

Her first school year was over.

The past seven months had been filled with many changes for her and so many others in Prosperity.

Emma Grimes and Sam had married two weeks to the day after she'd arrived in Prosperity. She had begged Jessica to help her with her duties at the schoolhouse, and Jessica had joyfully accepted. The decision turned out to be a wise one when Emma Grimes Jenkins realized she'd be having a baby two months after Jessica.

The Sunday afternoon reading classes had become so popular, Jessica had added extra classes on Tuesdays and Thursdays. Ross and Sissy had been her most able students, surpassing all her expectations. They soaked up all the knowledge she could teach and more. Sissy had even started talking about becoming a teacher herself one day when her children were older.

The school's enrollment had swelled to twenty-three by the spring. The children enjoyed having two teachers, and all thrived.

Jessica shook off her thoughts of the past when she saw Ross walking toward her. He raised his hand and smiled at her as she waddled down the three steps and picked up a ball and bat the children had used earlier at recess. His powerful legs quickly ate up the distance between them.

Ross took the bat and ball from her and wrapped his arm around her shoulder. He pressed his lips against hers and hugged her against him. "I love you."

She chuckled, nuzzling him with her nose. "I love you."

"Where's Patrick?"

"At Miller's Pond fishing with Billy Crumpet. The two could hardly sit still during the math lesson this afternoon."

"Now that school's out for the summer, there'll be no excuses for you not to rest."

"But there are so many things Emma and I want to do before the children come back in the fall."

Ross's eyes gleamed as he stared at her. "I still can't believe you talked me into letting both you and Emma teach next year. If I were in my right mind, I'd hire another teacher."

"Sissy's going to be helping us this fall, and you've got to admit, the situation is perfect. I'll watch Emma's baby when she's with the students, and she'll watch our baby when I'm at the school."

"Just make sure you let me know if it ever becomes too much for you. You're too precious to me, and I don't want anything to happen to you."

"I will." She hooked her arm in his and they started to walk home. As they strolled down Main Street, waving to their neighbors, she said, "It's hard to believe I wanted to leave this place."

"When you signed that piece of paper, I knew two years would never be enough."

"Perhaps we should write a new contract with a lifetime guarantee."

Ross hugged her against him. "Lifetime, eh? I like the sound of that."

*   *   *   *   *

Take a trip to Merry Old England
with four exciting stories from

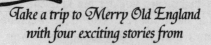

Harlequin® Historical

Return to the charm of the Regency era with

GEORGETTE
HEYER,

creator of the modern Regency genre.

Enjoy six romantic collector's editions with forewords
by some of today's bestselling romance authors,

**Nora Roberts, Mary Jo Putney,
Jo Beverley, Mary Balogh,
Theresa Medeiros and Kasey Michaels.**

Frederica
On sale February 2000
The Nonesuch
On sale March 2000
The Convenient Marriage
On sale April 2000
Cousin Kate
On sale May 2000
The Talisman Ring
On sale June 2000
The Corinthian
On sale July 2000

Available at your favorite retail outlet.

HARLEQUIN®
®
Makes any time special ™

Visit us at www.romance.net   PHGHGEN

COMING NEXT MONTH FROM

HARLEQUIN HISTORICALS

- **THE BONNY BRIDE**
  by **Deborah Hale,** author of A GENTLEMAN OF SUBSTANCE
  Love or money? That is the decision a farmer's daughter must
  make when she sets sail for Nova Scotia as a mail-order bride
  to a wealthy man, and finds the love of her life on the voyage.
  HH #503 ISBN# 29103-5 $4.99 U.S./$5.99 CAN.

- **A WARRIOR'S KISS**
  by **Margaret Moore,** author of THE WELSHMAN'S BRIDE
  In this captivating medieval tale in the *Warrior Series,* a knight
  aspires to make a name for himself at the king's court, but finds
  his plans jeopardized when he falls in love with a woman who is
  a commoner.
  HH #504 ISBN# 29104-3 $4.99 U.S./$5.99 CAN.

- **ONCE A HERO**
  by **Theresa Michaels,** author of THE MERRY WIDOWS—
  SARAH
  A reluctant hero finds himself on a wild adventure when
  he rescues a beautiful woman and loses his heart in
  Theresa Michaels's dramatic return to her *Kincaid* series.
  HH #505 ISBN# 29105-1 $4.99 U.S./$5.99 CAN.

- **THE VIRGIN SPRING**
  by **Debra Lee Brown**
  This talented new author makes her debut with this stirring
  Scottish tale of a young clan laird who finds an amnesiac beauty
  beside a mythical spring.
  HH #506 ISBN# 29106-X $4.99 U.S./$5.99 CAN.

DON'T MISS ANY OF
THESE TERRIFIC NEW TITLES!

CNM0300